Deep in ancient Darkness where seed and spore and root and sleepless worm commingle—Xibalba awaits. Human life has become a disease destroying the earth and Xibalba is coming to feed on the good and the evil alike and scour humankind from the face of the earth . . .

THE GHOST-SNAKE clenched her, clamped her into herself, and she knew the earth around her, remembered all her long years of life and knew their tininess in this swallowing earth. This earth was a throat, a knotty tongue, a root-veined muscle clenching and tasting her, and Quetzal became a rivering knowledge of everything within the planet's embrace.

She knew with awe this planet, a Titan's hand cupping her in the palm of forever. She felt terror and joy at the wonder of time without end. Dense granite made their passage through it arctic, almost frozen, till, pierced by veins of water, the brute rock yielded swifter transit. Then came strata of clay, and coarse jumbled gravels, gravels even more richly veined with water . . . and they were in the aquifer, the deepest base of the ancient river-course. Here was where their Adversary would be rooted, in this catacomb of waters . . . .

APRICOT BRANDY

APRICOT BRANDY

LYNN CESAR

JUNO

APRICOT BRANDY

Copyright © 2008 by Linda Cecere

Cover art copyright © 2008 by Timothy Lantz
www.stygiandarkness.com

ISBN: 978-0-8095-7204-5

Juno Books
Rockville, MD
www.juno-books.com
info@juno-books.com

To Della, Jake, M. and all our Woodland Creatures.

I

At long last, on a cold golden October afternoon, Karen Fox came home. The tires of her pickup crackled down the long gravel drive, around the bend, and there it stood: the big old two-story house, her childhood world.

A broody brutish old house, Karen thought, with its thick-pillared porch, deep eaves, and gabled windows that resembled hooded eyes. Crouched like a gate-keeping troll, it dared her to enter the orchard beyond it, dared her to open its door and step into the first sixteen years of her life.

Karen killed the engine and propelled herself out of the cab. She faced the house which she could enter for the first time in nineteen years, but it was no use. After all her furious rush to get here, on freeways, highways, county roads, speeding from sun-up to high noon, it all came to this. She could not climb those porch steps, could not open and walk through that heavy black door.

It stunned her, the power this house still had over her. She felt like her face had been slapped and the breath punched out of her, to stand so helpless against her fear and grief. Dazed, she looked around her and saw the plum trees in their ranks.

She would look at the orchard. It was hers now and she could at least do that. Turning away from the house, Karen walked past the packing sheds and up along the first of the picking lanes. She went up to where a rank of oaks screened the orchard from the county highway.

Here it was, the vantage she had liked as a kid. You could see acres of plum trees descending in gentle undulations. When she was ten or so she would perch here and gloat over the green wealth of her universe, the braided leaves, all gemmed with purple fruit.

She drew a half pint from the back pocket of her jeans and took a pull. As she drank, her forearm showed the etched muscle fifteen years of swinging a framing hammer had put there; her posture showed strong shoulders in her loose Pendleton and breasts large for her leanness. The sun, just declining, picked out the first wisps of gray in her loosely ponytailed blond hair.

She licked whiskey from her lips and addressed the trees. "This is a goddamned shabby turn-out, men! Look at you! Like a bunch of savages! Degenerates!"

After Mom's death, three years ago, Dad had not pruned nor picked them. The trees were spiderish in the gold light, crooked and hairy with untrimmed shoots and suckers, the lanes between them full of weeds and fruit-rot and clouds of flies. The scent of the decay touched her nostrils and, somehow, it filled her with memories of fear. Would she never understand Dad's crime against her? Would she never be free?

Groping for a gesture of defiance, she thought of a game she and Susan liked to play. They would sit around drinking wine and talking to one another like characters in a romance novel. Draining her half-pint with a flourish, she flung it out into the orchard.

"Now, at long last," she declaimed to the trees, "the comely Karinna Foxxe was the mistress of all she surveyed! She stood alone on the crag, a bit long in the tooth, perhaps, but with her willowy limbs and her swelling bodice, still a striking figure of Womanhood. But as Karinna gazed upon her new domain, ample though it was, she felt there was something lacking, something hauntingly absent from her grand estate! For where, oh where, was *He*? He who had so benevolently ruled this Fairy Kingdom of delight? Where, oh where, was Dear Dead Dad?"

Shouting this, her voice broke and she wiped away unexpected tears. "How she and Dad had haunted these verdant acres together, these nooks and bowers! But now, though she harkens, Karinna hears no sound of Him!" More tears came, so hot and sudden. "Oh, my plummy troops! Oh, my poor bedraggled army! Dear Dead Dad, your general, is no more! It seems he blew his fucking head off!"

It hit Karen then for the first time: though she had shunned Dad for twenty years, she had all along hoped to hear his voice just one more time. To hear him grieve for what he had done.

The breeze shifted, wrapping her Pendleton around her like a shroud. She looked skywards and saw a magnificent red-tail hawk—a female by her great size—crucified against the flawless blue. Karen's mind was lifted to the raptor's viewpoint and she remembered what a wide green world surrounded her, all the hills and groves and silver streams of Gravenstein County. Outside this place, outside these acres which still held her heart staked to the earth, there was a another world. One filled with peace and joy. There was a whole life to be lived, if she could just be free.

Back along the oaks she walked. There was the house and Karen tried to imagine she *had* been able to go inside it after all, imagine she was in there right now, in Mom's kitchen, maybe, where all the warmth her childhood held could still be found. Looking out the windows into the back yard, where Dad's private fruit trees stood, the ones for his brandy. But no, not till she knew through her own eyes that Dad was truly and unarguably dead.

So back she drove through hours of sun-washed terrain, seeing again the bright red barns and white-railed fences she'd passed coming out. Bales of hay studded just-mown fields, each bale casting the same parallelogram of shadow. Green slopes were dappled with harlequin herds of black and white cows.

But when night came and the towns became sparse islands of light in the long darkness, she stopped for another bottle of bourbon and drove drinking it. Pretty soon she felt simplified enough by the booze that she could pull off to a thinly-neoned country motel, crawl into a bed, set the TV screen flickering with murky shapes to keep her company in the dark, and deeply, simply sleep.

II

Karen woke late, got a six-pack for the road and fired up the truck with a brew between her thighs. She came into the metropolis' web of freeways just when they were starting to clog with afternoon traffic. The mortuary lay deep in the old downtown. She had picked Chapel Grove from the Yellow Pages three years ago, when Mom died. Had told Dad's old army buddy, Dr. Harst, who'd called with the news, that Dad could send Mom's body here, that she did not choose to come any closer than here to Gravenstein County, or to Dad himself.

Three nights ago, when Dr. Harst, weeping this time, called and told her of Jack Fox's suicide, she'd given him the same directions.

The mortuary was an extensive one-story structure, in dirty pink stucco with a pseudo-Spanish façade. The last direct sun had slipped off the building and was retreating across the parking lot. Freeways on their colossal pillars surrounded it on all sides, their rivers of traffic snoring and rattling through orange smog that was just beginning to be tinted with violet. Karen thought of Dad's so-different world, the one he'd never seemed to want to leave, save for a tour in Viet Nam, and later, in Central America—thought of the orchard with its cool, creaky country silence, its long corridors of shadow . . . .

Old Dad was a plucked root now for sure, warehoused amid monoxide and endless traffic. He was stacked like cargo in this downtown depot, "You're boxed and docked, old man. We say this one goodbye and I ship you to the flames."

But, at first, it was like yesterday all over again. She couldn't step forward, couldn't approach the mortuary's pompous façade, her legs cold and sluggish. And, Karen didn't really have to go through with any of this. She could tell that bitch on the phone just to burn him and send her the paperwork. Then head back to Frisco. From there, she'd sell Dad's house and all the ground it stood on.

Yeah. Back to San Francisco. Back there, things were really swell. *Tongue 'n' Groove Carpentry* limped along on what sub-work Karen could scrape from a few old friends. More often than not, Karen's partner Susan was paying all the rent. And meanwhile Susan had to go on living with Karen Fox as she was, right here and now, and as she had been all her adult life: a drinking, brooding grief-maker.

There was no other way, she had to face Dad, to tear her heart free of him.

Walking towards the entry, Karen tensed in anticipation of the opposition awaiting her. This business of viewing Dad, dead by his own shotgun, had been hard-won and had taken a good deal of almost-shouting on the phone two nights ago.

False columns ennobled the walls of the wide reception chamber, where a thick carpet of doeskin hue obsequiously received her feet. A beautiful black woman sat at the gleaming barge of the reception desk. It had been an older white lady three years ago when Karen had come here to see Mom. This woman was helmeted with lacquered hair and had sloping, bird-bright eyes.

"How may I help you?" That lilt, the *help* almost *'elp*. This was the musical voice, Haitian or something, Karen had encountered when she called.

"I'm Karen Fox." With a lift of her eyebrows, she referenced that telephone chat. There was a pause between them, the woman's slightly dreamy smile seeming to recall that conversation fondly.

Karen had said, "I'll have to see the body, of course, and then I want it cremated right away."

"Miss Fox," this woman had said solemnly. "It's not a good idea to view the deceased. His condition is very severe."

"Miss. You think I'm just gonna take the word of *strangers* that he's really dead?"

"Miss Fox, we can assure you. You can be absolutely sure. *Absolutely.*"

"Miss, you're not listening. The body is released to *me*. And what I'm telling you to *do*, is to arrange for me to have a last look at him and then burn him, in that order."

"Of course we wish to follow your instructions, Miss Fox, but this is a very unhappy thing you are choosing . . . ."

It had gone on from there, back and forth. All of that echoed for the two of them now as they took each other in. The woman's hands lay gracefully crossed on the desk blotter. Such polished, pointed fingers she had. Something in the way those hands lay crossed told Karen that the woman was still not willing to concede. "Ms. Fox, will you please permit me to say something to you? Your father's death is absolutely real. Again, *absolutely*. But when you do this, regarding his terribly damaged body, you make it more real than it ought to be. You are endangering . . . your peace of mind."

Karen had to laugh at that. *Her peace of mind* . . . "I'm very sorry. I know you're trying to be kind. Please, just tell me the room."

Though smiling again, the woman did not look like a particularly kind person when she answered. "You go left down that farthest corridor and turn right where it ends. It's room 311." Her eyes had an ironic glint: a fool had been warned and had chosen as expected. "And if you would just sign this release for the cremation, please?"

"Gladly. As soon as I've seen him, you can burn him. I don't want the ashes."

Karen passed the entryways of tasteful parlors and viewing rooms, but at the far hallway, all glamour sharply ceased. A many-doored white corridor stretched to either hand, its garish floral carpet short-napped and much-trudged. She turned left. This was a sizeable building. Someone whispered behind her. She turned. The hall was empty. She walked on. In the land of the dead, of course things whispered. A dark man in a long white lab-coat emerged from around the corner ahead and walked serenely towards her, the open coat delicately flaring as he came. He was Latino, his sculpted Mexican hair veined with grey. Had an elegant black suit under the lab-coat. He paused by a flight of stairs that led down to a lower floor and let her come up to him.

"Are you Ms. Fox? I'm John Rubalcava." He had a hard smooth hand like oiled walnut, a calm face carved of the same material. "You are going to view your father?" A quaver of hesitation on *view*.

Karen looked at him for a beat, trying to convey non-aggression. "I have to say goodbye to him. Think of it that way."

"You have to know that he is dead." Offering her own words back to her, spoken to the Haitian on the phone.

"I have to see, Mr. Rubalcava."

"I respect your courage, Ms. Fox. But you know, all the looking in the world doesn't change death. It remains what it is, stare as you will. You must excuse me. I'm so very sorry for your loss."

"Thank you."

Rubalcava's step got strangely lively as he descended the stairs, which led down to a remotely clangorous region. Things faintly slammed, stainless steel clashed and a sneaky chemical whiff came up from that stairwell. He spun gracefully round the turning and his coat flared almost festively. The wings of it had reddish-brownish smudges here and there.

The transecting hallway down which she turned was even more behind-the-scenes, more frankly funky. The walls bore waist-level skidmarks from gurneys and the loud floral carpet was balding in spots. That muted clangor she'd heard from belowstairs was audible up here as well and the smell was stronger too, that haunting, industrial-strength perfume.

Another door: 311. She stood in front of the door like she was staring it down. She muttered, with all the sarcasm she could muster, "Karinna Foxxe had come at last to that last doorway, beyond which lay the last remains of that dark, unknowable man, who had for so long . . . "

Oh, just fucking do it.

III

The first shock was the different carpet; again floral blobs were the pattern, but these screaming-loud in cobalt, marigold and scarlet. The floor's ugliness filled the whole bare cube of a room. Its only contents—the gurney along the far wall and the plastic-sheeted oblong shape it held—seemed to float upon the Hell of color. For an instant she thought it impossible to take these last few steps, but then found herself crossing over to him with the weightless, unwilling compliance of a commanded child.

Here he was.

The body was tightly scrolled up in the kind of tough white plastic she'd seen on construction sites. Its cocoon, like the wrapping of a bouquet, was flared open at one end to display Dad's neck and head, and at this flared end, the plastic was smudged and spattered a muddy red.

Still the commanded child, she leaned over him. *Take a good look at me, Karen. Look at the last thing I have to show you.*

The dome of his head had been blown out and his brow shattered. That he had been *shortened* was how it kept hitting her, a hideous joke had been played on him, taking four inches off his height. How he'd towered, when she was small! Now his eyes were wider-spaced by the fissured brow and the left eye seemed to strain upward, disbelieving, at this ragged crown of bone he ended in. His jaw gaped, the hinge blown. Most of his upper teeth had left him along with his brain.

Leaning there, breathing his aura of refrigerated decay, Karen could not help but pity this obscene vandalism to a man once so handsome.

Dad. It's me. Karen.

She had foreseen pain in this moment, but she hadn't foreseen that its cruelest edge would be love. The first years, when he had been Daddy, when she had been weightless and safe in the crook of his arm, had sat in his lap for stories—how he seemed to love to read to her!—his chest her trusted backrest and a favored bed if she should drowse. Somewhere down in its root, her heart still held these things, was partly made of them. As she discovered this, the cruelty of what he'd later done to her stunned her, seared her as if it were brand new and her first blood not dry from it, while at the same time, she yearned like a little girl for the loving father she had lost.

Resting both hands lightly on the gurney's side-rail, she leaned down to kiss his cheek. If she ever hoped to find that earlier undamaged part of her, she had to say goodbye to all of him.

Cold putty took her kiss, stubble nibbling her lips like frost crystals, chilled putrescence filling her nose. She straightened slowly, eyes still searching him, searching herself for the seam where this man's life left off and her own life, whole and inviolable, could at last begin.

Her left wrist felt the clamp of an ice-cold hand, a crushing grip and freezing to the bone.

Explosively she wrenched free and spun around. There was no one else in the room. All her nerves were firing in a cascade that drained out the bottoms of her feet and into the floor, while the floor itself was plunging, plunging into the earth. She stood in the same room, but suddenly it was deep, deep underground, unreachable from the world overhead . . . .

Dad lay there, mummied by the plastic, limbless, yet surely it had been his hand upon her wrist, just the way she had felt it in her youth, when he dragged her down to the fruit cellar, deep in the earth then, as she was now, in this deep hell of color and corruption.

She backed away from the gurney, taking slow steps, to show she still defied him, did not flee him. She tried to face him down as she withdrew. She closed the door behind her and leaned against it, rubbing her wrist to erase that grip it still remembered. Karen stood in perfect silence, all subterranean sounds were gone.

It seemed impossible to tread the swollen blossoms of the corridor's carpet, but she had to walk out of this nightmare. She lurched and staggered, till her legs came back to her. What festering wound had been revealed in herself? For the first time in her life, she had hallucinated. What had been torn in her brain, to bleed madness into her thoughts? Dad was finally gone, but was it only to leave her forever damaged by the booze he'd cursed her with?

No one appeared in the corridors, the Haitian's gleaming desk stood empty. She stepped out into the last light of the day and was glad, the hugeness of the city around her a balm. Glad to be above-ground, as if the city might erase that room from her mind, the growl of traffic replacing its awful silence. Standing down there in that room, death's antechamber, confronting what she had confronted . . . after all, who would not have gone a little crazy?

"Karen Fox," she said with quiet determination, "is going to be all right." But please dear Jesus—she started, still unsteady, across the parking lot—how could that be her last vision? Dad in his spectacular death, printed on her mind's eye. His crime against her scorching her heart. If she did not find strength and defiance somewhere, she would come away even more broken, even more crippled.

The door of a white pick-up opened as she passed, one of those new oversized brutes, and out stepped a tall, lean man in a deputy's uniform. A clipboard and shades, even in the declining light. As he moved to intercept her, Karen had a qualm of premonition.

He confronted her and took off his shades. "Hello, Karen."

"Marty Carver." A gulf of years had just been bridged. Marty's hair and his tufty eyebrows, like two vertical brush-strokes, were dulled to ginger from the red they'd been in high school. The plump mouth, still smug, was set in a chin a bit squarer now, somewhat pouchier underneath.

"Are you on an official mission, Marty?" Karen noticed that his armpatch said GRAVENSTEIN COUNTY SHERIFF. He *would* have stayed in their hometown and he *would* be a cop. "You're a long way from home here."

"I've got some errands of my own, but I'm here for you too. This is kind of a personal gesture, Karen. I called to find out when you'd be here. You didn't show yesterday, so I stayed over. I wanted to let you know personally about the Medical Examiner's Report."

"You mean the autopsy findings?"

"That's right. It's a sad thing of course, but I thought you'd be reassured to know that there was no foul play. Definitely a suicide. GSRs on his right hand."

"And those are?"

"Gunshot residues." He showed her some stapled sheets on his clipboard.

She noticed the signature. "Dr. Harst filled this out?"

"He's been our County M.E. for fifteen years now."

"Of course. He called me about Mom, before." Army buddy Harst, weeping on the phone three nights ago, had been a comrade-in-arms whose life Jack Fox had saved in combat. Marty was also Dad's old friend, though a generation younger. As a teenager, Marty had, in some wordless way, idolized Dad. Dad's tour in Viet Nam, and afterwards in Central America, seemed to have something to do with it. Marty had done a lot of hired work in the orchard throughout his and Karen's high-school years, though at school he'd never pursued any personal acquaintance with her. But near the end of their senior year he'd begun making a big deal to Mom about wanting to take Karen to the prom. Poor Mom knew that no one else had asked her daughter, that her daughter was set on not going at all. In the end Karen accepted for Mom's sake. She brought a flat of bourbon in her purse and got rowdy on the dance-floor. When Marty managed to get her out to the parking lot, she smashed the windshield of his car with her bottle.

"Well, thank you, Marty. It was very thoughtful of you. But you know, there was never a doubt in my mind that he killed himself."

This made something flare in his eyes and Karen realized she'd meant it to. Did he guess her accusation of his hero? Had Marty maybe, even as a kid, sensed her father's crime?

"You know," he said, "I wonder, Karen. After your Mom died, I made it a point to call and check in on your Dad every couple weeks. Did you ever call him once that whole three years? I didn't get the feeling that you ever did. I got the feeling you were just too busy with your lesbo friends out in San Francisco to give a damn."

Karen smiled. For a couple years after leaving for the coast forever right after high school, Karen had now and then come back to visit Mom. Always at some diner in the county seat, Gravenstein, twenty miles from the orchard, but still within Mom's driving range at her timid, invariable thirty-five miles an hour. Karen had brought an early lover on one visit. Both had more than a few drinks in them. Marty was there with some scared, docile girl. Karen had taken her lover to his table and introduced her at length.

"Hey, Marty. You just don't get it. I haven't called, I haven't talked to my old man for *twenty years*. Do you understand what I'm saying?" She had laid the ugly truth right there, just one question away from good old Marty, if he dared to ask it: Why not?

Real anger now in his yellow-brown eyes. But he didn't dare. Put his shades back on. "Your life, your choice."

"My life, my orchard." She was furious now, enraged he'd backed away, hadn't let her spit it out, and she grabbed the handiest thing, remembering how Marty had always loved the orchard. "You know, I think I'm gonna have some fun with that orchard. I think I might just burn it down tree by tree."

He didn't even nod. She'd got to him though, she could tell by the way he almost slammed his truck door closing it.

As he drove off, and she stood there waving after him ironically, it hit her. If Dad, with half his face, were not to out-face her, and drive her down into fear and pain for the rest of her life, she *had* to go into the house after all. Had to go back home and face it all again, till she had faced that bastard down and, once and for all, thrust him and his crime down into the earth, and finally set her spirit to mending.

AFTER MEETING KAREN, Marty killed some time in the city till Dr. Harst should arrive. A uniform meant something whatever jurisdiction you were in, and he drove like it. Smooth, peremptory, decisively claiming his space.

He liked the city's decayed old core. Lots of heavily-grilled mom-and-pops, run by ragheads and slopes. He liked immigrants—they kept their heads down and *worked*. They were usually easy arrests, too, and too poor for anything but Public Defenders, so they kept his production level high at the Gravenstein County Correctional Facility.

Why did winos like to camp behind dumpsters so much? Because they knew they were trash, Marty guessed. He could've gotten a ninety-day bit for public disturbance out of every one of these people. The city had too much real crime and the police, no doubt, had a harder time beefing their budget out here than Marty did back in Gravenstein. People in rural county seats knew each other and how things ought to be run. They worked together.

Marty wished he'd worn his civvies when he passed the porn shops. He'd had a good piece of Helen this morning, after the boy left for school, but you could never get it just right with Helen. If you tied the ropes too tight she'd start to whine and nag and break the mood. He was forced just to accept with his wife the more fictional degree of bondage and make the best of it. When he returned to the mortuary, it was dark. Among the four or five vehicles left in the lot, Dr. Harst's old dirty, battered, olive-drab station wagon had arrived. The doctor's big baggy profile was visible behind the wheel. His head was slightly cocked, as if he were watching something very distant.

The old man had gotten distinctly dreamy, since Jack Fox shed his mantle with a Last Supper of double-ought. Harst and Jack Fox went way back, to those jungles in Nam and Central America. My God, wouldn't *that* have been something! Marty honored them both for it, honored them still, but this was no time for dreaming. He and Harst had an appointment, a life-and-death matter.

"Hi, Doctor. How was your drive down?" Looking down through the window at him, watching, behind the thick glasses, those pouchy old eyes, yellowish like tarnished cue-balls, coming back from far away . . . .

"Hello, Marty. The drive was fine." Such a bleak little smile, saying that. The old man looked like a cartoon vulture; with his weak jaw, the puckers of his face flowed right down into those of his neck. A man who'd aged a lot more severely than his lifelong friend Jack Fox had done before his death. But Harst straightened and flashed a sharper smile. "It's time to join our friend."

They walked together toward the mortuary, Marty slowing his pace to match Harst's limp so that their advance was measured, almost ceremonial. This difference in their gaits made Marty realize what a crossroads this was for both of them. With Jack Fox in the earth now, the relationship between him and the doctor was going to change.

They pushed open the great front door and Marty slipped his shades back on: it felt right. Funereal.

The wide carpeted spaces were deserted. Beside the reception desk, a gurney gleamed, supporting a bulky blackness—a thermal body bag. They stood in the silence beside this plastic sarcophagus till Dr. Harst said, roguishly, addressing the body bag, "We'll have to haul ass on this, won't we, Jack? Have to get you back while the frost is still on the pumpkin, so to speak?" And laughed. Marty resented the old man's impiety with this powerful corpse. Envied it too. Harst, so much closer to him, could get away with it.

It was strange to wheel Jack Fox out under the big-city night. Rolling him across the asphalt, the body bag seemed like Jack's spacesuit for crossing an alien wasteland, on his voyage to reach the dark earth and deep roots that were to be his new mansion.

"I've cleared the back of my wagon—" Dr. Harst began.

Marty's nostrils flared at the sight of that old wreck. "My truck bed's better, Doc—we can secure him better there." The doctor was so dreamy-clingy about Jack Fox's mortal remain . . . and might have thought so himself . . . for he acquiesced at once. They bungied Jack Fox snugly in Marty's truck bed.

ALL THE WAY back out to Gravenstein County, Dr. Harst's eyes clung to the only love of his long life, a cocoon in a truck bed that was dancing through traffic ahead of him. More than once those red-rimmed eyes leaked tears. Oh Jack. How long we have shared the same world! It was everything, for me.

The doctor's grief at the loss that lay wrapped in that bundle filled his heart. He was in mourning. But in another part of Dr. Harst's mind there was calculation and the ant-like first tickles of fear. Now that Jack had moved on, was the doctor's own term near?

But, as always, Harst forgot calculation and came back to his tears. Forty-five years of almost hopeless love. At least there had been their friendship, unfaltering friendship.

Dr. Harst had seen Marty's distaste for this old station wagon. He'd never know the reason the doctor still drove it. It was because Jack, with the power upon him, had taken him into the back of this old wagon— pulled off on a dark country road—and sodomized him there, for the last glorious time in Dr. Harst's life. Again, his tears flowed.

IV

The motel room offered one towel, one micro-bar of soap, one plastic glass, one blanket, one dim TV that got three channels, and one picture on the wall above the TV—a trite sad-clown print, very dusty. Except for the tiny nook of the bathroom, this room was very near as bare and square as Dad's room this afternoon.

She hadn't chosen the motel with this penance in mind, but instead for the liquor store one block away. A brisk walk down a boulevard of sleepless traffic, a brisk walk back, the crisp fracture of a half-pint's seal as you twisted its head off . . . and then solace.

Karen lay and sipped and watched the news with the sound off, the blow-dries making their pretty faces—how long now? Soon it would be too late to call Susan. She had to call Susan, but sipped again from her spiked Seven-Up and put it off. From time to time she glanced up at the clown print. When it hung too long at the periphery of her vision, the vague smeared face hinted at a more dreadful one. And as she watched, her fingertips traced her wrist. She should not be drinking. Not ever again. Because her wrist which had been gripped . . . was sore now to her touch. Her wrist which *she* must have gripped. Her wrist which *she* had gripped . . . though she so clearly remembered both her hands resting on the chrome rail of the gurney when that cold clench had had melted every nerve in her body.

Except, of course, an alcoholic "clearly remembering" was an oxymoron. She should not be drinking. Not ever again.

The thing was, there was still tomorrow, and the orchard, and the house to go into, and what she had faced in the mortuary had settled nothing, had laid no ghosts. The thought of going into that house was as frightening as it had ever been, going in and staying there. And she had to stay there without drinking, facing everything and beating it cold, if she was to free herself at last and forever. So she should flush this bourbon and start not drinking here and now.

But she took another pull of bourbon and wryly thought that perhaps the real reason for her drinking was, if she ever got totally sober, she would finally realize she could never quit drinking . . . .

Must call Susan or drive herself crazy. She dialed. It was picked up so quickly, Susan must also be in bed, snatching the receiver from the nightstand, "Karen?"

"Yeah, hon, it's me. Calling from the land of the dead and the dead-tired." Trying to take the edge off things, sound amused about her mission.

"You saw him, huh?"

"I saw him. He—" a giggle rose up in her "—he's a lot *shorter* than I remembered him."

She could hear Susan trying to join her laughter, but not really succeeding. Susan would be waiting to get past the bravado and closer to her lover's pain. It irritated Karen. She didn't *want* Susan to get closer to her pain.

So she added, abruptly, "I know I mentioned it before and said I wasn't going to, but I think I *do* have to go back to the place, deal with it face to face. A couple days, maybe, is all I'll need . . . but I have to. I'm sorry."

"Hon," Susan began, striking a note that gently urged they get to the heart of their feelings. This was a flash-point between them. How angry Karen had let it make her in their earlier days. But Karen had learned since then how wrong an angry answer was. "You've got to forgive me, Karen. I've got to say this. Will you let me?"

"Sure. It's nice just hearing your voice."

"You shouldn't *do* this alone! Move back in there alone! You don't need to. Please let me be there with you and help you through it. You were defenseless when you lived it; now you have an ally."

Karen imagined it: she and Susan bedding down together in the dark of that house, Susan's lovemaking voice singing out in the silence of those rooms, those halls.

"Sue, if I can't do this alone, it's not *facing* him. Not by *our* rules. And he'll never leave me then. He'll just keep eating me hollow. But maybe, after just a little while, maybe things will look different . . . ." Thinking to herself that maybe even this was too much to be yielding and with half her heart whining *Yes! Be with me. I can't go in there alone!*

"*Your* rules? His and yours?"

"Don't ask me to make sense, Sue. It's just that to face it I have to relive it and I lived it alone. Mom just refused to know."

". . . You'll call me tomorrow when you get there?"

"Tomorrow afternoon, yes. Tomorrow afternoon or tomorrow night." She might not be up to talking to Sue right away. She was damned sure going to arrive there in broad daylight, though.

AND SHE DID. It was in the blaze of noon that her tires sizzled up the gravel drive again. And, amazingly to her, she was bone-sober. She took her foot from the gas and let the truck coast to a stop, confronting the house once more. Sitting bemused, Karen was amazed by what she had just accomplished. Waking before sunrise, she'd jumped out of bed, peed, washed, and changed, flung her things in the duffel, the duffel into the truck and roared onto the freeway.

It was *whoosh* all the way. An off-ramp down to a liquor store just ahead? *Whoosh*. It sank behind in a blur. Pure onrush had kept her panic bottled. (*You can't go there sober! You can't go in there with your mind naked!*) But now here she was, sober in fact.

What had she done? Had she lost her mind?

Momentum. It was her only hope. She flung her door open and surged from the truck. Jumped up those steps (worn round-edged by the years) up into the Stonehenge shadow of the massive porch roof, her key already out. She stabbed it into the lock like a dagger, shouldered open the heavy-boned door, and plunged into the dimness where armchairs, armoires, tables, door-frames, crowded her eyes with their ancient, intimate anatomies, sending through her a ghostly rout of childhood days and nights.

All urgency vanished. She stood there accepting what had dawned on her yesterday: that she had already been living here all along, had never lived anywhere else. All the fear and pain and ancient sweetness that breathed from every door and wall and chair around her now, had been the air she breathed every day of her life.

Moving slowly, she began to engage the place. Downstairs first. She pulled back the curtains, opened all the blinds and windows. Checked the closets, meeting in the hall closet a twelve-gauge shotgun propped in one corner, not surprised that Dad would have more than one, as the police must have the one he'd used on himself.

The kitchen, its sunny utility porch . . . . These were Mom's domain and brought Karen warmer memories. Her big stainless steel sink was on the porch in her canning nook with its worktable and shelves of jars that breathed out an aura of luscious jams and jellies. And here by the pantry door was her chopping table, its whole top a heavy cutting board which whispered a breath of tomatoes and onions and beef, precursors of Mom's stew.

It was harder to go upstairs, to those bedrooms and closets. She did little more than look into Mom and Dad's bedroom and her own, but in Mom's sewing room she lingered. It echoed with all Mom's years of patient—maybe desperate—labor, as if she sometimes had to work down her fear of what might be happening to her daughter, stitch that fear down tight and fold it away. She had to have feared, at least . . . whether or not she'd successfully avoided knowing? All the silence Mom had suffered here. Pity filled Karen's eyes and she wiped them angrily with her knuckles.

She went back downstairs. The dining room, the living room, the hallways—all had become Dad's in the three years since Mom's death. There were even more hand-guns and rifles showcased on the walls than she remembered. There were other beefy hand-guns in unexpected drawers, like that of the telephone table and the silverware drawer of the dining-room breakfront. And booze of course, even more booze than before. Bottles of quality whiskeys and brandies occupied every sideboard and end-table, occupied the mantel over the big field-stone fireplace.

And here was the door, the one to the basement. Standing before it, Karen tried for some bravado and declaimed, "That dark-browed, masterful figure, that brooding, elemental man might now be gone forever from this earth, but Karinna Foxxe felt his presence still in the long, echosome halls and chambers of Foxxe Hall!" It fell flat. It didn't work without booze in her to bring it off.

She toughed it out and, though cold to the bone, she opened the basement door and stepped down, experiencing that same twinge she'd felt here so long ago as Dad shepherded her past this point: up there was Mom's kingdom, there in the kitchen with its warmth and good smells. Down here, where Karen had to go, was Dad's much darker world.

The basement was unchanged. When she was six, it had been a half-spooky playground, gloomy in the corners with spiders and racks of big weapon-like tools, but basically safe because there was Daddy at his bench, fixing things, making life work right for all three of them. When she turned fourteen it became a true dungeon, where Dad grotesquely punished and shamed her ignorant body with his own.

Still, one level deeper was a place that was worse than this: the fruit cellar. Its door was at the basement's far end. Why were the times he'd taken her down there the most frightening?

Do it and be through the worst.

She opened the door, switched on the one yellow bulb, then sank down the steep wooden steps into the deepest part of the house. The close air was honeyed with preserves. The shelves of dark jars breathed a complex sweetness just bordering on spoilage. These jars had walled her on either side when she was sprawled beneath Dad's weight and though it was Mom who had filled them, there was no help from Mom in those moments and her bright jars just blindly stared at Karen, reflecting her fear.

But there was something else about this place that had made it the worst place of all. Something about its being down at the level of the roots of the orchard. As Dad rooted in her, she felt them all around her, just outside the buried walls, those millions of greedy roots reaching toward her like sharp, hairy fingers . . . .

Karen had come all the way home now.

Hello, again. It's me.

When she came outside the sun was already halfway down the sky. It shocked her. Well . . . night was just going to have to be faced. While the light was good, she'd explore the orchard, for the orchard itself was one of the witnesses to her long-ago destruction. This army of trees in which the house stood, their roots reaching beneath the house. The bigness of their silence had always been a part of the house itself for her, a part of its scariness at night when she was small.

She got in the truck and set it to rolling slowly down the lanes. The weedy, draggled trees looked best in this slanting light—burnished, bursting with foliage and fruit. Their battalions rode the gentle, down-trending slopes of the land. The whole spread sank towards its southern boundary. She saw it now ahead, down there near one end of the huge plastic-cocooned compost heap: Dad's shed, his study and distillery in one.

Maybe she'd been wrong. Maybe there was a worse place than the fruit cellar, though Dad had never taken her there in his shed. Karen had rarely even been inside it.

For a while she rambled left and right down the harvesting lanes, dropping southward a lane at a time, glimpsing the shed now and then through breaks in the trees, until she found the nerve and the anger to take the next turn straight down to it.

A faded plywood shed with a raked tar-paper roof. A big old 'fifties Chevy pick-up crouched under a shelter built off its side. That gray brute of a truck . . . . With a shudder—of fear, of course, but also fascination— Karen walked to the bangy old screen door. She pulled it open a few inches and let its spring pull it back to the jamb with a soft clap.

Way up there at the house on certain quiet summer afternoons, lying in the grassy yard where Dad's personal fruit trees grew, Karen could hear this screen door bang from almost half a mile away. Flopped on the grass with some comic books, Karen might be absorbed, only half hearing the far faint summery stir of the ocean of leaves around her. Mom was gone into Gravenstein for shopping and the girl, restlessly trying to get at the gist of one of those encyclopedic Superman thought-balloons, might be only remotely aware of the wide-scattered outbursts of birds or the wandering hum of a bee.

Then, far out across that sea of leaves, would come that remote tiny *flap-clatter* of this door. The minuscule distinctness of it, a micro-noise of wood clapping wood! This the child could hear as clear as thunder. Dad had gone down to the shed some hours ago. If he went down, he stayed drinking till dinnertime. Except some of those times when Mom was gone somewhere. Would she hear the microscopic truck next? Firing up to come up here?

. . . Yes, there it went. So faint to be so unmistakable! But already that young girl knew how quick its roar would grow as big as life, its tires come clawing to a stop at the yard's edge, Dad booming from the cab, "Karen, get over here to me! Double-time, girl!" And if she was not quick enough, he would grab her wrist and haul her up aboard . . . .

Half-consciously Karen touched her wrist and found again last night's tenderness, though lessened, it seemed. If only that memory of being gripped were fading, were not still so stark, like madness, in her brain. Of course, it was only memory she had felt in that mortuary room—the memory of what had happened here.

Only? What was the difference between a delusion like that and the full-blown DTs? Oh please, please don't let my brain already be that crippled by alcohol. Oh that son of a bitch. That cruel black boar.

She yanked on the screen door and shouldered the inner door open.

She was surprised by how well she remembered this interior, though it had all been so much neater, those few times she'd glimpsed it as a child. Dad's desk-and-armchair corner, with all its miscellaneous freestanding shelves and files walling it in, was now snow-drifted with papers, magazines, and books in sagging stacks. The other half of the space was occupied by the still. The benches and sinks, the trellises of copper tubing, the domed copper cookers, the cooling fans stationed along the coils, the little bunged kegs of oak—all looked orderly as ever, but dust-heavy cobwebs extravagantly festooned them.

She took a few steps towards the desk. Crowded with so much else, there was still a place on it for the brandy cannon, its muzzle aimed at a forty-five degree angle at the cobwebby roof-joists. A cut-glass howitzer that fired booze.

She turned back and stood looking out through the screen door. Dad's view.

As a child, most of Karen's visits down here didn't bring her inside. She would trot down across the acres in the late afternoon, important and pleased with her errand, admiring the gold light on the swelling plums. She would knock at the screen door and call, "Daddy! Mom says dinner is in one hour exactly."

From inside, his preoccupied, cheery voice. "Okay, Punkin! I'll be up!"

What had *happened* in those years that came after? Those years when he would step out of this shed and go up to find his daughter? She shoved open the screen door, stepped out, and let it clap shut behind her. And stood there looking up towards the house. You could just see the tops of Dad's prized brandy-trees in the back yard, the peaches and apricots under which his daughter lay reading. Because Dad, after the door banged, always stood looking for a moment, didn't he? Because there was always that uncertain interval between the far, tiny door-noise and the miniature engine-growl that followed it.

Yes, she was sure he had stood here, eyes probing that green skyline for her, for that faraway long-ago girl. Stood staring here and thinking . . . what? Could she ever know? Perhaps, if she could, it would kill her to know it. That brutal shit! He had murdered her heart here, buried it here so many years ago. Now all that she had was his sickness, but none of his reasons.

She snatched open the screen and slammed it wildly three times back against the shed wall, as if she could shatter it. Then she went back into the shed and flung herself down into Dad's big tattered leather armchair bought at some yard sale before Karen's birth. At

first she thought she was going to root through his
books and papers, search there for some fragments of
his thoughts, but she found she had eyes only for the
brandy cannon.

It was a long-spouted two-gallon jug of thick faceted
glass, notched to rest on an axle between two wheels of
carved wood. The neck of the spout was wreathed with
an almost indecipherably fine-cut design, something
with perhaps a dragon in it. It was filled only and
always—filled now—with Dad's own hundred-proof
apricot brandy.

Karen reached and plucked out the glass stopper. A
gust of Dad's breath stung her eyes and nose, soft and
stunning, a vaporous smack in the face. For an instant
his huge weight crushed down on her again, smothered
her smallness in that sweet stink of poisoned apricot.

"You really messed with me, didn't you, Cannon?"
Her voice was breaking, hot tears were sliding down
her cheeks. "You shot me full of holes." This was what
she had come here to face. Right here. To hell with
logic, resolutions. This was the demon she had come
here to wrestle.

No less than three dusty glasses stood near. She
plucked the least sticky one, polished it on the tail of
her Pendleton. She pressed the cannon's muzzle down
and poured it—a generous tumbler-sized glass—full of
gold. And she took it down in a breath, in three long
golden gulps.

V

"I'm heading home now, Dr. Harst—okay?" Fiona Billings, his clerk, poked her head into the morgue. Looking up from the dead Pakistani he was working on, Dr. Harst beamed her a look of kindly dismay.

"My goodness, Fiona, it's after six! You should have left an hour ago. Phil and Jed are long gone."

Plump Fiona scowled her pleased scowl. "Well, shame on them, then, with all this work you've got in." Last night a van of Pakistanis had hit a tree and four were now residents of the morgue. When Harst and Marty Carver had arrived after midnight with Jack's body, the Pakistanis were just being brought in. "At least you've got three of your reports typed up now, Doctor," she said. She worked from the tapes he made while performing the post-mortems.

"Fiona," he said, "you're an angel." Meaning it, too, feeling, with a rush of sentiment, how long and faithfully she'd worked for him. Wondering suddenly if his own long career here could really be nearing its end? "I'm going to check your time-slip very closely this month—I want to see plenty of overtime billed there."

"Oh, Doctor." She flapped a deprecating hand at him and withdrew.

The sound of a distant door closing announced her exit, then silence filled the building. Harst murmured to his mini-recorder, completing his observations on his subject's severe thoracic damage which included

the penetration of the pericardium and the heart itself
by the ends of two of the crushed ribs. That had been a
harrowing moment, pulling into the rear lot, with Jack's
body-bag in plain sight in the bed of Marty's truck, and
finding the station was like a kicked anthill. The meat
wagon and three sheriff's patrol cars, deputies standing
around talking, EMTs rolling bodies inside. Marty
parked a short way off and advanced aggressively,
keeping them away from his truck. But when he'd
talked to the responding officer—Bud "Burly" Babcock,
looking very ill at ease to encounter his Assistant Chief
Deputy here at this hour—Marty found the situation
was going to be marvelously manageable.

Pursuing Sheriff's Department policy of letting no
immigrant agricultural workers pass unscrutinized,
Babcock had "initiated a pursuit" when the van failed
to pull over for a tail-light violation. He indicated that
he "might have fired a warning shot" just before the
van hit the tree.

"You *might* have fired a warning shot? Let me see
your sidearm."

"I did fire one, sir. I already reloaded. I was, ah,
confused after the crash."

Marty let just the right rectum-puckering pause go
by. "Are you telling me this, Babcock, because you
think we might find a bullet in one of these men?"

"Sir, I fired in the *air*, I shot way high, I *know*—"

"Shut up. Just shut up." Marty pantomimed
deliberation, letting the moron's balls contract a few
more notches. "Have you filed your report?"

"No sir." Already the ox was feeling a stir of hope.

"I want it on my desk first thing in the morning.
Leave the warning shot out. If we don't find anything
in these bodies, we'll leave it that way."

"Thank you, sir. I just—"

"Just shut up. Leave us what ID you've got on these guys and all of you get out of my sight. And Babcock, even if this blows over, I'm not going to forget it. I'm going to be thinking it over and thinking *you* over."

So, when they were gone, Harst and Marty had installed Jack Fox in one of the freezer-drawers and locked it. And all day today, through the last ten hours, the doctor had felt Jack's secret presence in that freezer drawer, a hidden gravitational center around which his thoughts had orbited during his toil on the Pakistanis. Their dark bodies had seemed unreal, like phantoms, compared to the reality of Jack Fox hidden so near.

As he loosely sutured the thoracic flaps and turned his subject over on the stainless steel table, positioning the throat on the pillow-block to present the back of the neck, Harst imagined Jack to be sardonically smiling. Jack had been familiar with certain small chicaneries the doctor had practiced here, for their mutual benefit, over the years . . . .

This fellow had been the van's driver and, yes, he had what looked very much like a bullet entry on the cervical spine. When the scalpel had flensed away a bit of muscle, *voila*. The third cervical vertebra was shattered and more than half ablated. Plainly the work of a bullet. He murmured into his recorder: "Laceration of the neck and damage to the cervical vertebrae consistent with impact injuries sustained in the collision."

He clicked off the recorder and stood sharing an ironic after-silence with Jack. Very soon now, when Carver came down here, the doctor would see Jack again—for the last time in his life. His tears flowed once more.

Eyes blurred, he opened the Pakistani's drawer, picked him up, carried him over and set him inside. He had never concealed his strength from his assistants. Foolish pride, no doubt. A man near eighty, with orthopedic braces on his right ankle, who handled cadavers like a youngster carrying his bride across the threshold. Power. It craves to be known, hungers for the awe of others.

He wiped his eyes. Was this purely grief over Jack that racked him? Or was it also a selfish dread that his power—and his life—might soon end together?

No, Jack. No, my only love. You're gone and all that's left of me is desolation . . . .

And thus it was that Marty Carver, stepping into the morgue, found him weeping afresh, leaning on the autopsy table, choking out rusty sobs, and mixing his tears with the Pakistani's blood in the table's gutters.

"Dr. Harst." Harst turned and met the Assistant Chief Deputy's chilly smile, his barely-concealed disgust. Harst wiped his eyes on his sleeve, polished his glasses. As Marty started for Jack's drawer, the old man blurted harshly, "Don't get near him! *I'll* carry him."

"Suit yourself, Doc." And Marty had to marvel a little in spite of himself, watching this codger lift the bagged bulk from the drawer and hinge it at the waist across his shoulder—all in one smooth hoist. The corpse, half-skulled and all, had to weigh two-thirty at the least. Harst faced him, one arm hooked over his burden.

"Jack Fox carried *me* like this, through a half mile of jungle, under heavy fire, and me with a thirty-cal round in my leg. You think you know some shit, Carver, but you *don't* know shit. You've got the keys—let's go."

The morgue occupied the west half of the County Building's basement floor, but the entire building was partly foundationed on an older structure. A big field-stone-and-concrete cider warehouse had been sited here, one of Gravenstein's first large municipal works, spring-ing up near the railroad line shortly before World War I. It was razed in the post-World War II boom, but the mas-sive walls of its big cellar offered support the architects of the County Building incorporated into their new struc-ture. The old civic center was found to occupy an ancient river bed. Riparian gravel underlay it, honeycombed, not far beneath, by major channels of the water-table.

Marty led the way through a door in the morgue's west wall. A short corridor past the darkened offices of Maintenance brought them into the utilities plant. Fuse-boxes, steam heaters, fans, generators, tool benches bulked in the shadows. Conduit, pipes and ducts branched up the walls and across the ceiling, like roots sent down by a forest of steel. Marty heard the implacable limping gait of Harst behind him and couldn't help glancing back at this gnome, face all wrinkles in the half-light, tirelessly bearing his great burden, the glint of his glasses accentuated, no doubt, by further tears.

From the utilities plant's far corner, another exit opened onto a dim-lit stairwell. At the foot of one short flight was a padlocked double metal door, cold to the touch. The chain rattled out of the doors' bars, Marty thrust both open, and touched a switch.

It was a vast space, feebly starred by bulbs along the girders raftering its concrete ceiling. The floor of the former warehouse—of much older, buckled concrete— lay twenty feet below. They descended an antique staircase of stamped black iron, the soft boom of their tread like distant funeral bells.

Marty hastened now as they set out towards the far wall, Harst lagging more with every step, hating the younger man's eagerness. Near the wall, the materials for their rite were already in place. Marty fired up a generator and switched on a pair of contractor's floodlights, spotlighting a portable compressor and a forty-pound jack-hammer against the wall. He turned on the compressor and over its stutter said, as Harst came up, "There's a spot right here—just like Jack said—that echoes when you tap it with a hammer. Took me less than fifteen minutes to find it."

To Harst, the Assistant Chief Deputy seemed to be babbling with excitement, with *greed*. Harst gently laid Jack on the floor. As Marty turned to say more, Harst reached out, seized his shoulder, and flung him sideways. Plucked his feet right off the floor, sent him tumbling over and over, punishing his knees and elbows on the concrete.

"SHUT YOUR FUCKING PIE-HOLE! SHUT IT!"

As stunned by the strength of the doctor's voice as he was by the strength of his arms, Marty gaped up from the floor. The old man towered trembling over him. "You smug little snot-nose, I read you like a book. You think your time is coming and mine is over. Maybe that's true, maybe it's not. But what you have no conception of, and what you *will* grasp, is the awe, is the *reverence* that you owe this man. This is a *great* man who has faced a Reality that you would shit your *pants* to face. From this moment, as long as you are in his presence, you will say absolutely nothing. You will humbly, mutely do your work like the acolyte, the altar boy you are, or I will snap your spine." Harst's voice had grown almost quiet. He pointed at the jack-hammer.

Marty rose and obeyed. He had his ankle-rig, a snub-nose .38, and a reflexive voice in him said *cap the old motherfucker and send him down after Jack* . . . but Harst's power had reminded Marty that he was working towards a kind of miracle here and that the old man was its only surviving gatekeeper. Marty's time *was* coming—he had provided enough brown victims to Jack Fox to pay his way, but until that way was opened, he must walk the line.

The jack-hammer's hysterical clatter filled the great chamber—how could the whole town not hear it?—but almost at once, deep cracks branched from the bit. He probed them here and there, and a shard of concrete vanished into underlying blackness. He circled the hole and larger chunks sank away . . . .

He killed the compressor. The floodlight fell through the ragged aperture and down the dank throat of a rocky fissure in the earth. A cold fetor of subterranean water welled up from it. He heard Harst, behind him, unzipping the body-bag, and stepped aside.

The old man approached the brink, Jack Fox's nude corpse cradled in his arms. The ragged-crowned head with its addled eyes and blown-in mouth rested against the Doctor's shoulder. Harst made as if to speak, but only a noise of strangled weeping came out of him. He kissed Jack's broken brow, knelt, and eased him head-first down the fissure.

Jack slid down . . . and got jammed in the earth just at the limit of the light's reach. A whisper seemed to rise from the narrow chasm. Jack's head turned, or sagged, his averted eye glinting as if he glanced below. The earth made a slick sound of acceptance and Jack Fox slithered down and out of sight.

VI

The sun set as Karen drove back up to the house, with a lidded jar of apricot brandy on the seat beside her. Out her open window, she declaimed, "How quickly the shadows gathered between the trees of the vast Foxxe estate! Soon the crickets' song would start to rise, leaking up here and there at first, like some strange subterranean gas, till the sound of night would be everywhere, chirring, chirring . . . ."

Karen laughed, delighted with her eloquence, her anesthesia. She parked at the side of the house, got out and looked up at it. The smooth eroded siding was, as the light turned violet, as expressive as wrinkled skin. And how wonderful to see it through glass like this, through the thick membrane of brandy. There was pain in every eave and molding, there was unbearable defeat in the gable-darkened window of Mom's sewing room up there . . . but Karen could laugh! She could shake her fist at it and mock it in the prose of a bodice-ripper.

Still, once inside, she felt her buoyancy colliding with the weight of all the dark rooms around her, all the years they held. So she went straight to the living room, put her boombox on the mantel and cranked up Bonnie Raitt, then set to building a fire in the huge fieldstone fireplace.

She'd meant to roust some kind of meal from the kitchen, but the feelings in there were too complex. She wasn't hungry anyway, the brandy tasting rich as food. This, right here by the fire, was base-camp. She'd return to exploring the house tomorrow.

With the fire roaring, she lay on the couch with her paperback thriller, the Stones now thumping away, her toes sketching the beat as she sipped and turned pages. The phone rang. She'd forgotten all about Susan!

But it was some man, deep-voiced, asking for Mr. Fox.

"He died three days ago."

"Oh. I'm very sorry. I'm Kyle. We'd arranged last week to cut some of his trees into cords for him."

"Which trees?"

"This is . . . ?"

"This is his daughter."

"Oh. Well, I'm sorry. Very sorry. It was a grove of oaks in your northwest corner, near the highway?"

Karen had played there. It was her special "forest" at seven and eight, wild and druidical, not like all the tame plum trees in their rows. It was where she and a girlfriend might "hike" to on a Saturday afternoon, with doll-dishes and real lunch in their backpacks. Dear Dad had done it to her out in the trees now and then, but never in her play-forest. Too close to the road, no doubt.

"You said your name was Kyle?"

"That's right."

"Hi, I'm Karen. Listen, I guess he didn't want those oaks, but I do. But there are some trees you could cut, some fruit trees in the yard. They'd make lower-grade firewood, but there must be seven or eight cords in them."

"Well, they'd still go for ninety a cord and if I could get that many, I could leave you three cords and still do fine."

"So when can you come? I basically just want them gone."

"Not for two or three days, Ms. Fox. Could we say Sunday around eight, just to be safe?"

"That would be great."

"Okay, then. Thank you. And please accept my . . . sympathy."

"Thanks, but none needed." She hung up wondering why she'd said that. It was saying a great deal, really, to a stranger. Remembered Mom telling her when she was small, "When someone calls, you say, 'Who's calling?' and after they tell you, say, 'How may I help you?' You don't start telling them your business." The recollection was piercing, a sweet touch of Mom's voice. Why was Mom so little in her memory?

Dad tyrannized Karen's memory, as his spirit tyrannized this house. Where in it now could she still feel Mom's sweet and concerned presence, the way she could feel Dad's lurking everywhere? Her eyes went to the breakfront in the dining room where, above heirloom dishes, a photo of Mom as a young woman looked out the glass door, but faint moonlight from the dining room window hid her image behind its reflection.

Well, if Karen started uprooting Dad, maybe Mom would . . . start coming back out. A nice first step this, converting Dad's precious brandy trees to firewood. His pet orchard in the back yard, whose fruit went down to his still. Start with those. Bit by bit she might do it, dig him up and throw him out for good.

She jumped up and began to dance. Dancing, she heaped split after split of cured oak on the fire. She danced over for a hit of brandy and her Ry Cooder disc, danced the disc back to the machine and popped it in, and set to boogying all over the room.

Karen could rock. She strutted, bucked, and swooped. She raised up and testified. She danced through the kitchen, out the back door, and raised her jar in salute to the brandy trees standing in darkness. "Say goodbye to your parents, Baby Brandy!" She drank a prodigious toast and danced back to the fire.

Disc after disc she danced in front of the roaring fire, till her body's movement seemed far, far away, amid the thud of the music more and more remote. And there was her friendly old sleeping bag spread on the floor near the flames. She dropped to her knees and fell into it.

SHE STOOD NAKED in the downstairs bathroom, in front of the mirror. Deep night was outside the window, the big house around her brimful of dead silence, and here she stood, both her hands squeezing her breasts till they ached, her eyes staring into themselves in the mirror. Her breasts hurt, she wasn't dreaming. This self-caused pain had brought her full awake.

Her hands stroked down her flanks, slid behind, and covetously traversed the curve of her buttocks.

She said to her reflection, "Nice tits. Nice ass. Come on. I've got something special I want you to swallow, bitch."

Her smile was playfully cruel, not a trace in it of the terror that was freezing her, icing her solid from crown to sole. She watched herself give herself a wink, then turned and sashayed with a hooker's gait out of the bathroom, down the hall, past the living room, butt still switching grotesquely, into the short hall before the front door. Yet, within all this movement, Karen hung bodiless, an icy axis of fear unlinked to the prankish body that carried her.

This body opened the drawer of a lamp-table near the front door and found a prize. Took it out—a massive,

blunt-nosed revolver, a .357. "Off to the dining room!"
she crowed. "Let's eat!"

Sashaying into the half-dark of the dining room, she sat
in Dad's old chair at the head of the table . . . and set the
revolver down to make a comic production of pulling the
chair up comfortably to the table, like an eager gourmand
settling in for the feed. Then Karen took up the gun again
and turned the muzzle up towards her face, lacing the
fingers of both hands around the back of the grip, hooking
her left thumb across the trigger and her right thumb on the
hammer. Karen could see plainly the domed slugs nested
in the four exposed chambers.

"And now," she said cheerily, "you degenerate little
bitch, *bon appétit!*"

She leaned down and took the two inches of the
muzzle in her mouth, while inside she thrashed with a
frenzy that didn't stir the least muscle of her body. Her
most extreme will could move no more of her than her
eyes, which she raised to the breakfront across the room
and found within the moonlit glass her mother's face,
visible after all. She looked helplessly at the deep-set
darkness of Mom's eyes, at Mom's young lips, parted
as if about to speak . . . .

She cocked the hammer with a sharp meaty click
and squeezed the trigger home. When the hammer
slammed into the cartridge her bladder let go as her
terror, in a surge, reentered the circuits of her body,
convulsing her, toppling her chair backwards.

Gasping, she found it was herself who drew these
breaths, that her limbs were hers again. She got to her
knees and knelt over the pistol on the floor. Reached
for it, recoiled, then forced herself to seize it.

Her legs shaking badly, Karen stood up, horror
and rage sputtering in her like a wet flare. Releasing

the gate, she swung the cylinder out. Six rounds, the chambered one pitted by the firing pin.

Lurching at first, still unsure of her power to act, but moving at a dead run by the time she crossed the kitchen, she sent the back door crashing open, and took aim at Dad's brandy trees. Speed-fired the pistol empty.

Five muzzle-flares geysered, five thunders merged into one and left her ears deaf and keening with pain.

Her flame-scared vision clearing, she broke out the cylinder again and emptied it on the porch. Five empty casings and one unfired round, dimpled by the pin.

Long afterwards, Karen lay in her sleeping bag, holding that round. The windows were just beginning to gray. A few hours ago she'd guzzled more than a quart of hundred-proof brandy, yet her body was as pure and sober as a child's. She'd never felt so clean of booze. The monster that had filled her had purged every molecule of it. The monster was Dad, the monster was alcohol, the monster was *her*, when she drank and let Dad in . . . .

She'd shot herself in the mouth with the brandy cannon to make some kind of discovery and now she had made that discovery, not foreseeing that the price of it was supposed to be her life. Because of that long, long chance—one in a thousand at least!—of a dead round, she accidentally still *had* her life. She had her discovery as well: that drinking was a hurt she did herself in homage to the hurt Dad had done her. A whiskey sour was a glass of Dad. And now that Dad had vandalized himself, a glass of Dad was a glass of Death.

Karen sighed out a long shuddering breath. She tenderly gripped that cartridge as, long ago, she had gripped her stuffed rabbit, and settled down to sleep.

At last! At long, long last! She could quit drinking.

She sank into a feeling of deep solace, the feeling . . . here suddenly was more lost memory. Precisely the feeling of snuggling down into Mom's arms, for a nap, when she was small. She remembered Mom's eyes, staring from that photo just before she'd squeezed the trigger. So . . . Mom was here, too.

VII

Awaking in the late afternoon, Karen gingerly re-entered her body, cautiously hefted her limbs. No trace of last night's unearthly tenant, no alien will in her muscles. That tenant had been pure booze and her own sick heart. Absent booze, that tenant was no more.

Still, she stood stretching timidly at first . . . .

Outside the living-room windows stretched her new horizon of plum trees, all of them heavy with ripe fruit. It vividly came back to her, just how it had felt, when she was six or so, to look out these windows and watch Mom and Dad when they joined the pickers in the harvest.

Up on their three-legged ladders, filling their hip-sacks with plums, while everywhere among the trees there were other ladders, and hats bobbing amidst branches, and crates on the grass filling up with purple fruit. What a glorious bright business it had all seemed! By the time she was eight they were letting her help and by the time she was ten, letting her up a ladder.

Not long after, though, her parents stopped joining the pickers. In his fifties, Dad began spending more time reading in the shed. He was still physically powerful and did everything necessary around the orchard, but no more than that.

Karen must put her hand to this place, must treat it as she willed and drive its ghosts back into the ground.

She would mess with those plum trees, pick some of them. See if Fratelli's was still operating in Gravenstein and might give her a few bucks a flat.

There was bread in the pantry, old, but toastable. She made toast and coffee, ate greedily, enjoying how the house felt simply like a house. A place where she planned a day's work, a place she could change any part of she chose. Eager—with the sun declining—to be outside, she almost forgot to call Susan before rushing out.

Karen was glad to get their answering machine, to make this quick. "Hey hon, sorry for not calling, it was . . . overwhelming here at first. But listen, it's going well now. I feel like I've crossed a line. It's going better than I hoped. I've got to rush out before dark. I'm gonna pick some plums! I love you. I'll call you."

THE BIG SHED, they'd called this, the roof's rafters twelve feet high. The picking ladders covered one whole wall and the others were hung with long-handled pruners and branch saws, the props also leaning there in standing stacks—notched planks for supporting branches getting too heavy with fruit. Packing flats were stacked on one end of the long central bench. The cardboard separators, dimpled like egg cartons, were there, too. Karen still liked the feel of this big interior, its dust-motes shot with rays of late sun through gaps in the siding. It felt full of a benevolent, earth-loving energy.

A pouch on her hip, some flats and separators, some parrot-beak shears for all the wild twigs and suckers—she brought these out to the nearest tree and went back for the ladder. Despite having years of experience carrying extension ladders hooked on her shoulder, she found the picking ladder, which flared at the base, a more awkward matter and was running sweat by the time she had set it, its third leg slanting through the bristly branches, and finally climbed up into the tree.

Karen kept on sweating after that, a good two hours and more. Wherever she leaned in, she was assailed by ear-poking, eye-poking, mouth-poking twigs. You thought you saw them, then *poke*—there was another one you hadn't seen. Her relationship to the tree quickly became one of attack and counter-attack, and repeated assaults with the parrot-beaks. Each time she climbed down with some plums, she stood in a litter of twigs and her tennis shoes trod a muck of fallen fruit mouldering in the deep weeds. Each time she re-set the ladder, she fought a new battle with the clippers, the smell of decay floating up around her.

When the sun set, there were four flats of plums to carry back into the big shed. And, under a sky half rose, half violet, she was glad she'd stuck with the struggle. She felt sweat-drenched and purged, felt so much herself, with the night coming on.

She'd get up first thing tomorrow. Could pick *Dad's* special trees in the yard, yeah—peaches and apricots should fetch more than plums. Go into Gravenstein in the afternoon with seven or eight flats. See how the town had changed.

Time for a shower. What the hell, she'd rinse down right here under the hose . . . . A little afraid of that bathroom at night, are we? Well, so what? Take things at your own pace, get your mind back, get strong.

Dropping her clothes on the ground, turning the hose onto her scalp, Karen sent cool water spiraling down her nakedness. Wonderful, this garment of water. She stood wearing it, stroking it on her skin.

She carefully wrung out her hair and scraped the wet from her skin, watching the dark just beginning to congeal around her. Suddenly it seemed terribly blatant, terribly reckless of her, standing naked in front of the trees like this. It seemed the whole two hundred acres, and everything in them, beheld her, *discovered* her there in its midst.

She shook her fist at the orchard and carried her clothes into the house. A nice clean T-shirt and jeans. Hot tomato soup, more toast, and a dish of plums.

Next, another fire. The night was cool, but it was really the movement and the noise of the blaze she wanted most. Karen settled into the couch with her thriller.

The story seemed terribly thin, but that was okay. She clung to the sketchy characters, their faint voices and unlikely actions, while underneath hearing and feeling the house around her, its shadows and silences testing her calm. This was to be expected. She would conquer the place one night at a time, by enduring it, defying it, coldly sober—

What was that she was hearing? Hard to separate from the fire's low noise at first. Far out on the drive . . . gravel crackling.

Dad. His truck rolling in from a night drinking in town, Mom out of the state, visiting her sister . . . .

Realer possibilities followed this deep-buried reflex of fear. Marty Carver, on some nasty personal errand. Or more likely that Kyle, a big-sounding man, laying the courtesy on thick, while realizing that now there was only a woman here, a woman alone.

An engine, drawing nearer, then shutting off just out front, as Karen pulled open the hall closet, plucked out the shotgun she'd found. She worked the slide and a shell sprang out. She retrieved it and threaded it back into the magazine as feet mounted the porch steps— thank god that old son of a bitch had at least taught her how to handle weapons.

But the knock on the door was delicate and the voice—calling, "Karen?"—was Susan's. In her relief, Karen pulled the door open with the shotgun still clutched in one hand.

"Karen, I'm sorry, but I just had to—" and then she took in the shotgun. Karen laughed, standing it in the corner, and wrapping her arms around her beautiful russet lover.

"Country living, sweetheart. I sit on the porch with my corncob pipe and the scattergun in my lap!" She held Susan at arm's length and looked at her. Susan smiled back, relieved at her welcome. Still half in the porch shadow, her faint freckles were darker. With her petite sharp chin and her sleeked-back tarnished-copper hair, she always struck Karen as one of those thrusting, searching small mammals, taut and graceful, a mink or marten . . . so alert to Karen's moods.

Remembering Susan's opening apology, Karen also remembered, with shame, those drunken times she had slammed doors in her conciliatory lover's face. "We've fought so much, hon, and I'm so sorry for it."

Susan smiled. "*You've* fought so much."

"*I've* fought so much, oh yes, but I'm so glad you're here."

Susan grinning now. "So why aren't you inviting me inside?"

Karen laughed . . . and yet still did not step aside to admit her. Felt the weight of the house at her back, holding her in place like a barrier. Or was it her own will, holding back the house's weight from falling on her lover . . . ? She forced another laugh. "Come on into the haunted manse."

Once Susan was inside, Karen felt instantaneous relief, felt her lover as a shield, an unclouded spirit that all the past here, her fears and imaginings, could not pierce. "A tour!" she proclaimed. "A grand tour! You will note the predominant decorative motifs—firearms and booze . . . ."

She saw every room over Susan's shoulder now and though the downstairs bathroom still gave her a qualm, she found everywhere a wonderful freedom from fear, everywhere saw a sad place where someone else had suffered long ago, a place she herself might soon lock up behind her and leave forever.

Susan responded cautiously, registered but never uttered a word about the gloom, the claustrophobic aura that filled this place, spoke only of Mom's touches here and there. Up in her sewing room Susan said, "You must have liked it up here. Did she ever teach you how to sew?"

"She tried, but I was never that interested. I did like to be up here, though, when I was small, watching her work. All this—" she touched the cabinet's miniature drawers of buttons, findings, needles, spools of thread "—seemed like treasure to me."

"I once asked my mother to teach me so I could sew clothes for my dolls. She told me it was peasant work— not in so many words, of course." They both laughed at their shared image of Mrs. Kravnik, a moneyed, oh-so-proper autocrat.

Down in the kitchen, more toast and soup, some canned green beans, strong coffee black, the way they both liked it, while Susan filled her in on the home-front. She had a week off from the law offices. Two of the gay contractors Karen worked for sent their sympathies, and one, DeWitt, a check from her last job. Bonnie and Letty, Karen's partners in Tongue 'n' Groove, had also sent their love and were going to give her a cut from their new remodel job with DeWitt.

While Karen did the dishes, Susan was slicing some peaches from the trees out back. "Want some?" she asked Karen.

"No thanks."

Susan cracked the seal on some of Dad's tonic water, splashed out half a tumbler, took a bottle of vodka from the shelf, and added a couple inches to the tonic. Susan drank wine occasionally. Maybe a cocktail at parties. Karen cocked an eyebrow at her.

"Did you want some?" Susan asked her.

"Not right now." The many times Karen had quit drinking, she never said so, felt it jinxed the resolution. And now, how could she tell her lover *why* she'd quit? They went into the living room. Karen watched Susan sink into an armchair and take a long pull from her drink.

It almost brought tears to Karen's eyes. She understood this was an attempt to be *with* her in her time of trouble. Sweet Susan, so moderate and abstemious, had resolved to abandon this long-standing separation between them, Susan standing outside Karen's affliction, exhorting her from the shore to come out of the whiskey river that carried them apart. Susan had decided that they would swim together and swim ashore together.

Karen bent to feed the fire and said, "It's nice to watch you have a drink and not have one myself. It's a novelty. It's . . . neat."

Susan laughed with pleasure, making Karen grateful and ashamed. Hadn't she just asked her lover to drink *for* her? Just like letting her into this house: standing Susan between herself and the demons in her heart. But that was just what her lover wanted to do. So . . . let her in. Let her help.

"Know what I've started doing? Picking plums. It's kind of fun. We could take some flats to town tomorrow. Maybe sell them."

"That sounds great! Count me in. Farmer Sue, at your service."

"Hoed a lot of rows, have you? Kicked a lot of cow-flop, back in old Mill Valley?"

And so they talked about Susan's mom and her latest phone call—from France, where she had gone on business. Susan mixed another drink and mimicked the formidable Mrs. Kravnik's latest exhortations that she go to law school, for heaven's sake, and do something serious with her life. Law school on the East Coast, of course, where the only good ones were (and where the unspeakable Karen-what's-her-name *wasn't*, of course).

Susan sipped, and laughed, and mimicked, and Karen laughed with her, and secretly sorrowed for her lover, this daughter who could always remember every word of her mother's criticisms.

They laid a pad of blankets on the rug, to sleep in front of the fire. Settling down, guilty Karen feared her generous lover, loosened by drink, would long for love's reward. They lay in one another's arms, kissing tenderly, Karen dreading, with each kiss, what more would be asked of her.

But even here, Susan's generosity shamed her. She sensed Karen's fear, even through her liquored languor. With a last kiss, she turned to snug her back into Karen's front. Soon, spoonwise, they slept.

VIII

"We're gonna whip some plum-tree ass, is what we're gonna *do*, Kare!" Susan felt great. She had never done anything like this before. Had never had a beer in the mid-morning, not long after breakfast. Had never helped carry two picking-ladders out into an orchard drenched with morning sun. Had never stood between her lover and a giant bully—and that's what this place, Karen's whole past, *was*—had never squared off with such a bully: *Put up your dukes, motherfucker!* Susan felt a nice glow from the beer, felt adventurous and more alive for Karen's sake.

"Steady as she goes, mate!" Karen laughed. "Now we plant this third leg here right amongst the branches."

This entire farm was the bully, a nightmare forest haunted by a dead ogre. This was the place where Karen's heart lived . . . always. No wonder she drank. But now she was here to help her—with the drinking and with cutting her way out of the forest.

Cutting was surely the operative term. They worked opposite sides of the same tree while Susan got the hang of it, then worked adjacent trees, Susan gung-ho to cut a wider swath. Her sweat ran and the clippers made her hands sore. Now, in the heat of noon, a beer seemed highly appropriate. She went and brought out the rest of the sixer in the cooler. Slipped one in the pouch of her picking apron, held one up to Karen before re-mounting her own ladder.

"Oh, not right now, thanks."

Susan recognized Karen's casual, noncommittal mode from the times she'd tried to quit before. "I'm an idiot! What am I *doing*?"

"You're a sweetheart. This is Beer-keg Fox here. It becomes second nature to offer old Fox brewskis."

"I *am* an idiot."

"You're my inspiration. Shut up and pick, darlin'."

And Susan did feel like her inspiration. Getting quite skillful at this work, it seemed to her—made those branchlets and suckers fly and each time she went down the ladder, laid new rows of gleaming fruit in the flats. She drained her second beer with gusto and climbed back up with a third in her pouch. She looked at Karen in the next tree over and willed herself to be a gift to Karen. An ally.

The sun was getting awfully hot, though. Wasn't this *autumn*, for Christ's sake? The smell of rot rose from the weeds and, with it, big bumbling flies, relentlessly molesting Susan for her sweat. From up on the ladder, the orchard looked more like an ocean, a perspective of green billows rolling away across the acres, dwarfing their labors.

What an awful place this was, to suffer what Karen had suffered. Susan thought of her own mother's oh-so-genteel form of abuse, her austere—no, *perverse*—denial of love. Whenever little Susan craved closeness, a simple, warm burrowing into love's arms, her mother found some mistake in her, some slovenliness, some violation of what a Young Lady should be. Some excuse to mask her void of love.

But how much more cruel to pour your hate into your child, to maim the organ of her love itself. No wonder Karen had to be half-drunk to make love, to attempt to make love. Now that she wouldn't drink, she would probably not even make the attempt, like last night. It crossed Susan's mind that if she were a man, she wouldn't be so shut *out*, could *enter* Karen's wound, and gently but insistently probe until she liberated that scarred and buried passion . . . .

Jesus, what was she thinking? Where did *that* come from? This whole place was sick. It seeped into your brain . . . .

Finding her bladder full, she climbed down, considered trudging back to the house, then pulled her jeans down and squatted in the lane. "Piss on this place," she said, feeling daring and slightly tipsy.

Karen laughed. "Amen to that," she said, looking down from her tree. "You wanna lie in the shade a while? Take a wee nap?"

"The hell with that!" Susan went back to work, a trace more clumsily than before. This was getting more tiring as the heat rose and conjured bigger and more numerous flies—flies and a dozen other breeds of bug the trees swarmed with. The clippers had raised ripe blisters on her palm, which popped. Her sweat stung them. The twigs, which she'd avoided more deftly at the start of her labors, started poking her face, as if counter-attacking from every side.

She grunted and toiled on. These trees—it was like wrestling with huge crabs or lobsters, scaly lower life-forms—the cut twigs yielded with a repellent succulence. They seemed to thrash as they fell and to twitch on the grass, like the sundered tails of lizards or rats.

Then, as she leaned slightly off-balance deep into the branches, something big moved, so close to her face it was out of focus. She flinched back and saw, inches from her eyes, a huge gold-and-black spider seizing a large moth that had just struck its web. With quick, darting movements of its obese abdomen—horribly sexual ass-thrusts they seemed—the spider bound the moth's wings tight, and pierced its head with its fangs.

Susan's revulsion exploded. She swung a blow with her clippers that tipped her off-balance and seized the ladder one-handed as she felt it topple. They came down together with a snapping of branches, Susan desperately extending one leg as they fell sideways. Her foot took the impact, her ankle awry, and buckled under her weight with a sickening crackle.

It WASN'T BROKEN, they decided. Seriously swollen and mottling with purple, yes. Excruciating to put her weight on, yes . . . but it would take her weight and with none of that grinding twinge that betokened a fracture. One of the closets yielded a cane, probably from Mrs. Fox's final, arthritic years. They applied some ice. Susan considered and thought that a glass of something might perhaps ease the pain. They finally settled on a Bloody Mary. Susan found it tasty and soothing.

She bent to stroke the hot eggplant of her ankle. It answered her heartbeat with echoes of pain. "You know what this orchard *really* needs, Karen? A forest fire." Said this devoutly—imagined, with bitter longing, the reptilian trees in flames.

"I think that's a swell idea, but let's sell it first. Come on, hon. While those aspirin kick in we'll scoot up to Gravenstein. Get meds, ice packs, Ace bandages. We'll sell some flats, too, and have some cheeseburgers."

Susan felt her habitual irritation at Karen's patch-it-and-truck-on attitude towards injuries. In Susan's Mill

Valley homeland, all injuries required the sacrament of a doctor's visit. She felt some irritation too at Karen's simple perennial faith in cheeseburgers as potent antidotes to all misfortune. But Susan mainly brooded on the thought that this whole foul place had *done* this damage to her in its spite. How right the Inquisition had been, to purge its demons with the stake and torch!

"That sounds great, Kare. Cheeseburgers. But could we drive around the orchard before we go? I haven't really seen it yet."

As they wound downslope in Karen's truck, the land's curvature slowly swallowed the house and sheds, and Susan felt herself in a sea of trees. And found it all a bit intimidating, really, the brute will and labor manifested by all these regimented trees, all this shackled, captive life. *Agriculture*. Look at it: an army of tamed trees. This was really Titan's work. Susan remembered her childhood fear of the troll in *Billy Goats Gruff*. Farmer Jack Fox was a monster just like that troll. That big, black-souled son of a bitch . . . .

"What's that? Compost?"

They had a view of a great worm-shape wrapped in black plastic and weighted with tires: a tube of compost fifteen feet high and stretching a full hundred feet to one side of Dad's still-shed.

"Why are those tires on it? I've seen that before . . . "

"Their weight keeps a tight seal on the plastic, keeps the heat in, it rots even faster."

"Boy. You could start a whole new farm on that much."

"And next to it there is the still-shed. Dad read there. And made brandy from those fruit trees back up in the yard. When the screen door of that shed slammed, I could hear it all the way up at the house . . . ."

Karen began telling about it, still meandering the truck through the lanes as she talked. Susan watched her lover's profile as she listened and saw that Karen could not quite believe she was saying these things out loud.

"Oh, Karen," said Susan softly at the end.

Karen swung them back upslope and shortly had them on the highway. After a visible hesitation, she said, "I think I understand what you're doing with this drinking and I love you for it. But hon, you don't have to drink *for* me to help me stop," saying this, she reached out and touched her lover's cheek.

"Hey, who says it's all about you? You always get to be the drunk and rowdy one. Asskicker. I'm little Miss Sweetness-and-Light. I keep our checkbook balanced and get you out of trouble. Maybe I like this. Maybe I just want to have some fun and kick some ass!"

A rusty laugh jumped out of Karen. "Girl, you may be kicking ass, but you sure fucked up your foot doing it."

Karen had really laughed. Sober. Susan blinked at sudden tears and thought: *Daddy Fox, I am gonna kick your ass. You're through hurting her.*

The highway to Gravenstein showed Susan a lot of countryside, twenty miles of it. The green life here was like a conflagration. Between the beef-lots and walnut orchards, everything was grass and wild trees to the horizon. Ivy clothed those trees, mistletoe studded them, and mosses and lichens bearded them. The undergrowth poured down both banks of every stream they crossed, as if stampeding for a drink. Here and there the vegetation was reclaiming clearings where decayed sheds, long-spined and roofed with shakes, buckled and sagged at the roof-beam, settling like supple-backed scaly old dragons into dense garments of blackberry vine. The dairy-farms, with their piss-rich hills of compost under the hot sun, packed a stench that was almost ethereal, the incense of a Natural Mystery, life's metamorphosis into organic soup.

And the roadkill! Animals in impossible flat postures flashed by. They looked like Cubist dancers, all their three dimensions, teeth, spines, tails ribs and paws, presented in a single plane. The highway was like a long narrow battlefield starred with red smears whose very species her eyes recoiled from determining.

"Boy, the country is so *real*."

"Rich, isn't it?"

"Hey! Are those *eagles* up there? They're so huge."

"Actually, sweetie, they're turkey vultures. Noble when aloft, but mo-fugly up close. Bald wrinkly red heads for rooting in carrion."

As they entered Gravenstein, Karen pronounced it "a lot bigger" than it used to be and told Susan what was new to her: outlying "townhouse" developments for the upper-middle, two new gas stations going in, new office buildings . . . .

"Lemme just hook through here for a look before the drugstore."

"I'm fine, Karen."

It was the older residential half of town, blocks sunk in big old trees, with overflowing gardens and root-buckled sidewalks where tricycles lay toppled. "Most of my friends lived around here. Girls I really liked. But when I went to their houses, I'd wear out my welcome with their parents, I felt so safe there. It was always hard to leave, get on the bus home."

They drove back to central Gravenstein to the drug-store and. in the store's parking lot, applied their medical

purchases. Susan stuck her leg out of the cab and Karen
bound it with the Ace bandage as snugly as Susan could
stand. "It'll cut down on the throbbing once you're used
to it. I'll get some ice for the pack at that liquor store."

"And . . . get me more beer. It helps with the pain."

A slight pause. "Beer it is."

Their next stop was Fratelli's Produce Emporium.
Near the tracks, in an older-looking district of shiplap-
sided houses and wooden power poles, Fratelli's still
thrived. They parked in its back lot. Outdoor produce-
stands under broad, pole-propped awnings adjoined
the big brick structure of the store itself, from whose
back door, as if they'd evoked him, stepped a narrow-
shouldered, big-middled man whose jet-black hair and
moustache were thirty years younger than his face.

"By God, old Fratelli's still clockin' away. No, hey,
just stay here with the ice on—"

"Using it's the quickest way to heal, how often have
you told me that? I wanna meet him."

The man stood at a kind of ceremonious attention as
they approached. Karen glanced at the Ranier can in Susan's free hand as she caned along, but Fratelli did not.
"Karen Fox! Shame about Jack. Whaddya got for me?"

"Mr. Fratelli. It's so good to see you . . . after so
long."

"You t'ink I was dead?" Mildly asked, but with no
smile.

"Never. This is my friend Susan Kravnik."

Only then did he look at her, the same calm, formal
face. "A pleasure. Whaddya girls got?" The question
sounded more searching to Susan the second time.
As if he'd heard something about them, was alert for
something. Susan smiled charmingly.

"Mr. Fratelli, what *would* we have?"

"Plums, Mr. Fratelli," Karen put in. "And I thought—" it seemed to strike her "—I could bring some apricots and peaches, if you wanted them."

"Plums I gotta lot of. For good . . . fi' bucks a flat. Apricots an' peaches . . . from Jack's brandy trees?"

Susan saw Karen blink. "Yes. The ones in the yard."

"Those, I don't gotta lot of. For good, thirty a flat."

"That's very generous." Karen sounded a shade more remote. "So, come take a look at the plums?"

"I trust you. How many flats?"

"Twelve."

Fratelli dug bills from his pocket, sorted among them. "Take eighty for you plums. B'tween fren's. My sympat'ies. Sal! Bring the cart!" He turned and walked back into the store.

Susan asked, "Is he always so . . . businesslike?"

"I remember him more chatty. But I was small then and he was younger."

"You don't think it's two dykes from Frisco that . . . stiffens him up?"

Karen laughed, but not like before. "I guess I wouldn't rule it out."

Sal rattled up with the cart. "Hey, Sal," said Karen. "You were this high the last time I saw you." Now bigger than his father, with some brawn on him, and livelier too.

"Hi Karen, who's your friend? What happened to her?" Big lips in a grin somehow conspiratorial, his eyes drinking them both in greedily.

Susan said, "I was practicing cartwheels and injured my foot against the ceiling."

He was giving them a goofy smile, just looking at them, not registering the joke. It crossed Susan's

mind he might be a little slow. Karen said, "Hey,
Sal, you think we look funny or something? Are you
memorizing us?"

"Huh? Hey, I'll get your flats. Bad bad news about
Jack, Karen. Really, really sorry."

Thoughtful pulling out of the lot, Karen said, "I
didn't even *know* Sal. He was like six the last time I
was here . . . . Hey, the Koffee Kupp's still open! If their
cheeseburgers haven't changed, you'll love 'em."

Susan did, in fact. Devoured two of them. Looked
fondly, as she sipped her beer afterward, on Karen.
"You've been so strong. You're facing so much. We
should do something just for fun."

"We should go camping," Karen said with a wry smile.
"Just to be on a piece of ground that isn't Jack Fox's."

"I say that's a great idea. Sleeping-bag cuddles! I
love camping."

Karen laughed more freely. "Dear love, you don't
know jack shit about camping, but I think I could make
us pretty comfortable. There's some beautiful places
down along the river."

THE SUN WAS just an hour from down when they got back.
And found a bulky blue pickup—decades old, and not
unmarked by ding and rust—parked behind Susan's
rented red rice-rocket. As they got out of their truck, a
man stepped into view from the far side of the house.
A wide guy in a faded gray flannel shirt, raising a hand
in greeting, coming forward . . . . an older guy with a
short, gray-shot beard, becoming wider as he neared,
appearing very solid.

"I'm Kyle, Ms. Fox—we talked on the phone? I'm
so sorry to drop in—I called but you were out. I had a

bid to make out this way and I wanted to grab a look before Saturday."

"It's totally okay, Kyle," shaking hands with him. "This is my friend Susan."

"Hi, Susan. I'm sorry to intrude."

"No problem."

"I also wanted to mention, Ms. Fox, that I just hired a helper . . . . so I expect we can be out of your hair in well under two days."

"Hey, whatever it takes, Kyle. Actually, we'll be gone camping when you do it."

"Oh." Susan thought he sounded pleased with the arrangement. "Where should we leave your cords?"

"Just pile them at the edge of the yard back there," said Karen. "I meant to ask you. How did you come to know my father?"

"I didn't. He answered my ad in the papers. I just spoke to him on the phone that once. Please do accept my sympathy." He had shaggy brows on a rawboned face with a lot of complex erosion around the orbits of his deep-set eyes. Somehow the word *sympathy*, coming out of this seen-it-all face, had an ironic ring to Susan. He offered his hand once more. Again she felt a callused palm and the gentlest of squeezes from an apparatus of hydraulic strength. "It was nice to meet you both."

IX

They were making dinner—or Karen was, while Susan sampled a Bloody Mary spiced with Louisiana Hot Sauce. She was enjoying the revelation that she was, actually, a person who could hold a surprising amount of liquor and function perfectly. "All I'm trying to say, Kare, is that I just get an uneasy vibe from him. Like he tells me he's sorry to intrude. Like, hey, I know you're gay and I'm not trying to muscle in here."

"Boy, are you over-interpreting. But suppose he was hinting that—isn't that just being sensitive?"

"More like being calculating. I felt a lot of very conscious self-containment in him. Like the way he always kept just the right respectful distance. And his voice pitched just so, like, I'm totally mild and non-threatening here."

"Susan. All these things from some slim guy in a suit, you'd like them. This guy looks strong and physical . . . it's just your upperclass distrust of the lower orders." Trying to jolly her a little.

"He *does* look strong. He looks skinny edge-on and a yard wide frontwards. Why is a guy that age in that kind of shape?"

"I sense that you're going to tell me."

"You have the same hunch I do. I think this guy's been in prison."

"Well, what of it? Two of the best framers I know have done time and come out smart and kind."

"See? I knew it. It crossed your mind too, didn't it?"

"Sure it did, after all my years in the trades? I thought there was a good chance of it and I trusted him anyway."

"Karen. I'm just trying to be the realist here. Let's just *entertain* the worst-case scenario. You hire two guys from *Deliverance* to come here while we're gone. They break into the house and discover a *fortune* in free firearms. They lie in wait for our return. They have some fun with us in the house for a while. Then they pop us, bury us and leave with the fortune, and there's no one to identify them. A good time has been had by all."

Susan was surprised to find Karen looking at her with something like concern. "Hey, Susie-Q. We'll stay here and camp afterwards, okay? They won't come into the house and we won't be worried, because dear old Dad taught me how to *use* these firearms. But, honey, don't let this place get to you. Drinking like you're doing and this place . . . they don't go together. The ugly vibes you felt are *here*, not in that guy."

After dinner Karen built a fire and got into her book. Susan recognized the tiredness that always overtook Karen on her first day or so of sobriety. Susan herself felt great, considering. She took her cane and started trying out Karen's theory that sprains healed faster the more you walked on them. From the front door, through the living room, into the kitchen, then back again—she caned. She got into it, found the pain lessening somewhat, the ankle accepting more weight. It could still be excruciating if she hit the wrong angle but, with just the right rhythm, she could move right along.

Back and forth she went, could do this indefinitely, it appeared. She liked, too, how it must break the gloom of the place for Karen, to have a life and motion for company. On her fourth or fifth turn through the kitchen, she noticed the shelf of brandy bottles.

She took one down. The white mailing label said only *Apricot Brandy*—written with a fountain-pen in handsome copperplate print. "The dead tyrant's private stock," she murmured. Smiled. "What was yours is ours now, old boy."

She found a corkscrew. The brandy poured with a satiny chuckle. Golden—blended with nectar, no doubt. The bouquet made her scalp tingle. One high-octane inch, down the hatch.

Its heat seemed to tendril through her whole body. Damn! She tested her weight on her ankle. It felt one whole notch better already. She left bottle and glass standing ready, then caned her way—with a certain jauntiness now—back towards the front door.

"Kare?"—as she passed the living room—"Would some tunes distract you? I'm getting into this. I need a beat."

"Don't overdo. How 'bout some Emmy Lou Harris?"

"Let 'er rip."

Back and forth. Got some upper torso boogie going, some sway in her gait, stopped sometimes on the downbeat to lift both arms and cane in hallelujah flourishes, winning sidelong looks and smiles from Karen. Back and forth. Every few circuits, she slipped some golden inches in the glass and slid those golden inches down her throat.

It became a kind of victory dance, the dead brute's poison her plunder, its fire tamed to healing heat. She walked a sentry's rounds. No ghost could pass to do her lover harm, her cane a club to tear its cloudy shape to harmless tatters . . . .

"Hon, come sleep. You need to rest now." Karen, she realized, was already nodding off, was waking herself to say this.

Susan shed her clothing on the floor, sitting on the couch to extract, quite smoothly, the hurt foot from its pant leg. "Your clothes, too, Kare . . . that's it, come on . . . just to lie close . . . just to lie down together as close as we can be . . . ."

But even nakedly entwined, Susan knew they could be closer yet . . . be so much closer still . . . knew that kissing Karen, kisses here and here and here . . . that these kisses were magical doorways, were entries into Karen's heart, entries through her tastes, her textures, into the great soft flame her body could become . . . .

At the same time she knew Karen was not present, was astray in this lovely body of hers, was lost in lonely corridors where outrages peered at her out of the shadows.

Susan could feel Karen in there trying to reach her, trying to bring this body into Susan's hands, into Susan's lips, this body full of love, instead of fear. Susan could feel Karen's failure in there, and her grief, as Susan reached her lonely climax. Karen had only her sad wish to give—and her tender struggle.

But not lonely, no, because now at least Karen was inside the circle of Susan's arms and nothing could touch her beloved without going through Susan's body first.

When Karen slept, then Susan allowed herself her anger at that hulking criminal who had haunted and poisoned her lover's heart for so long. Lay a long time hating this house, hating every plank and beam of it, every wall and doorway. And blamed herself. How could she have tried to take love from Karen here, where Karen's love had been gutted?

She got up silently and dressed, her ankle now hurting with a vengeance, an agony to work through the pant leg. In her rage at Jack Fox, her memory roamed his acres, seeking some purchase. She had only an image in mind, a weapon still lacking a target: in the big shed, on the ground by the wall where the chainsaws hung, she'd seen a big red gas can . . . .

She caned into the kitchen—it was agony to manage it quietly—to restore her mobility with some of the ogre's brew. Three . . . hell, five golden inches. Her throat seized them down and they worked like a charm. Her pain melted away as she put on her armor of fire against fear.

Oh, lord. Oh, yes. She smiled, was a functional biped again with some help from the cane. As she re-corked the bottle, the amber inch remaining winked at her. Suddenly, like inspiration, it came to her. An object for her anger.

The still-shed. The heart of the place, in a way. A fire, the only sufficient exorcism, would be self-contained there, nothing to spread to but a heap of compost. Then sell this place, pluck its foul roots from their hearts, and walk away.

She caned out the back door from the kitchen, easy down the three porch steps, into the night-black grass, under Dad's fruit trees . . . while the night passed through her clothes and took a cool and perfect grip on her nakedness beneath them. Her body felt impossibly distinct and distinct in the darkness around her she felt all the other monstrous shapes of life, a mighty army, that shared the night with her,and whose exhalations mingled with every breath she drew. Terror or exhilaration shimmied down her spine. Fear fell away. Her distinctness was not that of prey. It was that of a conquering flame.

She headed around the house, toward the Big Shed. Her cane's alternating piston-stroke felt like a cyborg enhancement—machinelike, her righteous anger advanced and she almost laughed aloud at this unsuspected power and competence in herself.

All open studs and joists, the shed was skeletal inside, its cool scent the ghosts of sun-warmed plums. The wide open overhead door let a wedge of weak moonlight in that touched shovel-heads . . . the downhung bars of chainsaws . . . and the five-gallon can. Outdoing herself now, Susan caned her way to the car with that dead-heavy counterweight and did it flawlessly. The can was as heavy as fate and she toted it like a carry-on to her flight.

Her rental, almost colorless under the chip of moon. The can on the passenger seat. Herself—cane in, butt in, right leg, left leg—behind the wheel.

She was ready . . . and how *right* this was. Like in some old play, murder must out. A heart's murder. It was *too much*. It couldn't be let stand without an answer.

She fired it up, pressed the accelerator tenderly, tenderly. The engine scarcely louder than at idle, she crackled off of the drive, past the sheds to the packed-earth lane and down the lane, into the orchard. Only then did she switch the headlights on.

In the headlights, the bristling trees that flanked her struck postures of stark deformity, like floodlit ghouls discovered at their work. The car sank past their endless battalions and fear scuttled everywhere in their shadows, but fear could not touch her. Her flame torched it to smoke.

She pulled up at a distance from the holocaust-to-be; she stopped and stood, armed with cane and can, facing the shed. The huge black tire-studded larva of the compost heap, all eyes it seemed, nosed up near the shed. Belatedly, she caught the scent of the heap—a big faint breath of plastic, decay chambered within it. Karen said it was hot in there . . . . Well, Susan had brought some heat of her own.

Setting the can on the ground, she woke the creaky hinges of the screen door. Shouldered the inner door, already ajar. Found the light-switch just inside the jamb. Bare hundred-watt bulbs came alive and she had the sensation of hitting water from a long fall: with a shock, she was right inside Jack Fox's blown-out skull.

His books and papers were a dirty snowfall, drifted lopsidedly on every horizontal cleft and nook, the shaggy dunes dripping from the edges of the desk and file cabinets—all this around the axis of that baggy, lived-in leather armchair, like a sagging old rhino that . . . yes, still gave off the brute's rank smell. And here was his brandy gun, cut crystal, the one thing of beauty in this lair. Over there the vats, the cookers and coils, the homey Frankenstein's lab of a country boy cooking up monsters who came lurching out of that door and up through the trees, to seize a young girl, long ago . . . .

She blocked the screen door wide open and left the inner door likewise, then brought in the can of gas and set it ceremoniously on the floor near the chair. Sitting, perched rather, on the edge of the chair, she looked back over her shoulder, out into the door-framed night. The night welcomed to her now and the door an aperture out of this bubble of madness, this hundred-watt hell.

On the desk was a not-too-dusty glass. She polished it on her shirt tail and unstoppered the cannon—what exquisite carvings in the crystal—and tilted herself some more armor of fire.

Susan was an inveterate scanner of other people's bookshelves. She was surprised at once by the anthropological tenor of more than a few of Jack Fox's titles: *The Brides of the Cenote*, a bulky condensation of Fraser's *Golden Bough*, Eliade, McNalley's *On Aboriginal Cults*, a work on Meso-American corn gods. *National Geographics* and *Smithsonians* abounded in teetering stacks, and biology, botany, and zoology texts were everywhere.

She glimpsed the edges of photos in a tattered manila envelope. The manila, much handled, had that furry suppleness of skin. She tilted the photos out.

Eight-by-tens, old black-and white glossies. The first was of a sandbar in a jungle stream, with a canvas shoe, the toe of it, jutting up from sand. And these dead branches, a little farther along the sand . . . they were the bones of an arm and the small web-work of a skeletal hand.

All the photos were of corpses, some new, some older.

She tilted the cannon again and drained this glass in a breath.

They were battle-dead to judge by one, a skull that still had its leathery skin and a collapsed tunic, with shoots and sprouts poking out of it like arrows and darts that had found their mark. Another sandbar shot showed a more recent death, a man sunk sideways, one reaching arm exposed, the open mouth, like a swimmer's taking a breath, half full of sand. Had died when the river was in flood, it seemed.

She thumbed through them, nearly a score of them. She stopped at a group-shot of living soldiers, posed in fatigues, backgrounded by palm trees. Jack Fox's platoon or company or whatever, because there he was, at the end of the front row of crouching men. It struck her at once he was older than most of the others. He had a grave, refusing face, giving the camera only so much. In his forehead, above the juncture of his brows, there was a slight knot. An inward grappling—even then—with some dark problem.

Susan lifted her face from the photos. Her will had ratcheted tight to the pitch of pure certainty. This Unclean chamber cried out to God for the flames.

She tipped some valedictory inches from the cannon and caught a flash of detail from the intricate carving around its spout. She leaned close, tilting the spider-fine web of incisions against the light. All at once, the pattern surfaced from the weave.

It was a dragon, sinuous, exquisitely scaled, circling the spout. Its tail did not quite meet its grossly fanged jaws, but both were buckled to the same human victim. The jaws engulfed the head and shoulders of a naked woman. The tail looped to present its dragon loins frontally and copulated with its meal.

With a hiss of outrage, as if scalded, Susan reached down to her side, uncapped the gas can, and toppled it on the floor. As she straightened again, she found the cannon suddenly quite near her face. She looked down its spout. And the crystal cannon, for just a nanosecond, was a pouncing insect, its crook-legs like diamond razors flexing, stabbing its crystal proboscis deep into Susan's neck. She became a nova of blinding white light, became a spike of pain driven home by a wrecking ball . . . .

And she was stumbling, falling, scrabbling on the floor for her cane, then flailing it, in a frenzy to get up on her legs.

An utter drunkenness had descended on her. The whole earth lagged massively out of sync with her least movement. Wherever terror thrust her—and she was purely terror now—her movement was too soon, or too late, to stay in plumb with universal gravitation.

There was the gaping door—a big hole she could pitch through, out into the night, out of here. Her left shoulder collided with the frame and she toppled around it. Somewhere between the door and her car, the cane fell away, because it ceased to matter. She made the car, fell inside, found the keys' dangle, and twisted.

At the car's first forward surge, Susan felt a remote burst of hope, but as the floodlit trees roared past on either side, understood she had not yet escaped, that this earth under her wheels and the green deformities that sucked their lives from it, were all him, were Jack Fox. That she was not yet emerged from his body, his will, and that she had taken his poison inside her.

She was staggeringly, metronomically drunk, toppling left and right, upright only on the average; the car plunging in and out of the deep ruts, but—veering— she just managed to keep the wheels in the lane. The tires shrilled, trailing a plume of dust like a darker night on her tail.

Here, dear God, was the house at last, almost out, almost out. She watched its shadowed gables skim past, a woman she loved in there, a woman she had to abandon to save her own life . . . and she was within seconds of saving it now, there were the gateposts, the whale's lips, gaping ahead, and escape just beyond. The gravel drive sizzled and snapped under her tires.

Keep it floored.

She almost didn't make the turn onto the highway, fought back and forth, came screaming out of a fishtail . . . and then she was on the swift asphalt, the river of escape, pedal to the metal, salvation-bound.

Out of nowhere, headlights head-on, two great suns filling her windshield. There was an impact so total it knocked her body right out of her.

Not much of her left, after. Heard something far away . . . the boom and clatter of steel . . . .

X

Karen awoke alone in the sleeping bag. Out the window was the gray before sunrise and a thin, milky mist hazing the plum trees.

She lay a long time, remembering last night's lovemaking. Feeling defeated, but then feeling something hopeful, too. Could begin to imagine, with Susan's sweet persistence, a cozy sunlight place for them, quiet mornings of love fulfilled.

She rose and pulled on her jeans. "Susan?" she called, tying her shoes.

And heard the gravel crackling out on the drive. Where could Susan be coming back from at this hour? She opened the front door. Susan's car was gone. A patrol car coming around the bend.

Karen knew right then, really, but at that point could still refuse to know, could step out onto the porch, brusque and puzzled, come down the steps as the car's door opened, displaying the county shield. She was expecting Marty Carver to emerge, but confronted a thicker brute with a waxed flat-top and a broad, bullock's nose.

"What's going—"

"I'm Officer Babcock, Miss. Are you Karen Fox?"

"Yes, what's—"

"Are you acquainted with a Miss Susan Kravnik of San Francisco?"

"Oh, Jesus, what's happened to Susan?"

"Are you acquainted with her?"

"What the fuck do you think, you moron? You know I am or you wouldn't be here!"

But the man was implacable, indulging his hate—with a straight face—simply by refusing to omit a single step.

"Did Miss Kravnick have a rental? A new red Mitsubishi?"

"Yes, she did." Knowing the truth past all hope now, but still desperately bargaining with it, telling herself she *didn't* know, not yet.

"We need you to come down to the County Coroner's office to confirm the identity of her body."

You could *feel* him, behind his straight face, loving that. An under-thug, this guy, but surely prepped by Marty Carver. For a moment, her hate of him and of Marty insulated her and held off the pain and the horror . . . .

But then the hate blew away like smoke and she was left with it: Susan was dead.

HARST POURED MARTY, and himself, a brandy. "So how have you been feeling, Mr. Assistant Chief Deputy?"

Marty didn't answer. He had been in the office ten minutes and hadn't yet sat down, had paced, had opened the inner door to the morgue and wandered around in there. Harst had followed him around with his eyes, enjoying the mismatch between the man's deep ignorance and the stoically masterful persona he tried to project. A tall, lean drink of water—Harst conceded he was cute. Recalled with pleasure hurling the man across the floor. A few years ago, he might have raped him too, just to teach him respect for his elders. It would have been a fitting ceremony for Jack's interment, but Harst was eighty now and it had seemed too much like work. Were his own final hours indeed approaching?

"I asked you a question, Carver."

You could see Marty didn't want to spill the beans about the premonitions of strength he had been feeling in the last two days, but that, like the punk he was, he also craved to gloat. He said off-handedly, "I might have something for you, maybe next week." This was their code for a cadaver that had to be legitimized by the Medical Examiner's Office.

"Oh, Marty, you randy scamp! It's like elixir, isn't it? And so it begins. So what's your assessment? Is Karen going to stay on?"

"My feeling is, she will. She really hates us."

"That surprises you? She will indeed stay. Rage and guilt will hold her there. Her squeeze-box died there, and of *her* disease, of drink. Would that be her now? I hear the rhino tread of Babcock."

A knock at the outer door, and there was Babcock, bulkily presiding over Karen's entry. "Thank you, officer," said Harst. "We'll call you when she's ready to go home. Close the door, dear, please. Sit there. I think we could all use a drink." He set Marty's glass by his and brought out a third. Filled all three, studying Karen under the cover of a condoling smile.

How well Harst knew that stunned slump of bereavement! She had her mother's gold-and-brown coloring, but her father's beauty, the lathed cheekbones, the jaw more delicately sculpted but just as unrelenting. Her body was stunned, but not her gray eyes studying Harst and Marty in turn, hate like a smoke in those eyes, looking down at the three shots of brandy and back up at Harst. "Smells like apricot," she said. Her voice, gritty from long silence, was almost Jack's voice. It made Harst falter in his answer.

"It's Jack's . . . it's your father's, of course. You know he was my dearest friend, the man who saved my life. When I drink his brandy, I commemorate my love for him, as well as my tenderness for his daughter. You've had two unbearable bereavements, Karen. I'm deeply concerned for your state of mind."

"You mean my sanity?" A mocking challenge here. He had not expected this alertness in her, this . . . accusation. He did want to probe her sanity, had hoped, thinking to find her helpless and afraid, that she might blurt out something *not* sane she had lately experienced and thereby pass on to him a sign, a message from Jack. She had picked up her glass and studied it before he could frame his answer.

"The kind of grief you must be suffering has nothing to do with sanity, Karen."

She ignored him. "Marty? Whaddya think? Should I knock back this hooch? Susan died with her blood running two-point-eight, according to Officer Ape." This with a bright smile and batted lashes.

"I'm not sure what you're asking." Marty a little blustery. "A drink in moderation, to calm you down . . . ."

"No offense, Marty," she smiled, "but you're such a moron. You boys want to stand me a drink—how not? Okay. I'd like us to drink, not just to Susan, but to my father. I know you two loved him like a father. Maybe more than a father." She paused, her gaze lingering on Harst. Saw pure poison glow in his lens-smeared eyes. She had guessed! "Such a man as Jack Fox," she intoned, "is not erased by death!"

The two men drank and Karen knocked hers back, thrust out the glass. "Hit me again, Doc." Slammed that one back, held out the glass again. "Three's the charm, and not so stingy, Doctor."

She stood up when she'd drunk this and slammed the glass down. "This the morgue through here?" She led them out.

Marty's eyes questioned Harst, who shrugged. He limped quickly into the lead, brought them to the drawer, unlatched and slid it out. Kravnik, Susan. Severe spinal and thoracic damage . . . .

It took Karen's eyes a long time to receive the catastrophic wreckage. She stood witnessing it, withstanding it. Then bent down to kiss her face, eerily lovely and undamaged above the broken ruin of torso and limbs. "Seems I'm always doing this," she said in a small voice to herself. And then, to Harst, "That's Susan."

She turned and walked back towards the office, then slowed and turned again. "Did I understand right? You don't know who she hit?"

"Not yet," said Marty. "It had to be a head-on—her car was found mid-road, crushed in half. The other vehicle was apparently able to drive away. It had to be something big. Naturally we've got everyone alerted for a truck or semi with frontal damage."

"Naturally. Tell Officer Ape I need to pick up supplies on the way out of town. I'm done here."

As Babcock slid back out the drive, Karen carried her forty-ouncer of Green Death—half empty now—over to the rim of the orchard. Stood looking at those six trimmed and picked trees, their litters of twigs on the weeds around them. There she had worked at Susan's side, just yesterday. Could almost hear the echoes of their voices in those trees . . . .

Susan was up in the Boys' Club now, up in the Monkey House. Was now the wholly-owned property of the he-chimps. Up there where everything was locks and keys, guns, paperwork, brandy, and smugly lying looks of sympathy.

When Harst poured her that drink, she'd almost slapped it from his hand and spat out in their faces all Dad's crimes against her. But they already knew! Their postures confessed it when she first walked in, the comfy way they watched her, sure of her, a victim, a psychological wreck already in their pockets. They thought they'd made her drink. *She'd* done it. Stepped willingly back in the trap that she'd let Susan step into for her. Poor, tender Susan. The chimps had her now. In a drawer.

Here she stood, all at once alone in the world. It gave her a flying, snatched-by-the-wind feeling, the way that first drink in Harst's office had felt. A wild letting go, an inner *yes* to the rage that was all she had protecting her from her grief. She had no reason to be careful any more. If anything, she owed Susan a death.

Yesterday had seemed almost summer, but this afternoon was wholly autumn, golden blue and chill, with a promise of night mists and shivers. Chug-chug goes the rest of the ale and smash goes the bottle against a trunk. She went into the house to get her old canvas coat from her duffle bag.

A drink back in town would be cheery, the 8-Ball, perhaps. But it would be wise for a single damsel to have some security at such a rowdy place. Hmmm. What would be appropriate for the 8-Ball in the fall? Why not Dad's .357 Smith here? It worked just fine, when the ammo was live. And here was a fifty-count box right in the same drawer! She thumbed in the six rounds, snugly planted seeds, and planted the Smith in one of the coat's roomy side pockets, with nary a bump showing, for all the piece's brute heft.

THE 8-BALL WAS both spacious and richly dark. The light was dim even at the bar. She took the most separate available stool—one stool away from a guy in a leather sports coat on the left and the same clearance on her right from two grizzled men—the nearer badly needing a shave—both of them in suspenders and worn flannel shirts sweated under the arms.

The old bartender, his wattled face sagging towards hound-dog, aimed at her shifty eyes that Karen still recognized: her first-grade pal Shelly's dad, Earl Sodder. "Hi, Mr. Sodder! Recognize me? Old Jack Fox's daughter?"

"Karen. Real sorry about your dad."

"Well, it turns out you can help, Mr. Sodder. A double Jack Daniels and a water back!"

As Sodder set it up, the bristlier suspendered man turned toward his friend. Karen heard, " . . . California pervert . . ."

She turned her stool to face him and addressed him brightly. "You'd be Jessie Rangle, wouldn't you? Sheep-rancher out on Vine Creek. Midge Adams' mom, Carla, she's your neighbor." This brought him around. He had a long chin, like an oversized gnome's, and tiny chips of gray eyes webbed in his sunburned squint-lines. He didn't hide his scorn, but showed his curiosity foremost. Karen, still smilingly: "Did you *know* old Jack Fox? Did you *fear* him?" She surprised herself with this second question . . . then watched it pay off. The troll-face contracted slightly, as if recalling a foul taste. The man blinked.

"The reason I ask," she enthused, "is that I *viewed* his remains. And oh, dear lord! The mess that buckshot made of my poor daddy's skull! The whole top was gone! I'm here to tellya that I, for one, have the greatest respect for high-impact gunshot wounds. Look here. Case in point." With unthinking expertise, she drew the Smith and set it on the bar. "See, I'm a woman alone, an orphan now. But praise Jesus, my daddy taught me to use guns real good! Do you know what I could do to the skull of *any scum-sucker I didn't like* who stepped his sorry, saggy ass onto my property? Why lordy-lordy! I could spray his redneck face across a full five acres of Daddy's plum trees!" Smiling and batting her eyelashes, leaning closer across the intervening stool, she said this.

A strangely peaceful silence followed, as if a golden moment of accord, of understanding, had settled on the room. The big-chinned rancher Jessie Rangle gazed at her as if she'd just hummed a melody that wakened poignant memories.

"'Ey. Karen,"—this from her left—"come sitta table wit' me, come on."

The man in the leather sports coat with the garish dye-job—was Mr. Fratelli. Pocketing the Smith, she knocked back her drink. "Why not? I didn't recognize you, Mr. Fratelli."

"You bring us the same to our table, eh, Earl?" He laid a twenty on the bar. Outside of his store, it appeared that Mr. Fratelli had an expanded public personality: the leather coat and slacks of costly-looking shimmery gray stuff like mob guys wore in movies, an inch or two piled up on the shoes due to his short legs. When Earl brought their drinks to the table, Fratelli said, "Keep da change!" with a grand wave.

"Karen," gravely, leaning close, "you got good dirt out there. T'ree hunnerd t'ousand."

Expanded, indeed. How long had it been now? Working the store in his apron, but on off hours, in his slick leather coat, buying whole properties. "Do you buy much land, Mr. Fratelli, or is it only my Dad's you want?"

"Huh! You be surprised, the lan' I own! But you got good dirt."

She wanted to see farther into this new Fratelli. "Well, current economy and all, that's a possible price for a hundred acres of trees. But that leaves out the house. A classic two-story whatever, good for a hundred more years. In California some wine-yuppie would pay a million. Even out here, another four hundred K for the house."

"I don' wan' the house, I wan' the dirt. I only pay you for dat. Move the house you wanna, take it witchoo."

"What would you do with it if I just left it there?"

"Tear it down an' sell the wood."

"Is that because you're afraid of it?"

He sat looking at her, not unpleasantly. "Karen. You ask me that . . . why *you* stayin' there?"

"I have things to do there." She stood up.

"You call me."

THE SUN WAS drawing westward when she returned to the orchard for the second time that day. She stood looking at the house, imagining herself asleep in there last night while Susan did . . . what? What had put her out on the highway at two A.M.? She found no clues in the living room, but in the kitchen . . . . Dad's brandy, an inch left in the bottle and a sticky glass. Of course.

She poured the remnant in the same glass, her lips trying to taste the memory of Susan's lips on the rim as she drank. Thought of Susan saddened by their lovemaking, getting up and getting dressed, coming in here for more of the brandy she must have been drinking pretty steadily since dinner. Then heading outside into the night . . . .

Here, near the big shed, was where Susan's car had been parked. Karen looked inside. A stripe of low sun lay along its inner wall and showed quite clearly a dust-shadow under the chainsaws. The gas can was gone, was it somewhere outside here? Then she noticed the faint scars of tires slanting across the grass and onto the picking lane. Of course. If Susan had meant to burn and purge, the shed would be a natural place to go.

The sun was one diameter above the horizon as Karen drove down through the acres. Dad's brandy shed was in the slanting shadow of the compost heap and through its gaping inner door she could see the bulbs blazing inside. She parked just short of Susan's cane, lying on the grass.

And with the screen door screeching, she stepped into a dizzying reek of gas fumes. Saw the toppled can, the toppled glass, the sticky spill of brandy across . . . nightmare photos.

Susan must suddenly have run for her life. Had sat here drinking, sifting the contents of Dad's desk, and then had run for her life, dead-drunk, reeling out of here, dropping her cane, firing her car up, rocketing away, straight out of the orchard, onto the highway, into her death.

Karen gathered the photos and put them in her truck. She went back for the brandy cannon, topping it off from a keg marked *Apricot* and carrying it as well to the truck. She had the last things Susan touched, the last things of Dad's to hurt her, before her final hurt. Now she should strike a match . . . but she was not done with what the shed contained. Dad's thoughts were here and some might be retrieved.

She left the lights on and closed the door—sealing in the fumes, leaving it all just a match-head away from destruction. The next time she left, she would leave it blazing.

MIDNIGHT FOUND KAREN in the living-room armchair. The cannon was down on the floor in her right hand's reach and her glass was asleep in her hand on her lap and no dreams were visible behind her sleeping face.

She had waited patient hours for the house to confront her, swallowing penance in the form of danger. Through it all, the house had stood silent. She felt snug as she went under. Snug in the belly of the whale.

XI

Just after midnight, Dr. Harst sat at his desk, idly studying his hands under his low desk lamp's small wedge of yellow light. His office was otherwise dark, its inner door open on the morgue, the morgue dark too, just a low gleam here and there along the tables, the banks of drawers.

It was in your hands, he thought, that you most poignantly saw the passage of your years and all their loss and bitterness. You felt no self-pity, but a more dignified, detached compassion, for these old monkey-paws now close to gripping their last branch.

These fingers, when they were smooth and strong, had clutched the back of Jack Fox's web-belt as Jack, a single great piston of uncrushable strength, carried Harst's younger self through howling, hammering, steel-shredded jungle. And just two days ago, these hands in their present knuckly, ropy, spotted shape, had delivered Jack Fox down to the furnace of the under-earth.

"I'm afraid, Jack," he told the darkness behind him. "It's just that I'm afraid."

Did his low voice wake echoes out in the corridors? Madly, he wished for that. Some night-shift Deputy wandering over here, into the locked half of the County Building. Someone from the *surface* world blundering in here, interrupting. But there was only silent darkness outside his front door's pebbled glass.

He'd come here two hours ago, because he could no longer pretend he didn't feel that low, insistent tugging in his spine that had nagged him his whole day at work. A meth-lab out on some decayed farm had exploded and he'd had two-and-a-half crisped decedents to examine for pre-incineration entry-wounds . . . . Throughout, he'd felt this fugitive touch along his backbone, like a gesture from the earth rippling up through the air.

But he'd gone home, made a dinner he didn't taste, sat down to his journal . . . and found, of course, that the only thing to be recorded was the demand being made of him at every other heartbeat in his ribs.

And so, at last summoning the obedience, squarely facing the duty owed, he had come limping back through the dim halls. Had entered his office, passed through it to the morgue, through the morgue towards the utilities plant. He'd brought a penlight, but turned neither it nor any other light on as he advanced, his pace dignified but unhesitating, a priest's advance towards the shrine.

Without light, not even down the blackness of the iron staircase, nor across the restless, buckled concrete floor, he moved blind as any mole, navigating towards the aperture by the scent of its cool, rank updraft and, when he was quite near, by the pull of it, the dizzying gravitation it exhaled.

Only when he had painfully knelt beside it, touched its ragged concrete lip, did he switch on the penlight. He was holding it at his chin, though, lighting only his own face. Leaned his lit face over the vent, self-presenting, and said, "I am here."

What he had expected, had come: a dizzy downward sagging of his body, a pulling of his heart towards his master. *Come down*, Jack told him . . . .

But Harst's terror had mutinied and taken back his will. He aimed the beam down the vent then. The fissure's wet throat had widened farther down there, a hungry gullet of ribbed clay and, still farther down, some movement dully glinted.

Harst had reared up, staggered back, and on fear's rebel legs marched back to the stairs and up them. The light beam, like a shaft of sanity, led him, and his shaky, coward's body followed until, coming back into his office, he saw this desk, the center and sanctum of his priesthood for nearly thirty years. All the power he'd had here, all the lust gratified . . . here, he found his better self again.

No further retreat. He took his chair, turned on the lamp. And murmured, "I yield, Jack. I do not flee farther than this. But I just can't meekly enter my own grave."

Thus he sat there through the hours. If he was summoned, let the summoner prove his power. He was sincere, believed the summoner *would* come, and so he sat here in good faith, in obedience. But there was also, sneaking at his mind's rim, a baser thought: that the summoner could not literally come, and required his self-delivery, his assistance, and in that case, the green hills, the sunlit sky, the sweet breath of the breeze . . . all these things might—just might—be his again tomorrow.

And so he studied his hands and, with a certain sense of ceremony, embarked on a journey of memory through the long years of his love for Jack. Jack was that rare thing, innately a hero. He'd always gone first into the Hard Places, was born to walk point. Harst thought again of that two hundred meters of jungle, the torn leaves spitting on all sides.

And how much farther than that Jack had carried him, through all their succeeding years together! Along a path both dire and miraculous. Harst's eyes filled and ran over. So much he owed Jack. All those raptures in the wild night when Harst, red-handed, had known the presence of Power Undying in his spine . . . .

But always underneath it was this unthinkable point: that immortality meant *transmutation*, into something so Other that the passage loomed like death itself. And again Jack had walked point! Had taken leave of his body with the brusque, imperative gesture of a king doffing his crown to seize up a greater diadem.

There was a sound from the morgue behind him. A sound? Yes: a drawer unlatched. And then . . . the steely whisper of a drawer sliding out. Shedding his resolve that he would not move from this spot, Harst willed himself up and away, but discovered he could not move. Could not stir the smallest muscle.

The drawer clicked and rattled delicately in its frame. Next, a soft smack, bare skin touching concrete. The drawer gave a last rattle as its burden left it. Just before Harst heard the next faint, naked footfall, a waft of air tardily touched the back of his head and flowed softly around to his face: a scent of cold and the beginnings of decay.

The moist chafe of foot soles on floor.

Could. Not. Move.

The cool waft teased him more insistently. He was already floating in the stream of its will and, in moments, it would set him in motion.

Was this that merciful shock they said the zebra felt as the lion ate it alive? This suspension? A sense that tearing jaws were already at work on him, but still far away somehow?

The air swelled more strongly against the back of his neck, displaced by a nearing mass. Cold blue fingers sprouted before his eyes, interlocked across his brow, their grip like winter stone. An effortless, inhuman strength bent him back in his chair.

What he saw above him was the eerie loveliness of Susan Kravnik's untouched face, above her shattered chest and limbs. Her hands took a grip on his cranium and *wrenched* his head, sending a complex, surrendering crack through his frame.

His body sagged, a long floppy thing, a Something Else he was anchored to. Harst's eyes scanned for the last time this odd little office he'd ruled from for so many years. One dead hand gripped the back of his collar and dragged him out of the chair. His legs and arms hit the floor.

Out of the light she dragged him, then down the length of the morgue. Facing forward, with a click and a hitch like clockwork in her tread (he recognized that brutally fractured femur on the right) she hauled him one-armed behind her. He looked around him, watched the trusty old tables passing, gleaming him goodbye.

Then down through the utility plant, its big gloom starred with small red and white trouble lights, lit gauges. Harst, his torso hissing across the polished floor, saw around him other old friends, these elemental servitors of his temple who had furnished him with the heat, and the deep cold, and the light, and the voltage for his handy little bone-saws . . . .

Goodbye, then.

Down the black iron stairs and into real darkness. His heels dragged drumbeats down the crusty risers, as he sank into the echoes, into the big, dank breathing of this stony lung. This was the buried breath of life itself, of life's relentless conspiracy against the universe.

They crossed concrete, its bucklings like a sine wave his limbs traced, a reading of the restless gravels, the fractured sediments, the snaking waters just beneath this earth . . . . Yet there was a node of light down here. He glimpsed it when a jolting cocked his head back far enough to see, slantingly, there along the farther wall, a low faint exhalation, a most delicate glow of the dimmest memory of green . . . .

When she had laid him by the aperture, he saw this nimbus, smelled its cold fetor, close at hand. It whispered to his nostrils of recycled generations, deep-layered ancestries of lives as remote and numberless as stars. The corpse, most awkwardly upon its shattered props and hinges, was kneeling at his side.

She gripped his clothing at the throat and tore it half asunder with one pull. Turning him, tilting him, gripping him, she tore his jacket and shirts to rags, and clean away. The thickest seams shrieked and yielded. As she worked, the unreal loveliness of her face made her seem to daydream, her gaze slanting up and away, inwardly following the landscape of death's discoveries, still so new to her . . . .

The livid fingers snapped his belt, stripped off his trousers and briefs, the cloth surrendering like dead leaves. Tore the stout leather cuffs of his leg-brace free, the aluminum struts ringing on the concrete . . . .

Harst lay, his clothes in a torn, placental scatter around him. He was nude as a newborn, but a *re*delivery, to be popped back into the oven of birth. Lay while she worked herself upright again on her broken frame, the surviving one of her small breasts rocking with the labor on her half-crushed thorax.

Collecting the litter of his torn envelope, she wadded and flung it down the fissure, seeming, in these movements, nightmarishly maternal, gathering his garments before tucking him in . . . .

No utterance? No promise? No . . . warning?

There was a moment of her face close to his and he saw then, hovering far back within its remoteness, a relentless purpose, an inexorable will. He saw Jack, the hand that worked her puppet frame, and saw the Master whom Jack served. Harst understood this was the only utterance that would be granted him.

She tipped him backwards down the fissure, fed him down—gripping his calves, as she angled him to the aperture. Harst was dangling, arms stretched like a diver's. His eyes flashed starkly, left and right, at the ribbed throat of swallowing clay that received him, and she let him drop.

Once more, on her Rube-Goldberg hinges, Susan's corpse knelt down. On her knees at last, still seeming to daydream, she leaned over the fissure, and dove after.

XII

Chainsaws woke Karen. The crackly *shusss* of a fruit tree toppling out in the yard, and she remembered Kyle. Karen Fox, brandy-tree slayer, her troops had arrived and she had begun striking back. And the world, again today, was empty of Susan.

In the kitchen she opened a can of pineapple juice and guzzled thirstily and, from across the room, watched them out the back window without showing herself. They had two trees down and were trimming off branches. Kyle's helper was like him, all shoulders and no stomach, but a good deal taller and much younger, with black hair sleeked back and a lupine, clean-shaven face that radiated handsomeness. There was something self-displaying about him, the postures he struck as he worked.

Well, they had their task, but what was hers on this Sunday, Day Two of Susan dead?

She knew, all right. Go back to the still-shed, where Susan had somehow caught her death, and get Dad's papers. He was the black hole that had sucked half the life out of Karen. She'd seen those renderings in astronomy texts: a dimming star, with a ribbon of its substance snaking off of it, into that gravity-pit. A dimming star, that was her self.

SHE SPREAD DAD'S CASUALTY PHOTOS on the kitchen table, in Mom's domain, in the morning light. It didn't help. Was

Karen's world from now on to be a world of corpses? Tears of self-pity filled her eyes; she wiped them angrily away and looked. Stills of the Dance of Death in the Central American jungles. The earth's unstoppable clockwork ticking away the forms and features of the dancers. Collapsed men, like flowerpots sprouting shoots. In what spirit had Dad made this record?

In an older black and white group shot from Dad's first war, Viet Nam, was dear old Dad younger than Karen had ever seen him, but still ten or twelve years older than most of the men around him . . . giving the camera the somber riddle of his gaze. He had gone to this war, though old enough to have skipped it, and Karen was born when he'd just been back a couple years. But six or seven years later, through some friends in the CIA who went back to his Nam days, back he went to the jungles of Central America. How strange to go back to war at almost forty like that.

Karen left the photos spread on the table and, weeping, came into the living room. She stood looking at Susan's suitcase, there on the floor by the fireplace. "Oh sweetheart," she choked, "what a shit hole I dragged you into!"

Willing the shock to wake anger and purpose in her, she took a cold shower, brushed her hair back and ponytailed it wet, and stepped into clean denim and flannel. Outdoors, Kyle was feeding rollers to the splitter. The helper was loading the splits into the truck bed, but as soon as Karen stepped out onto the back porch, this younger man turned towards her and exclaimed, "The lady of the house!"—and came striding toward her, snatching an apricot from one of the standing trees he passed. "I've gotta tellya, this is crazy, cuttin' down these trees! There's still good fruit on 'em! Look! It's delicious!" Standing in front of her, he took a bite, chewing noisily, demonstrating the fruit's goodness. He wore a mock-innocent expression, while behind it, in the flinty black eyes, was a genuine stupidity, a simple ferocity.

"Wolf." Here came Kyle, stepping between them, holding Wolf's eyes with a faint smile. "I'd call that truck loaded."

Wolf stepped back, theatrically smacked his forehead. "I'm outta line again! I'm sorry, Miz Fox! I get excited, is all. I haven't been outta the joint long, is all. I'm just really grateful, you lettin' a couple cons work for you like this!"

Something she didn't catch passed from Kyle to him and Wolf was comically backpedaling, making showy haste toward the truck. "Yessir, Kyle, I'm outta here! I'm gone!" He gunned the truck out, splits bouncing in the bed.

"I apologize for him, Karen. He looked me up a week ago and I owe him some help. I was glad when you . . . when I thought you wouldn't be here. He's one of those people who's never really *out* of jail. Myself—"

"You don't owe me any explanations, Kyle."

"Yes, I do. I've been out three years now and I *am* out. I have never, and would never, hurt anyone, except in self-defense. Wolf's only here because he helped save my life once, or what amounted to my life. Does this sound like I'm trying to . . . intrude my life on you?"

Karen saw in the fitful movement of his eyes—going inside, returning to hers—an unaccustomed labor. Saw he lived alone and found a curious comfort in his isolation, a kind of relief from her own. "You say what you want, Kyle. I'm listening."

"I want to put Wolf on a bus tomorrow night, with the money I make from these cords. I can keep him in line, but he's very obnoxious. Can you, and your friend, stand having him around? Because if not—"

She held up her hand to stop him. The man was a noticer. He had sensed Susan's upper-class discomfort with himself, clearly saw what it would be—would have been—with Wolf.

"My friend is dead."

"What?"

"My friend Susan is dead. She was killed two nights ago in a crash."

"I'm so sorry."

Her eyes were running over. She wiped them on her sleeve. "Look. That asshole doesn't bother me. I trust you. And I'm going to take his advice. I'm gonna pick that fruit. Lot less work this way, actually."

"I'm so sorry."

"Just cut those fuckers down, Kyle. Every one that falls makes me glad."

She brought stacks of flats and dividers from the big shed and began to harvest fruit from the branches heaped in the trim-pile, stacking the filled flats in the cool north shadow of the house. This was better than leaving the fruit rot, as she'd thought to do. Better to convert Dad's darlings to dollars. Transmute them and squander them. All hers, now.

Wolf returned and the trees continued to fall, shed their limbs, be bucked into rollers, split, and loaded— but the majority of the actual work was Kyle's. It was fascinating, tracking Wolf from the corner of her eye as she picked. His most important product was Attitude. Anything served for a pretext. She watched him manufacture ten solid minutes of attitude from a cigarette he bummed from Kyle. He commented on the crumpled condition of the cigarette. He expounded on its smell and feel. He bummed Kyle's lighter, then went on about its sorry condition and low fuel level. At last he lit the cigarette, with a flourish, and the doubtful air of a connoisseur. He smoked two puffs, with infinite skepticism, and crushed it out, pronouncing it unsmokable, expounding for a further three minutes on its sorry taste, and the superiority of other brands. Through it all, Kyle worked steadily, tossing cigarette, and then lighter, with a practiced smoothness that didn't break his stride, and smiling a bit, maybe, at the performance. Kyle was a graduate in this game, after all, and recognized it as the entertainment cons offered each other, stand-up comedy manufactured from nothing

Wolf was a live exhibit of the brutal barrenness of prison, that null environment where all talk must be improvised from emptiness, while silence meant madness. This poor asshole *was* in prison. He lived in an utterly unfurnished mind.

At the same time, there was a choreography in the two men's movements. For all Wolf's arm wavings and postures, he never once got in the way of Kyle's unrelenting labor and whenever Kyle came to some two-man phase of the work—moving the splitter, for instance—Wolf was always, somehow, right there at hand to help. Here was the reflex of mutual accommodation, effortless for men who had lived years in small boxes together.

The lopped branches they heaped up surrendered their fruit to Karen's hands. When she'd totally plundered them, she'd burn the pile right here on the lawn, spray it with diesel, and leave a black scar in the grass beside the stumps.

She could burn this whole place down, though, and still be in prison here among the ashes. Would still have nowhere else to go, but into the black pit of Dad. She'd let Susan face it for her and somehow Dad had killed her. If Karen failed to face the same herself, her shame would kill her just as surely, though more slow . . . . Shouldn't she, after all, sit down to that desk in the dead of night, as Susan had done? Pick up the thread of Susan's life just where and when it had ended . . . ?

She looked at the stack of flats she had filled. She felt ridiculously tired by this slight work, she who could frame for ten hours straight and strike every sinker true. Karen Fox, butch babe extraordinaire. Not much left of her now.

Back into the kitchen, walking through it, her eyes refusing the glossy black-and-whites still spread on the polished tabletop. Out to the fireplace, the cannon, and her glass . . . . Mellower, Karen decided on the comfort of the two men's company without the contact: from the window of Mom's sewing room. She took her refilled glass up the stairs.

Entering—as she'd always done when young—she ran her hand along the smooth curve of the sewing machine's case. Everything in here was so neatly shelved and shut away. When she was six or so, this was a universe of magical little drawers, glittery treasure in each one. She sat at Mom's desk by the window overlooking the yard and again found comfort in watching the pair work. Kyle there implacable, Wolf dancing his attitudes, their isolation seemed to offer her strength to face her own. You could almost forgive Wolf his stupidity, you could *see* the man dancing around inside invisible walls. In Kyle's relentlessness she sensed self-constructed walls, a careful channeling of himself . . . toward what? Some bitter, private form of justice?

It jarred Karen, though she'd been watching them pack up for the last quarter hour, to realize they were climbing into Kyle's truck to leave for the day. The sun had westered, slanting in shafts of saffron and marigold across the stumps and trimmings of more than half Dad's brandy trees.

All around her now, the house began to reassert itself, the rooms seeping full of their individual emptinesses. The truck swung out onto the lane, out of view, and headed its long way out the drive . . . . Hello, walls. Hello, Mom. Did you *never* see anything from this window? Never any sign or clue?

Realizing she was absently fingering a tier of drawers in the escritoire, finding the bottom drawer was open just a crack . . . she slid it out. And saw two thick letters inside it, their envelopes much handled and browning with age. She took out the topmost. *Mrs. Emily Fox,* at this address, typed with a worn ribbon. It was postmarked in Mexico City in December of 1980. An unknown someone in Mom's youth?

When she unfolded the sheaf of pages, the dense lines of Dad's frighteningly legible handwriting hit her like a slap in the face.

> *My Dearly Beloved Emily,*
> *A friend will mail this for me, probably from Mexico City. You must have the whole truth now, while I am still resolved to tell it.*
> *Something in this jungle has found me and entered me . . .*

She slammed the letter face-down. Here it was, in these pages right under her hand: Dad's sickness. Here

was what she'd come back to find, what had found her
that first night *(something has entered me)* and had
come within a hammer-stroke of killing her. It was
what Susan had gone looking to destroy and what
had crushed her. It had lived here in Mom's drawer
for more than half a century. Karen had reached out
unthinkingly and, just like that, it had crawled up her
hand and into her mind, a spider rushing out of its hole.
Mom had known something then.

Karen remembered the somber, private man from
the platoon photo. *You must have the truth while I am
still resolved to tell it.* Dad talked like that sometimes,
that curious formality. How would a rising madness feel
to a measured mind like his? What a terrible loneliness!
No wonder, in these pages, he cried out to his Emily,
his only companion. Oh Daddy . . . And Mom, alone
up here—if not knowing, then at least fearing, fearing
through all those years.

Her eyes traveled around Mom's sanctum . . . and
froze. There was a yellow dress draped over the top of
the sewing machine case. Surrounding the shock of its
presence (she had *stroked* the bare wood of that case
when she'd come in!) there was a halo of something
else, something more frightening than the thing's
undetected advent while she sat here. It was familiarity.
Because she knew this dress, this pale yellow dress with
a border of blue sewn along the hem. The remembered
feel of its fabric crept across her back, her breasts,
and flirted with her knees. This was the dress she was
wearing the first time Dad violated her. The one with
the bloodstain on the back of the skirt, the one she had
thrust down into the trash barrel in the big shed and
told Mom she had thrown away because it had been
bloodstained in a different way.

This dress, exactly the same one. The fabric spoke to her fingertips across a quarter of a century, chaotic years half shrouded in darkness and full of drunken noise. Under here would be where the stain was . . . *still* was! Bright and wet! The blood still red . . . and sticky to her fingers.

It was like that time a sleeper wave had seized her off Point Reyes. Karen had been peering solemnly into the tide pools when, suddenly, she heard a hiss behind her and felt the whelm of an advancing mass. Then, inside of an explosion, she was racing, tumbling out to sea within a huge foaming fist.

Plunging down the stairs and towards the hall closet, she swept into and out of the closet, lifting the Remington twelve-gauge pump. Tucking the butt to her shoulder she hoisted the muzzle and blew a plaster-spraying crater in the ceiling beneath the sewing room. Her hearing gone, her shoulder stone-numb, with four more muzzle-blasts she harpooned the darkness of the bedroom hallway and punctured the living room's walls.

In the perfect silence of her deafness, the dress echoed in her mind's eye. Its yellow paled, its fabric soft with launderings, draped there with that scary emptiness of yourself that dropped clothes sometimes had . . . *Something has entered me.* She threaded five new shells into the magazine. Pocketed more, fearing if she stood too still, her heart would go out like a blown candle. Something has entered me and it's telling me I'm already dead, that I was destroyed thirty years ago. But here I *am*. I'm a drunk. I have the DTs. But here I *am*.

She remembered the taste of a steel muzzle in her mouth. You could not back away from what was inside you. You could only move to meet it. The brandy went down her throat like a wrestler throwing a hold on her. Come in. Come out. Show me.

Karen patrolled the house with gun and bottle, the gun for dealing with apparitions, the bottle a far more familiar weapon. How many times had she shot herself in the mouth with one? How big would the exact number be? She went to every room, but not back upstairs. Went to the basement, the fruit cellar. Went outside to the big shed, the yard, the picking lanes, and back into the house. Into every room, but not back upstairs, not again tonight. Everywhere else she went, and stood, and dared him, or whoever was doing his work, to step forward. As the sun set and dark came on, she tried to call Dad up before her.

When at last she felt her strength crumbling, her thoughts blurring, she went back down to the basement and sat on the floor, the shotgun across her lap, and leaned her head back against the wall.

ONCE AGAIN, chainsaws woke her.

She wasn't quite sure she was awake until she had understood her surroundings, for she found herself lying on the floor of the basement and hugging the shotgun, curled against the wall near Dad's workbench. The light slanting down from the ground-level window was late, near noon, she thought.

She propped the shotgun against the wall and struggled to her feet. She held her right hand in the sunlight slanting on the workbench. Whorls of a dark stain, half worn away, etched the pads of her fingers. She put her tongue to them and they yielded the taste of her own blood.

Outside the chainsaws insisted, insisted, the dogs of terror snarling at her, hounding her to take up a weapon.

XIII

Wolf asked Kyle, "Is that another saw?" Kyle held his own at idle. Yes. Another chainsaw roared beyond the house. Wolf looked a question, but Kyle just stared back at him. After a moment, they went back to work.

Wolf kept listening. "I hear trees falling," he said, giving Kyle a sly smile. The older man again returned his gaze without answering and they went back to work.

Wolf got to look at last when he drove the new load out. The bitch was a wild sight. Hair in witchy strings, the muscles standing out in her neck as she back-cut a plum tree and toppled it with a frontal slice. She had a dozen trees down, the squashed clouds of their branches entangled with each other, the raw butts of their trunks red in the sun. She had started the slaughter right in the middle of the row—just plunged in and started dropping them. *This dyke was hysterical . . .*

Karen turned in time to catch Wolf's eyes as he drove past. She saw the excitement, the joy of chaos in them, and didn't care. Just turned again and attacked the next tree in the line, working until she ran the chainsaw out of gas. Stood sweating, swaying on her feet, and knew the approaching footsteps were Kyle's.

"Karen?"

"Hey, Kyle!" Watching this careful man trying to decide what he could say to her.

"Are you okay?"

The trite question brought tears to her eyes and made her laugh at the same time. "Am I okay?" She dragged her sleeve across her eyes and put on an expression of honest bafflement. "Why, what makes you ask that?"

He smiled, almost a laugh. In her misery, it warmed her to find that this winter face, so shuttered against the cold, still knew how to laugh. "I'm worried about you, Karen. I think you're a kind person, you've been kind to me. I . . . like you."

"You know I'm queer, right?" Karen, grinning, feeling friendly towards this guy, was surprised by the hostility she heard in her question. His eyes held hers, a little sad now.

"I don't see anything queer about anybody loving *anybody*. And . . . when I tell someone I like them, it's not because I want something from them. It's just because I like them. I only bring it up . . . in case there's some way I might be able to help them."

"Help them," echoed Karen, nodding, with a forced smile she meant as an apology. Looking back over her shoulder, she gazed up at the house, its windows blinded by the noon sun. In her life-long aloneness she had always lived there, had never for a moment lived elsewhere. She turned to see Kyle looking at it, too. Thought, maybe wishfully, that he felt what she did: that this house was a monster.

"Kyle. Would you . . . come over for dinner?"

He smiled. "I'd be pleased to. We could talk. I think you're like me. Talking about the hardest things can seem pointless. But sometimes it loosens their grip."

"What time is good for you?" Already she felt helped. Another person would be with her when night fell. Another voice to listen to, instead of the squeaking of her own brain in its squirrel-wheel.

"When we've got our last load, I'll take Wolf to get some cash and put him on the bus out of state. Then I've gotta drop the load, clean up. If we finish in another four hours, let's say between eight and nine?"

WHEN MARTY FOUND Harst's office empty at nine A.M., found his big swivel chair lying on its back and the drawer that had held the Kravnick woman open and empty, a terrible joy began tingling in him. That the woman's body would be gone was not in itself remarkable. Over the last few years especially, Jack had required offerings which Marty and Harst had been deputed to provide.

No. It was the toppled chair and the drawer left jutting open, that sent the prickling up along Marty's spine. Some upheaval, some peremptory will had erupted here. Jack had required *two* offerings last night. How had Marty's dark master executed his will? The Assistant Chief Deputy of Gravenstein County actually shuddered, just detectably, as he stood imagining the century-old basement below him, the fissure in its floor . . . imagining that what he had helped slip down into that fissure, might have the power to climb back out of it, in the dead of night.

There was terror in this image, but there came an exaltation with it. He'd felt hyper-alive all morning. He'd come sharp awake in bed just at sunrise, sensing a conversation going on quite near him and found it was his body speaking within, a murmuring of joint and muscle, a rumor of change cadenced by a new authority in his heartbeat. He'd dressed, breakfasted, driven here—and all the while, this rumor of rising strength was running through him.

Calling Harst's house from the phone on his desk, after six rings he heard: *Dr. Harst is either occupied or away. Please leave your message.* As Marty listened, his heart began to gallop. It felt like a mighty engine he drove. A new gulf echoed around Harst's canned voice. After the beep, he said, his words ringing like an epitaph, "I think you're both occupied *and* away." Smiled. "*Can* you get back to me?"

In the morgue he slid the long drawer shut. Whatever had happened here last night, it had been a changing of the guard. Marty remembered Harst's hands, hard as oak, hurling him across the floor. Those hands' strength had now passed into Marty's own, or was beginning to . . . .

He went up to his office and patiently, all morning, he played Assistant Chief Deputy. The two morgue workers, Phil and Jed, came on-shift at noon, and he went down to talk to them. Phil was young and plump, with evasive, intelligent eyes. Jed was fifty and plump, with a perfectly dead-pan face. Phil kept nodding as he listened, busy projecting conviction and comprehension. Jed just listened.

"The doctor was working late and I stopped in," Marty told them. "Just after he gave me the paperwork, we got the call. Transatlantic, from Paris. A hired van was already on the way out from the city. Got in at midnight and took her off. I guess the doctor is sleeping in today." Babcock alone had brought Susan's body in. Susan's mother was as ignorant of her daughter's death as she was of her whereabouts.

Phil said, "Such a sad thing. A daughter, the mother so far away . . . ."

Marty went into his office and emerged in boots, jeans, and a cowboy shirt. Told Contos, the day captain, that he was out on personal business the rest of the day. Fired up his pickup and headed out to the Spaith walnut orchard, twenty miles east of town.

The trees were years untended, ragged and shaggy. A paving of walnut shells popped under his tires as he drove through the acres to the fieldworkers' shanties, a web work of bleached barracks and battered sheds, all of them shedding a dandruff of shingles. The shanties were the only gainful enterprise left on Spaith's acres— rental housing for migrant hands employed at other ranches and orchards. At mid-day in harvest season, the shabby complex was as empty as he had expected. He parked behind an outlying shed.

A Mexican woman opened to his knock. She was somewhat stout, but her neatly muscled frame was equal to the weight of the big breasts that swelled her shirt. A face in its thirties, burnished by hard work, broad but still exotic, lips cushiony and curved, her sloping, thick-lashed eyes reminiscent of Central American bas-reliefs Marty had seen.

He held up before her a packet of twenties and a pair of handcuffs.

"Okay, but make hurry please, I don' wan' . . ." Any of her neighbors to know, of course, or at least to directly observe. She shut up quick at his glare, though. The wordlessness of this transaction, his implacable looks, her mute submission—all these were essential erotic elements, as he had taught her.

He came out two hours later, leaving another packet of twenties with the woman on the theory that well-greased wheels didn't squeak, no matter how hard they were run.

Looking around at the yellow leaves of the walnuts blown like flames in the late-morning breeze, he exulted in his newly revealed power. Harst had surely gone under and the mantle was Marty's now.

A wooden door clapped. Turning, he saw a short, lean old woman crossing the leaf-strewn ground with a hatchet in one hand and a red rooster by the legs in the other. A tiny gaunt and seamed mahogany woman with thick white hair crowding out from under a battered gray fedora and down onto her ancient denim jacket.

Her gait was purposeful as she headed for a stump that was stained by previous bloody work, but she stared at his face as she passed, seeming bemused and then astonished at something she saw in Marty. Was his new power so plainly manifest to others? But when she came to the stump, she was suddenly businesslike, whipping the bird down on the wood, which stretched its neck out under her quick hatchet. The head flew away and the body jerked, spraying, still gripped in her brown fist.

And when her eyes came back to Marty's, he thought he saw fear in them. Then he thought he saw measurement and solemn purpose. He made himself taller, staring his authority back at her. She smiled and gestured the truncated rooster at him. Offering it to him? He waved it away and headed for his truck. He should have summoned her to him, made her feel the weight of his presence here, but he couldn't be bothered.

He rocketed back to the highway, walnuts exploding under his double-wides. There was another new-born power in him that he was eager to demonstrate, this time to his brother, Rodge.

———————————

THE OLD WOMAN KNOCKED at the cabin Marty had stepped out of. When there came no answer, she opened the door and went in.

The younger woman tiredly raised her head from the pillow, told her elder in Spanish, "Leave me, grandmother, and take your bloody rooster with you."

The old woman answered, "Aren't you afraid that animal will kill you?"

"Him I don't worry. I leave here soon."

"You say you're leaving a year now. You not leaving."

"Why would he kill me?"

The little lean old woman looked at her. "To feed you to something."

"Quetzal, you ancient daughter of a whore, leave me alone."

"Lupe, you young daughter of a whore, you should leave here."

RODGE HAD BEEN a classic big brother, country-style. He'd thumped young Marty pretty good during their early years, teaching him to jump to it and keep his mouth shut. But Rodge had had a sense of responsibility to Marty, too, and had taught him very solemnly the things Marty needed to know to be a man. That there were two kinds of men in the world: beef ranchers and sissies. Rodge was totally sold on good old Daddy. Daddy was his hero. Marty, like everyone else, saw the old man for what he was, an incompetent half-drunk with a pitiful three hundred acres.

But Rodge was a believer. He worked other people's ranches all through high school when Daddy's sorry spread offered no work. And right out of high-school

had begun his long campaign to marry Marsha
Maitland, ten years his senior, daughter of Maitland's
Super Market. Cal Maitland was judged the cagiest
old sonofabitch of his generation and his daughter
was a wholly self-focused and intrinsically combative
woman who was genuinely bemused by handsome
Rodge Carver making calf's eyes at her and constantly
pestering her to go dining and dancing.

For six years Rodge mooned and squired her,
sweated to look love-struck, and stoically endured
the hoots and gibbers of his drinking buddies, while
Marsha pursued her entrepreneurial passion to build
Maitland Meats, a regional distributor, on the platform
of Maitland's Supermarket, whose success in town had
rested on its excellent butcher's section and old Cal's
connections with local beef ranchers.

After six years, though, Marsha told him that marriage
was a step that still needed thinking on. She hired Rodge,
at a derisory salary, as the market's assistant manager.
Four years after that—a period in which the embryonic
Maitland Meats had built its first warehouse and then
slid inexorably into bankruptcy, throttled by Marsha's
incessant feuding with her suppliers—Marsha married
Rodge and made him manager of the market.

Marty parked behind it and strolled to the rear door
of the big meat room. This was the part of the store
its manager always gravitated to, mooning over steaks
and roasts and his soured ambitions. There he was at
one of the drain boards, trimming a roast. Rodge was
pretty porked-out these days, looking tubular in a blue
smock. He turned.

"Well, howdy, *Shurrf*!" Rodge always called him
that, like Marty was a small-town tin-star and Rodge a
famous outlaw.

"Hey, Rodge. You got a minute? I've got some good news."

"No shit?"

"Well, good news for me. Wanna hear it?"

"You're gonna tell me if I want to or not."

"You got that right. First off, just stand there while I show you something."

Marty went to the walk-in freezer. Stepped in, reached up, and gripped one of the beef sides. Gripped it by its fat-waxy edges and lifted it off the hook. Two-twenty-five, maybe two-fifty. His arms hefted it with the inexorable ease of a forklift.

He stepped out of the freezer with it and grinned at Rodge, whose jaw was hanging open, his eyes wide. "Watch this," Marty winked and hurled it at him from fifteen feet away. It was a crowning moment of Marty's life, watching that great parallelogram of raw meat sail into his brother, slam him back against the drain board, and drag him to the floor beneath its weight.

Marty knelt beside him, flipped the side one-handed off his body, and smiled down into Rodge's dazed and bloody face. "Everything I've wanted to say to you over the years, Rodge? I think this just sums it up. You know what else I can do? I can tear off more pussy in two hours than you can in two months. I'm not making it up! See the thing is, I don't really want to hurt you, because I don't *need* to. I just want you to understand what's happened to me. I'm someone else now. I'm a new thing, like you've never met before. And what it boils down to is that I run this town now—I mean really run it. Now you know some old boys that thought the world of Jack Fox, don't you?"

Here he saw a new understanding begin to dawn within his brother's terror. This too was sweet, seeing that Rodge at last had to grant that all Marty had hinted about Jack Fox over the years was true. "I want you to tell them what Mr. Fox just gave me—tell them from me. I wouldn't tell anyone else though—they'd think you were crazy. Lemme help you up . . . looks like you hurt your back pretty good there. Here, I'll hang this back up for you."

XIV

Marty took the highway right back out of town, to call at the home of his superior officer, Chief Deputy Karl Rabble.

Twenty years ago Rabble had been a young star down at the Fair Valley Spring Rodeo. Mainly broncs in his first two years, but then, in his glorious last year, bulls. By the time the bulls were done with Karl, he got one of his legs so extravagantly broken, he still hitched around in a full leg brace, like some salty loveable old Deppity in a Western.

All the good old boys loved him. The man was born for a high post in the Sheriff's Department. He was Chief Deputy within five years of entering the Department. The Chief Deputy ran things, because the County Sheriff himself spent ninety percent of his time in the State Capitol advancing his political career.

But even the best men have some weakness. Karl Rabble's weakness was orgies. He liked an evening with a bunch of friends, a bunch of bought girls, a bunch of hootch, and a bunch of comfy furniture. Karl liked the kind of entertainment where everyone was guilty at once and more or less right out in front of each other. His band of chosen cronies, who included some powerful local men, had a special gleam of the eye for each other. Marty had known about it all for years.

Was it only three years ago that he had dared to *do* something with it? Marty had been born then, nothing less. Born. He had seized the envelope and torn it. He had dared to achieve heroic stature.

He owed it to Jack, of course. Had begun by going and whining to Jack. Jack's wife was not long dead, but, worked up with his personal crisis, he barged right in on his mentor one late autumn afternoon. Found him down in his still shed and implored him to reveal what to do. "I'm stalled, Jack. I'm *forty*. My life is in a rut." He wanted to be initiated, to move forward, to participate in the Mystery. Hadn't he been loyal to Jack all these years? Hadn't he had an unfaltering faith in him?

Jack still held the book he had looked up from when Marty entered, still wearing his gun and his Detective's badge on its belt-clip. Jack had looked him tiredly up and down, stared at his badge, then glared up into his eyes. His seamed face seemed hewn from a gnarled trunk. Laughter lurked in his eyes, like something stirring deep in a tarn.

"Take control," he said. "Come talk to me then." And waved him imperially away.

He had fretted over Jack's meaning for hours. And then, thinking of Jack's look at his badge, saw it was obvious. As Detective, Marty was a high-level grunt, but still a grunt. He must take control of the organization that presently controlled him.

Once his mission had been shown him, the way to accomplish it came in one smooth rush of inspiration. As he sat down to work out the details, he discovered himself to be a master at the kind of planning that was called for.

Karl Rabble's revelers never omitted their Halloween Party, always holding it in Karl's rambling ranch house eight miles outside of town. Marty personally rigged seven cameras and recorders in the place over the course of two days while Karl was in the office. The artfulness of his placements and their angles was revealed in the tapes when he collected these afterwards, but before he did, he laid some further groundwork.

The orgiasts were at least half-smart. They always brought their females in from the distant metropolis and brought them back on the same night. This Halloween's entertainment was no different. In the small hours, two vans of "poontang" rolled out of Chief Deputy Karl Rabble's place.

Marty was waiting. He called for immediate back-up, put the flashers on them just at the edge of town, and pulled them over. The drivers were Warren Bibbs, who controlled twenty thousand acres of fruit in and around the county, and Harry Knacker, whose wife's family had developed three of the new gated townhouse communities outside of town. Both Warren and Harry gave great Breathalyzer results and were sequestered in squadcars. The girls were taken to the station and booked for drunk and disorderly, their prints, pictures, and IDs computer-checked. Half of them were hookers and half of them enterprising drugged-out runaways. No less than five of them under sixteen. When it was all securely in the bag, Marty apologized to Bibbs and Knacker, realized the mistake he had made, gave them back the girls and sent them on their way.

Karl Rabble called him into his office next morning. Marty had come in late—he'd gone into Karl's house the moment the Chief Deputy left it and retrieved and copied all the tapes. When he came in, the smoldering Rabble had limped over to lock the office door and commenced roasting Marty's ass. Solemn and respectful, Marty apologized for his mistake. "But sir," he said, "the reason I came in late was someone left these on my porch last night, with a note that said I better look at them. It appears someone's taped your Halloween Party. I think you should run these right now, sir, because I think we have a problem."

Karl watched it on his Sony, leaping forward to kill the volume when the party-roar leapt out with the images. While he sat there watching, Marty provided a voice-over. "The nasty thing is, we booked all these girls, they're all in the database, and five of them are juveniles. In fact those two you're with right there? *Both* of them are juveniles. Those photo matchups with these tapes would be perfect—shot the same night! If this is some kind of blackmail, whoever made these tapes could have you and at least four of your friends sent up for statutory rape, and *all* of them for aiding and abetting."

Rabble was a fool, but not a retard. As Marty talked he could see, by the sagging of his shoulders, that the Chief Deputy realized what was coming.

"Well, Karl. We're both on the same page I see, so I'll just cut the shit. I could just blow you out of the water and maybe get your job. But it would be much better for both of us to do it this way. You will take a limited disability status—some developments with your bad leg, let's say. You will get me a two-grade pay raise to occupy, in an acting capacity, the currently unfilled post of Assistant Chief Deputy. You'll remain in charge and officially active; I will run the shop. Just say yes or no."

"Yes." Not turning around. Not even moving.

"Good choice! Get up. Get on over here and shake on it, Karl. Look me in the eyes."

Rabble stood up. He had a broad, square brow, a big, broken, jovial potato of a nose. A tanned, intrinsically convivial face, but slumped now, sagging like an empty garment. Marty took a powerful grip on his hand. "Hell," he smiled, "you never cared about running the shop anyway. Too much like work." And, still gripping his hand, took a step back from him and delivered a powerful side-kick to the meat of Karl's damaged thigh. The bone gave loudly and Karl collapsed to the floor. Marty pulled open the office door and shouted at a passing deputy, "Reg! Get the paramedics! Karl's taken a fall on his bad leg!"

The whole floor mobilized for the well-liked Rabble. Still Marty found a private moment at his side. "You're in, Karl. Obey me and you'll have it all—your reputation and your job and your poontang, and no prison walls. You with me?"

The pain-filled eyes found his and acknowledged servitude. Marty nodded benignly. Re-breaking Karl's leg had been an inspiration of the moment, but how right it had been. Only this crudest form of subjugation had staying power, to teach a slave his place. "Decide how you fell, Karl, and stick to that story."

WHEN MARTY PULLED into Karl's drive, he had to smile. The poor old gimp sonofabitch. Rabble thought he'd been in slavery to Marty these last three years? He was about to meet his new, superhuman master.

The day was still warm, so he knew he'd find Karl out back by his trout pond. There was the rodeo-hero, in a chaise lounge. The pond was a pretty Dogpatch affair. The spoil from his sloppy bulldozing had been left heaped beyond the pond's farther rim and now formed densely overgrown hillocks of shrubs and thorny berry vines. Along its western rim was an automotive graveyard—a pick-up and flat-bed chassis in various degrees of decay, bulky engine parts woven with weeds scattered around them. Other dingy furniture flanked Karl's lounge. Flattened beer cans and cigarette butts mosaiced the trampled dirt. Karl had a whiskey-bottle on his lap.

The disabled Chief Deputy offered that careful pretense of amity he'd developed for dealing with Marty over the last three years. "Pull up a chair, Marty! Wanna shot? I'd rather sip beer, but I have to get up to piss too often."

"No thanks. Getting around okay?"

"Pretty good. The new pins help. It's tiring, though."

Marty turned another lounge, so he could recline facing Rabble. "I stopped by to tell you, Karl, that you have to start paying your taxes."

"My taxes. I guess you're gonna tell me what that means."

"You knew Jack Fox, didn't you?"

Knew something. His eyes got uneasy. "Not much. People would talk about him . . . ."

"Jack and I were close, Karl. We *are* close. No, just listen. I'll make it very simple. There are powers in the earth, Karl. Powers in the earth. And thanks to Jack Fox, I *have* those powers now. And the thing about these powers that I represent now, is that if you don't pay them their taxes, they take *you* instead."

"Marty, no disrespect, but I can't believe you're really—"

"Hold up." Karl cringed at his sudden movement, but Marty was just springing up and heading over to the automotive boneyard. "This old Chevy engine block. What do you think it weighs, Karl?"

"Three or four hundred? I dunno."

Marty picked it up and hurled it fifty feet into the pond. A great columnar shaft of water sprouted from its impact, rose gracefully, and crumbled down onto the pond's heaving surface.

It was like kicking Karl in the leg three years ago— worth ten thousand words. Rabble gaped up at him, awed. Marty scooted up his lounge so their faces were even closer together when he sat back down. "See? Do I *look* like the circus strongman to you? Something very, very serious is going on all around you, Karl— right now. And you have the choice between *feeding* its power, or becoming its food. Now. This is the piece you're going to use." And he produced a Glock which, along with other guns, he had taken from Jack Fox's house, on the night he went there with the meat wagon that took Jack away.

XV

Karen stood listening to Kyle's chainsaw restart, recommence its gnawing at Jack Fox's darlings . . . looked down at her own saw and her half-full mug of brandy. Tipped over the mug with her foot and watched Dad's precious blood-additive melt—wrinkled gold—into the weeds. But the saw she took up again and refilled its tank. She'd begun this work in panic, and rage at her panic. She would focus on the rage. Do this coldly and well.

She walked back to the stump of her first victim and realized, from a crushed crate under its branches, that she had begun with the tree Susan had fallen from. Susan up on her ladder, sweating, eyes bright . . . Susan alive, just three days ago.

She began to cut her way up toward the start of her row near the highway. She carefully aligned her notch-cuts to the picking lane, to drop the trees square across it and, if their branches tangled with the trees across the lane, went in and cut them apart so the victims lay flat, their red butts aimed at the house. She made her back-cuts perfectly horizontal and tried to leave the neat, half-beveled stumps all of a height. The soothing sweat, the all-obliterating dance of hard, careful work . . . it was almost like peace.

She had to refill her gas can twice from the drum in the big shed before she reached the head of the row. She brought a box wrench and a new chain out with the second can and knelt in the weeds to slip the dulled one off the bar. The old man left half a dozen chains on a nail in the shed wall. Every one of them was sharp, though the whole place was years overgrown.

An idling motor came up behind her. Wolf was back with the empty pickup. "Maaaan! You're runnin' some sweat! You're pumpin' out some juice! You havin' a good time here, or what?" His handsome face was beaming with moronic glee. She saw that he had only that one smile, really, a tool to work closer to people, leverage more liberties, his flinty eyes checking you meanwhile for cracks in your façade, places where he could move in closer to you.

"Well, you tell me," she said. "You're doing the same thing."

"Well, yeah, but . . ." And he waved a hand at all the acres of trees rolling down slope from the house: *I'm* cutting firewood. *You're* insane!

She smiled at him and, overriding a deep fearful instinct, let him see her dislike in her smile. "Got a ways to go, don't I? So I guess I better not stand around jawing." She turned and knelt back to installing the new chain, heard the truck slip oh-so-slowly into gear and roll on inchingly, taking forever to be gone, the man telling her through the engine's growl how his eyes were lingering on her back.

She went back to the other end of her cut and began to finish off the row. She had worked her way almost to where she could see around the house to where the men were working, when she found that they had done working. The truck swung out onto the drive carrying its last load and towing the splitter behind it. Kyle gave a farewell double toot on the horn. Wolf didn't look at her, was turned talking to Kyle. Was on his way right out of the state, thank God.

When they were gone, Karen saw how low the sun was getting and, feeling a sharp chill in the air, went in the house and got her canvas work coat, came out and sank back into the chainsaw-trance. Something in one of the coat's pockets bumped her thigh as she worked. She realized she still had the .357 in there and then forgot it.

Half an hour before sunset the whole row was down, a huge segmented serpent of glittery foliage speared in the flank by shaft after shaft of sawn trunk. It was something. It didn't help against the silence of the night to come, though in a few hours Kyle would fill some of that emptiness It didn't help against all the nights to come, but still this serpent was a good thing to have made, was bold and beautiful, a shout of defiance against him, dear dead Dad.

Night fell outside the bright-lit kitchen as she chopped mushrooms into spaghetti sauce and set it simmering. Then, though at night the bathroom was hard to enter, she went into it long enough to pee and wet a towel with warm water. With this she went out into the living room to undress by the fire she'd built and wipe her body clean. But nakedness was frightening anywhere within these walls and she was quick getting into clean jeans, clean Pendleton. With her running shoes back on, feeling herself once more fight-or-flight ready, she was easier again. And thought: You *cut down his trees bold enough—now go back upstairs to that sewing room.*

She went back in the kitchen, chopped up a salad and put it in the fridge to stay crisp. Then turned on her heel and went to the foot of the staircase—faking out her terror and trying to give it the slip. But found it right back in front of her as she stood at the foot of those stairs. Was that dress still up there? Was that letter? Were they both hallucinations? Even if they were hallucinations, they were still Dad talking to her, Dad still right in there, owning her brain and her bowels. Did she have the spine— Did *she* have the spine to go up there anyway and see what he would tell her?

She started up the stairs and found herself climbing ever more slowly, felt each riser lifting her into a whole other atmosphere of fear, where she had to pause and learn if she could breathe it . . . . The light from the living room sank behind her foot by foot, while the upstairs darkness inched down, bringing her the smell of its old, worn carpet, of the ancient varnish on its dark, closed doors.

Far outside, she heard the sigh of an engine on the highway. Was it decelerating? She could not tell . . . and then couldn't hear it any more.

She stood waiting. Waited a long time and no sound followed. Her heart was hammering. She looked up into the darkness.

Not tonight. Tomorrow, in the daylight. She could give herself that much—her heart was still bleeding from Susan's terrible wounds. She could not bear more terror, not this night. She would give herself the solace of Kyle's company, try to take some hope and courage from him, a man who had lived at least as hard as she had. Tomorrow, by daylight, she would climb all the way up these stairs and go into the sewing room.

Karen turned and went back down the stairs. Kyle would be another hour. She slipped her canvas coat back on and stepped out the back door into the autumn chill. A waxing gibbous moon was up, its moonlight filling a strange new void, a field of stumps where Dad's special trees had stood all through her childhood, all through her life.

The devastation she'd ordered shocked her, then the shock grew on her, became hope, even a first stir of joy. This wonderful emptiness she'd created caused her to shiver. All Dad's crooked old poison-mothers, vanished at her will, only beautiful moonlight here in their stead. Breathing it in, it felt like pure freedom.

All the trimmed branches, still studded with fruit, lay in a big pile to one side. Karen wanted some gesture to proclaim her victory, a rite of defiance. Stepping off the porch, she came to the trim-pile, a shaggy mound as high as she was tall. A bittersweet smell came off it of sheared wood, sap, and bruised fruit. Unbidden, a memory flooded her of how she'd loved these trees as a little girl. Of how she'd stood small beneath them, looking up into their sun-drenched splendor.

It took her several heartbeats to find her rage again, her vengefulness. "Hmmm," she murmured. "How 'bout an apricot?"

She reached into the heap for a handsome pair as a trophy and slid her grip around a plump pair of spheres. But what greeted her palm was the cold, slack elephant skin of a hairy scrotum, which holstered balls like eggs of ice. The alien flesh stirred and its slow, reptilian wrinkling tickled her fingers.

Recoiling so powerfully her heels snagged, she toppled onto her back. The wind knocked out of her, she lay gasping and just then heard, beyond the house behind her, the crunch of gravel far out on the drive. Footsteps.

Kyle would be driving his truck . . . .

The steps came on, a purposeful stride. . . someone big.

Dad was her first thought, her palm still tingling with the nightmare it had gripped. But another thought followed, one more urgent than nightmares, one that put the hard earth back under her and set her struggling to her feet. Instinctively she shunned the house—now was not the moment to be boxed inside it.

Her legs steadied as she ran to the house corner, crouched and peeked around it. The footsteps were still beyond the curve in the drive from which she would be visible. Darting across to the big shed and working her way around it, she crouched down and peeked from that corner.

It *was* Wolf. *Crunch, crunch, crunch*—here he came, high, wide, and handsome, and just detectably unsteady from the booze he'd been drinking. The big asshole climbed the porch, opened the front door, and walked right in.

She had to get a grip, had to get cold and clear, fast. Her truck was out, the keys were in the living room. What about Kyle? Kyle wouldn't have told him he was coming back, or Wolf wouldn't be here. He thought Wolf was gone from the state and Wolf thought Kyle was gone from this place. All Karen had to do was stay hidden till Kyle showed up.

Wolf would know from the set table that Karen was here—that she'd spotted him, bolted, was hiding and, after a while, he'd know she wasn't hiding in the house. How long could she elude him? She knew these acres and he didn't.

If she should get into the orchard a dozen rows deep and hide in the weeds, she could watch both doors of the house. Turning, Karen saw that the trees she had felled formed a wall of tangled boughs she couldn't crawl through without considerable noise. She would have to go up or down the open truck-lane, in the moonlight, to get around the felled row and into the standing trees. And then she wouldn't be able to watch the house.

Meanwhile—it struck her—Wolf was poking around in that house, where every handgun known to man was on display and every form of booze would make him more reckless. It was like Dad at his worst had come back in this goon's body. Dad was back in the house. She remembered Wolf noisily smacking on one of Dad's apricots.

Then, like an earthquake her mind's eye showed her the twelve-gauge pump shotgun, with five rounds of double-ought in it, leaning against the cellar wall beside Dad's workbench, right where she'd left it when she woke up this afternoon. It was the worst thing for Wolf to find before Kyle got here and the best thing for her and Kyle to have when he did get here.

But what if—an aftershock here—a slower and deeper jolt than remembering the shotgun, was she sure she wanted her *and Kyle* to have it when he got here? Kyle: I'll make sure she's home—cooking dinner. You go in and make the grab. I'll come by and join the party . . . .

Could *that* be true of him? She'd seen Kyle laugh— you could trust that, couldn't you? When you didn't know someone at his core you unconsciously waited for that, to see how he laughed, before you started trusting him . . . you looked to see if he really liked laughing. But some people knew all the moves and could fake them. Especially sharp-minded, older men like Kyle. Could do anything with their faces, while their guts were cold. And in that case it was twice as urgent that *she* should have the shotgun.

But—did she dare? Even as she asked it, she saw a light come on upstairs—Wolf was poking around in her parents' bedroom. She dared not think, because from this instant every thought was risk, was lost time. And instantly she was up, running in a crouch, creeping as she neared the side of the house.

Finding the ground-level basement window above Dad's workbench, she prayed that the sash would move, and planted the heels of her hands under the thick wood mullion, heaving upward. The sash faintly groaned and gave with a chalky whisper—came up perhaps a foot before binding. It would be just enough, but she had to be infinitely careful not to make noise putting her foot down among Dad's tools. Better to thrust in head-first, explore the dark bench top with her hands, and draw her legs in after her.

She eased head-first into the dark and musty cellar air. It was laced with a cold ghost of the fruit-cellar's terrifying scent. Light from within limned the cellar-door—had she left the light on down there?

Her hands found scarred wood clear of obstructions. She put her weight on her palms, brought each leg in and gingerly planted its knee on the bench top. All her nerves were prickling for the least noise from the house above her, especially for the least creak of the floor-joists just over her head.

Learning how well she moved under extreme fear— she dropped down softly, square on the balls of her feet. Not a sound, from anywhere. Two stealthy steps to the end of the bench and she thrust her hands into the shadow where she'd left the gun standing. It wasn't there. Her eyes, adjusted to the greater dark, could see her hands groping emptiness.

The side of her head exploded; a concrete avalanche hit her shoulder and punched her skull again from the opposite side. From above her came a bray. Her stunned brain grasped it was words: "Looking for this?" The cellar door was kicked open and she was hauled by her belt into its spill of yellow light.

She lay with her head tilted back off the lip of the steep wooden steps; her vision steadied enough to show her Wolf, way up there, smiling down his one smile. He set something down—the shotgun? She couldn't move, couldn't seize the moment. He took her up by the belt again and threw her down the steps like luggage. The risers slugged her shoulder, chest, arms, head. Karen found she still had reflexes and kept her head tucked to her chest, her arms hugged to her. She came to rest face-down on the cellar floor, skull ringing and her left hand in agony, something surely broken there.

Wolf came down to stand astride her. Between his bracketing legs she felt the grind of his weight against the earth—hopelessly bigger, hopelessly stronger than she had ever been at her strongest. With a groan, she freed her left arm from under her and laid it out across the floor. Something definitely cracked in the hand.

The muzzle of the shotgun bit against the back of her neck. "Now you hold still, bitch, and don't give me any trouble." It was almost Dad's voice that came out of him, gritty and deep.

Reaching under her, with some difficulty, he undid her belt, shucked her jeans to her ankles, and then pinned them together with tight wraps of the belt. Jailhouse love. Straight and to the point. She couldn't stand up, but her legs could be spread, and he wrenched them apart, kneeling down between them. She felt the crush of his sharp shins across her calves

Scraping her face against the floor, Karen looked to either side and saw the dusty glint of the dark jars on their shelves. It seemed to her these jars were filled with rot, pure jellied poison. They had watched her taken apart decades ago and it was time for them to watch it again. Wolf was working at his own belt and britches, having trouble and muttering, *shit*.

He laid the shotgun on the floor and as she felt it knock the earth she lay on, she realized that her right hand, sandwiched between her belly and the ground, was pinched between two different hardnesses—the floor and something metal in her coat. Sucking in her stomach, she found the lip of the coat pocket with her fingertips. Her hand gophered into it, fingered a checked grip, swarmed like a spider around the full shape of the Smith . . . the web of her thumb on the hammer . . . her forefinger crossing the trigger.

She pressed her broken hand on the floor, its agony a remote fact, as she levered her chest up off the floor just enough to free her right hand, bringing it up, swinging it back. And with one liquid trigger squeeze, she squirted thunder from the blunt, brute barrel and blew a hole through the center of Wolf's throat.

XVI

Kyle drove up an hour later, his headlights flooding Karen on the porch steps. He took in her damaged face and dead eyes, the bottle between her knees and her hand laid across them. Her other hand, holding something, hanging down between her thighs . . .

Killing the lights and the engine quick, he got out and stood there a moment before approaching her. Finally, carefully, coming close. He seemed to consider touching her and decided he shouldn't.

"Karen?"

Her gaze wandered, as if everything around her had changed. Both amazement and bitterness in her eyes, as if she'd foreseen what it had changed into. When she saw him, she seemed to be trying to make him out from a distance. Absently, she brought up a big-bore revolver and rested it on her thigh. A bruise on her head peeked out through her tangled hair.

"Tell me what happened, Karen."

Her eyes moved from him to the orchard around them, like he was part of it all. With the bottle, she gestured behind her, "Go down to the basement, the door's near the kitchen. Go down to the fruit cellar."

He climbed the porch and entered the house.

Following him in her mind's eye, she sat there. Mentally watching Kyle approach the fruit-cellar enabled her, at last, to possess what she had done. Her very own homicide lay down there dribbling blood on the packed-earth floor. Karen Fox had fired and sprayed the life out of that body. Slowly, oh so slowly, her heart began to rise within her, her spirit lofted, exulting. The terror would come, but first she had this all her own. It was joy. It was Justice.

Beyond this moment loomed Marty, Harst, Babcock—they'd love it, they'd eat it up, they'd make sure she spent the rest of her life behind bars. But first—now—was this genial sun rising inside her, a wound unwounded, a murder of the soul avenged before it could be committed against her. Tears of silent gratitude ran down Karen's face.

Kyle came back out of the house, looking older, haggard. She looked up serenely at him. "Karen, I was in prison for killing a man who tried to kill me, in a fight of his making. I did seven years, but I did no wrong. Neither have you, you have done no wrong. Do you hear me?"

"Yes. I'm amazingly lucid, I know exactly which bone in my hand is fractured. I know who's in the cellar and what I did to him. I'm *calm*. I just don't have the least idea what I'm going to do now."

"I'll help you. Let's be clear about this, though. If you hadn't killed Wolf and I'd been here, *I* would have. You don't have a killing on your hands—I do. I never trusted Wolf, but I thought I had his measure. I fatally underestimated . . . his hollowness. I thought he had some friendship in him. I've fucked up your life with my mistake. I owe you anything at all I can possibly do."

"Like what?"

"I know the criminal justice system. Even innocent, in a situation like this, you're grist for their mill, you're product. We'll do whatever you want, but I think what we really must do is clean up everything and make the body disappear."

"You're just like I thought you were," said Karen dreamily. She was still somewhere in the ozone it seemed, still high on Justice, on deliverance. "You're like . . . an Upright Man, like in a Victorian novel." She smiled.

He smiled back, but sadly. "An upright man is what I'd like to be, but I am saying that we must commit a major felony and not give even a moment's thought to obeying the law. If you choose otherwise, we'll go to the Sheriff."

Karen shuddered. She considered where they might hide Wolf's corpse . . . and an image came to her. Yes, give Dad his own, make it *his* murder. "I know where to put him," she said. "That piece of shit will be clean bone in a week."

SITTING ON THE COUCH by a fire built high and hot, Kyle wrapped her hand and forearm, splinting them with a scrolled magazine, making a sling from bandanas. He cleaned her scrapes and cuts and smeared them with antiseptic ointment, brought her water and a prescription bottle of Mom's old Vicodins, relics of her months of dying.

For all the gentleness of his ministrations, it was like being flayed. It stripped her down to her pains and under the pain was the cold. Her exhaustion was absolute. The intoxication of justice had left her. At the center of her mind was terror—of the corpse she had made and the prison bars to come from it.

She sat sweating and trembling as Kyle disappeared for a while. He came back with Wolf's clothes in his arms and spread them carefully, piece by piece on the flames. The shirt and jeans were sprayed with the blow-back of tissue and blood that had geysered from the slug's entry—all the gore was stark-lit for an instant before it blackened and shriveled.

"Karen . . . Karen? . . . Listen . . . . He's wrapped in the tarp. I'm going to be down there a while—doing a wipe down and full scrubbing with rags. We'll fine-tune it later . . . . You hear me? . . . *Listen* . . . . When those are ash, lay more wood and put his boots on top, will you do that? Keep stirring it, burn everything down. We'll bury the ashes tomorrow."

KYLE STEERED HIS PICKUP into the back yard, parked by the kitchen door, and switched off the engine. They sat in the dark a moment. "We've got about four hours to sunrise," he said. "I wish I didn't need your help."

Karen just shook her head. Her body seemed mere mass, as void of movement as a stone. "Karen, I don't really know you. A few things, maybe, I know. Important things, but not what I—not what *we* need to know right now. So I have to ask, and you have to be sure of your answer, because the rest of our lives depend on it."

"Yes. Okay."

"Are you your own woman? Can you bury your own dead and keep silence? Can you carry the knowledge of that secret grave for the rest of your life?"

Karen looked once more down the corridor of her alternate life, should she turn away from this black rite before them: the arrest for murder by Marty Carver was a given. If Marty suppressed evidence, she might never get out of prison. If he merely obstructed and dragged

his heels, she would be years at the toil of proving her
innocence—would grow older and dimmer and drunker,
a caged animal in that pompous circus of the law. All
this, while justice was *hers*. She had *been* justice.

"I can keep silence."

He touched her arm and nodded—slipped out of the
cab and went in through the kitchen door. And came out
with the long tarped bundle folded over his shoulder.
When he dropped its weight into the truck bed, Karen
flashed back on the childhood sensation of sitting in
Dad's truck and feeling it sag when he climbed aboard.
She looked at the heap of lopped branches that Kyle, and
the corpse in back, had left from Dad's brandy trees,
and her hand remembered what it had found dangling
from one of those branches a lifetime ago, three hours
ago. It struck her that this orchard was the arch-Gothic
setting. If she was the heroine, as she had jested the day
she first came back, then this, Dad's Manse, was the
ultimate Dark Castle, where dwelt the male energy at
its most murderous . . .

Down the lanes they drove, the tools rattling in
the truck bed, Wolf's shifting weight slithery in its
tarp. The plum trees were startled green beasts in the
headlights, surprised in their deep communion with
the night, bristling like spiders at the intruders.

They arrived at Wolf's tomb. They stared at it, the
compost heap's black, tire-studded bulk lost in the darkness to either side of the headlights' white splash. Unfed
for three years now, the great worm's plastic sheath was
shriveling like old skin. The offering they'd brought it
was so small, a mere morsel to its hugeness . . . .

"We spread the plastic at that seam, then fold it back.
I'll toss the tires down—can you carry them out of the
way? The less we drag up the dirt here, the better."

"I can carry them."

Pulling the truck tight alongside the heap, Kyle climbed onto the roof of the cab. The tires he couldn't reach he pushed aside with a branch prop they'd brought. He pried up the edge of the sheeting and Karen peeled it back. The wall of rot exposed—black as the plastic—steamed in the night air.

Kyle aimed the idling truck's lights at their niche. Near the shed were flat-topped hand-carts for hauling picked fruit out of the lanes and they pulled these over. "We'll pile all the spoil we can on these. We can hose 'em off after. Let's spread out that tarp for what has to go on the ground."

And so it began, axe and spade, axe and spade. Not all the sinew of twig and branch in the compost had quite dissolved. Kyle had to chop free a wedge before his spade could bite it out and heap it reeking on the carts. As he dug deeper, thick steam wrapped him till he seemed to be melting into the headlights' radiance. He worked like a demon and mulch collected on the tarp to either side of him. The urgency of this work swept Karen up. It was like surgery on a giant worm, tissue to be removed and replaced at urgent speed, so that sunrise would find the giant whole and unscarred.

She took up a shovel and unslung her left arm. Found she could use her left forearm for a fulcrum on the haft and socket the haft's butt against her right shoulder for added shove. She shoveled the spoil onto the carts, ducking in and out of the rhythm of Kyle's much more violent labor.

When they were piled high she trundled the carts aside . . . positioned the emptie . . . . shoveled, shoveled, shoveled, with the scorching wet breath of the crypt drenching her. Kyle's voice welled out of the steam.

"Christ! It must be a hundred and twenty in here. It's a sauna!"

Two hours had passed before Kyle slit Wolf's duct-taped sheath and unwrapped his nudity. So complete Wolf seemed to her in his nakedness, if she didn't look at his head . . . All the detailed symmetries. It seemed she looked on an alien species, such was her sense of revelation. They carried him inside the smoking niche, Kyle with his shoulders, Karen with his knees. Between them he lay. The bullet had broken his neck and his head lolled. A dreamer, Wolf floated to his steaming bed.

In a deep angle of muck, soft and hot as just-cooked pudding, they tucked him. A shaft of the headlights struck him there, as white as snow by contrast with the black rot. Kyle tucked his legs up and Karen remembered photos of Neolithic burials, knee bones tented against ribcages, bony toys put away after their brief dance millennia ago. They were hiding Wolf away in the distant future . . . .

The filling-in went faster. Kyle made the muck fly into the hellmouth of mist. Karen shoveled in tandem, a sense of victory growing in her. She had never worked at such a sweating pitch and still felt so *cold*.

She couldn't help at the end, when Kyle had to toss it high enough to restore the compost's upper curve, so no betraying sag showed in the plastic when it was scrolled back in place. Then he once more moved the truck, climbed on its roof and, with Karen's help below, re-draped the black shroud. He replaced all the tires, used a rake to drag the higher ones back into position.

Mucky tarps and tools back in the truck-bed, the carts hosed clean beyond the shed—Karen was no help at all now. She leaned against the truck, her consciousness ebbing and then returning with a shock. The east was just getting gray.

She was back in the cab of the truck, rocking up the lanes towards the house. "Karen? Karen?"

"What?"

"We made it . . . . But you're hypothermic, you're almost in shock. I've got to undress you and get you in a tub of hot water. Trust me, please. I've got to get your temperature back up."

She nodded, or maybe only thought she did. She was gone.

She was naked in Kyle's arms and he held her like a lifted bride, his arms and chest all muscle, like knobbed and padded wood. She lay in the air on these strange supports, then was sinking, sinking into searing heat, unbearable heat . . . no . . . *luscious* heat, embracing warmth, salvation.

KAREN WOKE in her sleeping bag on the couch, morning light flooding the windows, smelled coffee and the fresh-soaped scent of her own body within the bag. Kyle was in the armchair. He smiled and gestured at the steaming cup on the table, toasted her with his own and sipped. His face looked battered in this light, scars on his cheekbone and brow she hadn't noticed before. The one on his brow looked like a side-ways slash aimed at his eyes he'd ducked just in time.

"You washed me," she said.

He looked embarrassed. "Not too thoroughly," he said. It made her smile and him, too, after a moment. "You were—"

"Hypothermic. You saying that's the last thing I remember . . . . Thank you, Kyle"

"No! I brought this on you. Don't thank me. Just forgive me."

He looked so desolate it made her danger dawn on her afresh: a corpse of her making hidden here. But she wanted to comfort him too, his guilt recalling her own for Susan. "There was death here . . . trouble here before you came. You walked into something, you didn't just bring it."

His eyes were fixed on hers, seeing something of what she wasn't daring to say. She had *touched* that dress and there had been black blood on her fingers the morning after . . . .

"What are you remembering, Karen? What's been happening here?"

His eyes seemed way too close to hers though he sat across the table from her. How had he gotten so close to her thoughts? But, how could he *not* have?

"Would you give me my pack? I need to get dressed." He stood with his back to her while she pulled on jeans and sweatshirt, wincing with the work.

Dizzy, she lay back down on the bag. "Okay," she said.

When he turned around, perhaps having sensed her pain, he handed her Mom's phial of Vicodins. She swallowed one with the coffee, meeting his eyes as she did, his eyes still close, too close. "What's happening here—" she felt she was following her voice out over an abyss— "is either that I'm insane, or what's *happening* here is insane."

He came around the coffee table, sat down on it. Then looked at her and held out his hand, palm up. After two heartbeats, she put her good hand in it. "You drink," he said. "And you're afraid you've gone past the point of no return."

"That's the first possibility."

Very gently, he laid his other hand on top of hers, his eyes never wavering from hers. "You haven't, Karen. I saw it last night. You're all here, you're whole. You couldn't have done what you did if you weren't."

Tears spilled out of her eyes and she blinked them away, still holding his gaze. If what he said was true, then she had been *living* a nightmare and not just *having* one. Susan was dead. Someone had killed her and vanished, and she knew damn well who that someone was. She pulled her hand free gently and wiped her eyes.

"Maybe I can tell you what's been happening. Maybe later . . . ." When she knew him better? The thought almost made her laugh. He touched her shoulder, got up and went back to his chair.

"I'll have all the time you need, Karen. But right now we have to talk about *details*. I've cleaned and put away all the tools and chain-dragged the ground down where we worked. All the dirty tarps are in my truck and I'll drop 'em in dumpsters on my way through town . . . because here's the hitch. I've got a parole review, down in the state capital. I have to go, be gone today and half tomorrow. Everything should be all right, but there's something you have to look into. When I left him at the bus station, Wolf had a gym bag with his gear in it. I haven't found it, but it has to be around because I don't think he planned to go back into Gravenstein from here." A bit of a pause. "You've got to make sure it's not here in the house someplace. He probably went from the station to some tavern, bought some drinks, chumming up the locals, and promoted himself a ride out here."

"And he was going to leave here . . . ?"

"Wolf wasn't the planning type. Now I see how little I knew him. I don't think we can rule out that he meant to kill you, Karen, and drive off in your truck. Keep that in mind and you'll find peace with what we've done."

"I am at peace with what we've done. I'm just not okay about the law, Marty Carver runs it, he hates me and he wants this place for himself."

"Okay. But Wolf came to town the day before we started here, stayed with me both those nights, ten to one Carver doesn't even know he exists. Just make sure his stuff's not somewhere around here. I found the slug and got it out of the wall—we were lucky there. I dug the blood out of the floor, re-raked the dirt and packed it, wiped down all the spray off the jars and shelves. I think I got it all, but if you're up to it, take a rag and some ammonia and make sure."

"Yeah."

"Here, take this." He handed her the .357. "I can't risk having this on me, or I would ditch it. Get rid of it, far from here. I think you have to sleep more before you start . . . but here's an alarm clock I found. Then please go and get your hand treated, out in Bushmill, or even farther. Say you hurt it cutting down those plum trees— get that in the record."

"Okay."

"I'm sorry I have to leave you now, Karen. Alone. But with my record, we can't afford the attention. Remember that we've *already* made this disappear, these are just details."

"Kyle . . ." What had already passed between them stopped her from thanking him. That he should have brought a man like Wolf here was part of who he was. But the whole of who he was, tears came to her eyes and she opened her arms.

He moved into them. The caution with which he embraced her recalled the first time he had shaken her hand—hydraulic strength applied with exquisite gentleness. She felt his voice through her breasts, her ribcage, like the purring of a gentle beast. "Karen, I brought this on you and I'll never rest until I know you're safe."

At the door he gave her a slip of paper. "Here's the number of the hotel I'll be at. Call me tonight from Bushmill." From the window, she watched his truck move out the drive, still feeling his arms around her. Together they'd buried Wolf . . . and buried Dad with him? But that thought made her shiver and the feel of Kyle's arms left her.

When he was gone, she resolved to start at once. She lay down for just a moment, reviewing the materials she would need to clean the cellar . . . and was gone.

AN HOUR LATER, she came full awake, weighing a thought that seemed to have come in her sleep. Last night, just before Wolf came crunching down the drive, she had heard the sound of a *motor* out on the highway. The sound tapered slowly, as if it might have slowed down not much beyond the orchard. What if the son of a bitch stole a car and drove it out here? And it was hidden just off road near the property?

There was a knock at the front door.

She was up and striding to it, swift confrontation her only remedy to her terror. The taped up hand? Hurt it cutting down those trees. The trunk of the last of them came down before she was ready.

It was Mr. Fratelli, short and upright, in the full pomp of his leather coat and gaudy black hair. "Karen!

I wake you up? You gotta get up wit da sun, run an orchard. Whaddya doin' to those trees out there?"

"Hi, Mr. Fratelli. I'm doing whatever I *want* to them, is what I'm doing." She made a wry face and raised her taped hand, on which Fratelli's sharp eye had already lighted. "I hurt myself cutting them down. I'm resting up, but I have to take off." Her relief at encountering only a greedy buyer for Dad's land was waning fast. Fratelli acted very familiar with the place, coming to the back door. She couldn't invite him in. She remembered the ragged holes the double-ought had punched in the living room walls, the ceiling.

But he showed no wish to enter. "You say you got apricots, peaches. I got Sal inna truck, we take some off your hands."

"I got thirteen flats already picked. Drive around to the back and load them up. And I'll do my own picking. I'll bring you the rest in a day or two, when I get my hand tended to."

Sal, with his occasional meaningless leer at her, loaded the flats. Fratelli gave her a wad of twenties. "Three hunnerd. I don't squeeze the pennies wit' friends." And he looked around saying this, an indescribable something in his face as he took in the stumps of Dad's brandy trees, the mountain of trimmings still jeweled with fruit.

"Were you really good friends with my Dad, Mr. Fratelli?"

Acknowledging the undertones of her question, he looked her in the eyes as if to say, *We both know something about old Jack Fox, don't we, Karen?*

Which, oddly, reassured her. He wasn't like Marty, or Harst, a disciple of Jack's. He was more a detached observer. He wanted to buy this place, but she saw, with instant certainty, that he wanted it to sell at great profit to those who truly craved it.

This brought inspiration. "You know the idea of selling this place, Mr. Fratelli, the idea appeals to me more and more. But you're way too low, number one. Number two, I have to talk with some business partners in San Francisco—settle some questions about my reinvestment plans. Bring me a better offer—a much better offer."

"'Ey. We talk again, I see what I can do, but you gotta be a realist here! Sal! Whadda ya waitin?"

She weighed what she'd done, watching them drive off, and hoped that she'd set invisible tumblers clicking around her. Some feelers must have gone from Fratelli to Dad's eager heirs and he'd be sure to make them aware of accelerating negotiations, if not of his purchase price. If Marty and Harst thought they had ownership in view, they would leave her alone. Hopefully, no more of Marty's poking around on this or that pretext.

But, she would *never* sell Dad's place now. Not until she could haul off the compost heap and dump it into the sea.

XVII

After Marty sent for Babcock, he sat at his desk, unlocked and opened a lower drawer. Nestled in there: a Smith .38, a Glock 19, an old but lovingly conditioned 1911 Colt .45, and a Ruger 9mm. He'd taken every one of them from Jack Fox's house the same evening he had learned the great man had set by the scepter and the mantle of his lordship and had sprayed some of the trees of his orchard with his skull and his teeth and his brains.

For each of these weapons, Jack Fox had made up all the loads. Jack Fox had fearlessly gone down to meet the Power. And, surely, had dragged down Harst, his high priest, after him. Look what Fox had boldly done! Look, too, at what Marty Carver must now just as boldly do! For Jack had placed the scepter in Marty's hands, to seed the earth with further sacrifice.

The guns awed Marty, they and his present duty, so that when Babcock appeared, puffing and blowing with outrage—word was the fool's personal car had been stolen last night—Marty never raised his eyes from Jack's weapons.

"Close that door, stand there, and shut up," he snapped.

The thing was, once Marty *began* this seeding of the earth, there would be no undoing it. The Power would reach up into the sun to feed, would start to seek its food at large. He would be great with the Power's greatness, but . . . in what kind of world would Marty stand so tall? Though for half his life he had dreamed of this threshold he now stood on, it seemed that he faced the question for the first time. It was a brave, great thing Jack Fox had done! How tall he had stood, how like a lion he had outfaced his death! But surely, an awesome passage was before Marty Carver in his turn and he, too, must become like a lion to confront it!

He rose and came around the desk, planting himself in front of the beefy deputy. "You think you're really something, Babcock. Always parking that stupid Mustang of yours with the keys dangling from the ignition! I've seen it a dozen times around town. You think you're so bad, so fearsome, that no one *dares* to steal it! Well let me tell you, you brainless side of beef, today of all days, I did not *need* a crime created by one of my own deputies because he is a moron. Step closer to me."

Babcock was visibly uneasy at this command, but he stepped forward, past his comfort zone, and into the aura of his superior's authority.

"Step closer."

Babcock stepped well inside of Marty's reach, in reach of an embrace, if Carver extended his arms. The Assistant Chief Deputy extended only his right hand and gripped his Deputy's shoulder. Babcock's knees sagged and he groaned aloud.

"Lower your voice," said Marty calmly. "Listen carefully. You'll take the unmarked Dodge." Added pressure, a shriller groan, a desperate nod. Sweat was pouring down Babcock's bullock face. "You know the bitch I've got out at Spaith's?" Another frantic nod, Marty's deputies were all aware of everything in the county that enjoyed the Assistant Chief Deputy's personal protection. "Turns out she's a murderer. We know, but don't have the evidence. You take her out into the trees and kill her. Stay there close by her body to make sure she's dead. Then leave her there and report back here to me."

Babcock groaned again as Marty released his grip. As stunned by Marty's strength as by his orders, he gaped at his master, who faintly smiled and added, "You'll do this, Babcock, or you'll spend twelve years in prison for the Pakistani. You shot him right in the back of the neck. Now, nod your head, or go to prison. Good. Take an unmarked car and take this weapon, it's cold. Be *sure* you kill her with *this*." He handed Babcock the .38 Smith. "Bring the gun back to me when you're done and from the moment you drive out, to the moment you return, maintain absolute radio silence. Do you copy? Stay absolutely *off* the radio. You got that?"

"Yes, sir."

KAREN PULLED on her jacket and slipped the .357 into the pocket. If she found what she suspected, acting fast would be essential, no coming back for anything. She went up to Mom's sewing room and slipped Dad's letter into her pocket. Mom's Vicodins, after she swallowed two more, went into another pocket.

Out the gravel drive to the highway; past the oak trees bordering the orchard. Following the remembered, stealthy motor noise where it had passed last night, not long before Wolf came for her . . . just beyond the Fox acres, where oak-scrub and berries grew thick up to the highway. Karen detected a torn seam in the vegetal screen. Heart hammering, she stepped nearer and, within the foliage, detected a hint of metallic blue.

A bright blue Mustang convertible, some restored classic from the sixties, stood roughly parked in a small clearing in the scrub. The keys were dangling from the ignition and there was an athletic bag on the seat. The asshole must have just gone out and stolen a car for his ride out here to rape her.

Driving this thing out of here she'd be bare-ass naked to anyone in the Sheriff's Department, who might have seen the car's description on the morning's bulletin. The cherried blue paint job was scratched by tough oak twigs, both doors scraped along their bottoms by the rocky ground coming off-road. The same harsh indifference Wolf had felt towards her body he had shown towards this ride, clearly somebody's baby. What a piece of shit!

It had to be taken and ditched, immediately. Wait till dark? It might not be reported yet, but by then it surely would. The pain of her fracture was sickening. Her body begged to for rest, but it had to be now. Climb in. Ditch it near town—ballsy, but the best place to hide it. Ditch it and hop a bus to Bushmill.

It rumbled alive like a dream and the roof came purring up over her. She closed the windows and accelerated in reverse. It bucked and wallowed, blundering backwards, taking more scratches, then jounced out onto the asphalt. Not a car in sight for a mile ahead or behind. Karen peeled out and set the Mustang humming at a comfy country sixty.

Taking the wheel in her hurt hand, she groaned as she unzipped the gym-bag. Out wafted a funky lair-smell. Pawing through the stuff made her cringe, but she got over it—she had, after all, killed the piece of shit . . . . A black nylon windbreaker, some jeans, T-shirts and briefs—all dirty. A 25-box of .38 rounds, but no .38. A comb. Not a scrap of writing, or paper. An awfully clean residue. It wouldn't have much to tell as trash scattered twenty miles away from the Fox place.

BABCOCK KEPT SQUARING his shoulders as he drove, each time bringing agony, but forgetting and doing it again. It was a habit of his when he was struggling to think his way out of a dilemma. It never brought clarity, but it was reassuring to remember the mass of his shoulders. Then the pain brought him back to his mission. His left hand still felt half dead. There was a sick twinge within the mauled meat of the arm itself. Carver had actually cracked his arm-bone! Just by squeezing! To do that, he had to have a grip like a *machine*.

Considering that inhuman grip, Babcock's agony of indecision disappeared for a while. This was some deep shit Carver was dropping him in, but Babcock was a devout believer in superior force and that iceberg Carver had it. Absolutely no question that he could and would put Babcock away for twelve years' hard time, making half the force lie under oath to lock him up—anything it took. His workmates only drank with him, and thwacked his back, because they feared him physically. He knew that and enjoyed it, but also knew that if he was tied up with a stick of dynamite poking out his ass, any one of them would gladly light the fuse.

But this was *cold*! It wasn't the way Law Enforcement *did* things. If you wanted to punish a killer, you beefed up the evidence and lied on the stand, or made someone else lie, and then sent his—no, *her*—ass to hard time or the death house! You didn't take her out into a walnut orchard and *cap* her! That wasn't Criminal Justice! The whole point of being a cop was killing people *legally*!

And just where was he going to shoot her? He knew the woman and her place, had on several occasions been sent by Carver to deliver her rent money. Babcock had seen those amazing Mexican tits she had on her and he recoiled from the thought of a chest shot. Burly Babcock discovered in himself, for the first, amazing time, a kind of . . . humanity. Killing men was fine, but he found he felt it was, like . . . *cruel* to kill a woman! He'd never known this kind of depth, this *complication* in himself.

As he approached the Oak Creek Bridge, his foot came off the gas. On a dirt turnoff down there, a blue Mustang was perched on the Creek's high bank. *His* blue Mustang! And that dyke bitch Karen Fox was standing beside it flinging clothes down into the fast-moving water.

Fury and righteous vengeance convulsed him. But as he moved to brake and throw a screeching spin-around, the movement sent agony through his shoulder—and he remembered his master, the man who had tucked the dynamite up his ass. His foot came right back off the brake and he kept on driving toward Spaith's. After all, he knew where the bitch lived. *Her* he could kill. And come to that, could kill this Mex bitch too . . . .

He swung through the weathered, hinge-sprung gates and the Dodge growled down colonnades of gold-leaved walnut trees, burst walnuts gunfiring under his tires. When he pulled up to the shacks, he stepped out into a surprising silence, only the whisper of hundreds of acres of leaves and nothing more. Then the door of her shack opened. She didn't step forward, just showed herself. That dark face, those Indian eyes that didn't tell you anything. In her skirt and her sleeveless shirt, she was one abundant woman.

"Ma'am," he said, "Chief Carver needs to see you down at the sheriff's station. Just get into my car, ma'am."

She didn't hide her hesitation, but then obeyed. When they were seated together up front, her scent was earthen and spicy and her femininity seemed massive, seemed to make the Dodge tilt to her side as they pulled away from the shacks. He felt almost intimidated. Was the Smith Marty had given him . . . a big enough gun to put down this mass of brown life?

Just as he was pulling out, he realized that a tiny old woman, wearing a battered fedora over her gray curls, was standing on the porch of a shack across the yard, gazing at their departure with grave, sad eyes. A panic of lost control, sudden disaster, rippled through him, but he didn't dare stop the car, his possession of Lupe felt too precarious, and the killing of her loomed too urgent and frightful before him. If he stopped now, he'd never do it. Should he come back and kill this old bitch? He would call Marty—but Marty had said *radio silence*.

What was happening to him here? Just keep a grip, keep driving . . . .

The picking lanes were spoking past them. This whole mission was insane! Why did he have to do it in an orchard? Anyone passing could look right up these corridors and see you plain as day a hundred yards off. Then, ahead, the acreage rolled into a broad depression. The carpet of gold trees sank, so that the lanes between them dropped just below view from this service road. He swerved and was suddenly jouncing along between the trees, down into the dish of low ground.

The woman recoiled, hugging the door. He looked into the tar-pits of her eyes—so huge her eyes were! "He's not at the station!" he blurted. Babcock was having another unprecedented experience. He was improvising! "He doesn't wanna go near your house. He's waiting in the trees. Sheriff Carver's waiting in the trees!"

That sounded strange. He pictured Carver up in a walnut tree, gripping the branches like a chimp. But the way she stared—did she even understand what he was saying? She was still hugging the door, but at least she wasn't jumping out. If she didn't jump out, he'd shortly be downslope there, invisible from the road. But was he really going to *do* this? A few seconds more and they had sunk out of sight from the service road.

Babcock hit the brakes and realized, as Lupe flung open her door and sprang out, she'd just been waiting a chance to bolt and, once she had her legs under her, this tough little bitch could *move*, could duck between the trees and dodge his fire. He got his hand on her ankle as she leapt, but the car, lurching forward again, broke his grip. He toppled out after, jarring his cracked shoulder to a blinding agony, got his feet under him and dove for her just as she had scrambled to her feet. Again caught her leg (as he heard the driverless Dodge crunch into a walnut tree) and again lost his grip, but caused her to fall more severely now, pitching her face-first against the earth, slamming the wind out of her.

He pulled the Smith as he leapt on her, was suddenly relieved to discover how easy this was going to be, done in the tumult of pursuit like this. Aimed and planted a slug in her upper spine as she scrambled to get her legs under her. In the leafy silence the steely slam of the shot seemed to nail her as much as the slug did, hammering her face-down to the earth.

As Babcock dropped to his knees beside her to plant a finisher in the back of her skull, she erupted, rose and flipped violently onto her back, fixing the black holes of her eyes on his. Her eyes transfixing him, his gun-hand froze. She lay staring up at him, her arms flung back as though she were pinned to the soil by some mighty acceleration of the earth towards the sky. Her terrible eyes seemed to be sucking Babcock's own right out of his head.

Kneeling above her in a helpless rapture, he beheld a nightmare. Her black hair, fanned out across the thick litter of dead leaves, began to melt. It grew, writhing like black roots, into the leaves. The leaves themselves liquefied, became a golden muck into which not just her rooting hair, but her flesh, too, intertwined, for her skin was blackening into a scaly branching hide that thrust tendrils into the liquefying earth that under her.

Babcock's own legs were sunk past his knees in the muck, but he noted it distantly, so enraptured was he by her utter transformation. Watching her clothing melt away, draining off her breasts and belly as the breasts and belly began to *swell*! Was he really *seeing* this? Her head had vanished in the steamy muck, while her breasts, thighs, even the tapering ovoids of her upper arms and forearms, bulged like baking loaves, reptilian loaves growing scaly as they grew.

Babcock was sunk to his waist in a bog that was *doing things* to his lower body. Fear for his life, already a remote paltry voice, at last roused him. He raised the gun again and emptied the cylinder into her scaly bosom. Each slug galvanized a spurt of elongation in the reptilian tentacles her body had become. Ropy with muscle, they plunged into the muck around his waist. Something was happening to his body under there, oh God! He was coming apart in the earth and she was pulling the rest of him down! Down into the earth!

THERE *WOULD* BE A CAR, just as she was ditching Wolf's stuff in the water. It didn't stop though. She flung the gym bag after the clothes, jumped in the Mustang, and raised a tail of dust cranking it back up onto the road. Done was done, all she could do was hide the car well and hope.

And about five minutes later, within half a mile of town and all its peripheral traffic, Karen came to the severely scary part. She passed other vehicles, half a dozen, maybe more, but none were stopped or even taking notice.

Outlying the new developments that fringed the town, there survived a few lanes of old houses sinking into their jungled yards, more than half of them abandoned. Gratefully she tucked the Mustang up the first of these lanes, eased back up to a big old derelict tucked back in the trees and sited against the wooded hills flanking the town.

She crept up the weed-cracked driveway, deep into where overgrown hedge and curtains of ivy dripping from the roof enveloped it. Though her hand was hurting big time now, cracked bone pain poking sharply through the anesthesia of Mom's old Vicodins, she wiped down the wheel and every surface with her sleeves, spending a long, careful time doing it.

Hooking her knapsack onto her shoulder, Karen struck out through the back yard and up into the hills, going slow, because of her hand's throbbing, and because she didn't want to be decorated with undergrowth when she walked back out of the hills and into town. When she was a mile up into the slopes above the house, she paused by a thicket and carefully buried the wiped-down .357 deep in the black earth.

After a half hour's careful walk through the overgrown hills, she had passed the edge of town and came down into one of the older residential zones, where empty lots gave her easy access from the woods.

Walking those thickly treed streets calmed her. She began to take stock of her escape and to exult in her conquest of Wolf, then of his corpse, and now of his gear and stolen car. All of them threatened her life in turn, all of them were behind her now. She felt strength and hope glow in her body—even her hand's pain, a battle-wound, felt like a badge of new courage. At last she had fought back against the ancient crime . . . and won.

As a girl she'd liked these streets, finding it hard to leave them and take the bus back home. There was May Tyler's house, her middle-school chum. May's parents were sweet, but God how tired of Karen they must have gotten, the kid just wouldn't *leave* at suppertime and catch her bus!

So unchanged, these blocks! Sidewalks buckled by the roots of the big old trees, a plastic tricycle toppled in front of a faded white picket fence, all the lawns and gardens lush, some a little shaggy. *Family* streets—how she'd envied all the classmates who lived here. Their houses didn't stand alone in the night, solitary in a sea of trees where a monster lived.

At the bus-station she learned it was an hour till the next bus to Bushmill. Settling down to wait, she noticed Fratelli's market, a few doors down across the street, seemed to be doing a pretty brisk business. Did that placard on one of the tables say "Fox"? She stepped out and walked over.

The old man sat at the register out under the awning. The placard in black magic marker proclaimed FOX FRUIT. It dominated a whole table of Dad's peaches and apricots. The flats couldn't have been out here for more than a couple hours and they were more than half gone.

Under his ambitious hair with its shameless dye-job, Fratelli's aging Sicilian profile grew more vivid to her. Big, thick, hairy-lobed ears, Old Country ears that caught all the rural rumors, were current on all the myths and magics muttered over a hundred hearths for miles around. Surely the old man knew more about Dad's place than Karen did. Knew that Jack Fox's produce had some rumored uniqueness, a rumor far wider spread than Harst's and Marty's clique of Jack Fox Disciples. That prickling sensation on Karen's back was the dawning knowledge of how many thoughts, throughout this whole big valley, were weighing her, the old fox's daughter, now alone on his acres.

"Ay. Karen. You got something for me?"

"As a matter of fact I do, Mr. Fratelli. I'm going to Bushmill to get my hand fixed."

"Bushmill. Why doncha go see your Dad's friend? Harst?"

"Because I don't *like* Dr. Harst."

So quick he'd thrown it at her, she'd answered on instinct and instantly saw she'd answered right. The tiniest crinkle of humor on Fratelli's face. He knew that all that was Dad's was her enemy; it was why he was sure she wanted to sell. "'S okay. I hear he's outta town f'a while."

"Anyway, I stopped by to tell you to pick all the rest off those trimmings from Jack's trees. I make it at least fifteen more flats. Just pay me now and take it whenever you want." *I've got nothing to hide. Walk right onto my property.*

He stared at her a moment, winked, and pulled out a wad of bills. "I pay you for *twenny* flats. Old friends here, ay?"

"Old friends, yes, Mr. Fratelli. But my partners back in 'Frisco and me, we don't see land values the same way you do. For Dad's orchard and the house, we're looking at least eight hundred thousand."

"Karen! You talkin' crazy! Look, I talk to *my* people . . . but you talkin' crazy!"

"Ah, Mr. Fratelli! It would've been nice to sell it to *you*, somebody that really knows the place, not some rich developer." She saw swift calculation in his eyes. "I've got to go. Just pick that fruit whenever you want."

And as she turned, she noticed, among the shoppers rummaging through Dad's fruit, was Helen Carver.

"Helen,"

"Hi. Karen . . . . I'm so sorry . . . about your Dad." She had a thin, pretty face, but an aura of exhaustion enveloped her, seemed even to dull her still-blond hair. As a girl in high school she had always been quiet, conventional, though never unfriendly, despite Karen's—even then—reputation as a drinker and a rowdy.

"It's okay," Karen said absently, looking in this tired face for the young woman she'd once known. "I didn't really like him much."

Helen blinked. Something like compassion in her eyes both galled and touched Karen in equal measure. She asked, "Are you a fan of Fox Fruit, too?"

"Well, Marty is, I guess." The cheerless smile she gave Karen saying this . . . . This Helen not as shy as that young woman had been.

Again Karen felt that touch on her spine. What had she drunk, when she drank Dad's brandy? "Helen, I'm waiting for a bus. Want to have a cup of coffee?" They had never been close, but Karen saw a furtive longing in her eyes. Life with Marty Carver had to be worse than lonely. He probably didn't let her *have* friends, it would be a kind of insubordination. "Come on. We can catch up, as they say."

Fratelli watched the two women walk off towards the Koffee Kup across the street. He called Sal over. "Go pick the resta those Fox trees, even the bruised. Get everyt'ing that ain't crushed." Sal roared off in the pickup. His father began restacking with expert hands the dwindling peaches and apricots, as he smiled at Duina Tyler, May Tyler's grandmother She was aiming her handsome, seamed face disapprovingly at the wares. "This is a sorry lot, Mr. Fratelli. Look at all the bruises!"

"Miz Tyler! Maybe you need glasses! Looka these apricots! Plump! Just ripe! Perfect! Mr. Tyler gonna love 'em!"

He watched her frowning some more, knowing what was coming. Mr. Fratelli understood the chill of age, the longing for some touch of that energy, that appetite of youth. Understood that it would have been Mr. Tyler himself who had sent her down here, once the word had gone round what was on sale.

"They'll do for jam," she said. "Gimme a flat of 'em."

"'At's fifty bucks well spent, Miz Tyler!"

XVIII

Sal Fratelli drove unwillingly down the Fox acres' gravel drive. He'd never liked this place. For one thing, everything to do with *agriculture*, dirt-farming, his old man in that apron stacking fruit all these years—he was sick and tired of.

Sal was a grower himself, true enough—on some private paths he had created in the wooded fringes of his neighbor's acres. But dope was different. Dope was cash, pure and simple, and cash meant *out* of this farm-and-cowflop town. Another season, and he and Cherry would have their hundred K, and get their nice little condo in the city. Growlights in closets then: contained, controlled growth. He guessed there was a kind of magic after all in bringing things up from the dirt, tiny green miracles spreading and branching, and fat rolls of green bills swelling in your pocket.

Cherry whined, quite a bit, especially near harvest. Sheriff Carver lives right next door! Blah blah blah. The sheriff's nearness worried Sal from time to time, but the reassurances he gave Cherry worked for him, too. These were wooded five-acre parcels and the crop was hidden across Mr. Kettrick's property line, in deep brush the old man hadn't entered, let alone cleared, in years. Trim a few suckers this afternoon when he got home and, in another week, all the buds would be boxed and locked . . . .

Turning onto the dirt road past the house, he pulled up next to the back yard and got his crates out of the bed of the pick-up, sighing as if they weighed a thousand pounds. Sal did *not* like being here. Karen was okay— who cared what people did in bed? She had nerve—he'd heard about what she'd said to that asshole in the 8-Ball. It was *Jack*, dead or not, he didn't like. People whispered things about him and Sal had never laid eyes on that dark-eyed brute without a shuddery feeling that they were true. Something about his land, something about this dirt under his feet that Sal didn't like.

He laid his flats by the heap of lopped branches and began plucking the fruit that studded them. All the apricots and peaches that he'd stacked for his old man, but he could almost swear these were different. They felt fuzzier, unpleasantly clingy to his hands, creepy to the touch, almost like skin. What a scary son of a bitch old Fox had been! Built like a brick shithouse, his mind always far away somewhere back behind his eyes . . . . Sal's hands flickered, deft amid the tangled twigs. Just get the hell done and out of here. He had his own crop to get trimmed before dark.

"Hello."

It was a little old woman, in a thrift-shop hat! Where did she come from? Dusty old Levi's jacket on her sparrow-thin torso. In road-worn jeans and tired black track-shoes as scarred as a blackberry-picker's arms.

"Jeez, Lady! You scared me—" He left it hanging, stopping himself from saying "shitless" just in time. "What're you doin' here?"

The old woman smiled a grave smile, showing a calm that slowed Sal's galloping heart. A kind of peace came off of her like a wave-front. There was a strangely heartwarming erosion around her bright eyes, as if her seamed face were a bit of cliff side, a small corner of your own land you'd come to love. He stared at her, thinking how wonderful her eyes were, as if they contained . . . stories. Yeah, a thousand great stories you'd heard as a kid, but had somehow forgotten since your boyhood.

"I'm here—what is your name? Is it . . . Salvatore? I'm here to look after the house. Will you be going somewhere after this? To—how do you say it?—to cultivate a crop of your own?"

Sal stood slack. How did she know his name? Had she come here to blackmail him? How did a housecleaner for the Foxes know his private business?

"No," smiled the old woman, as if he had spoken aloud. "I do not care about your crop. I am afraid for *you*, Salvatore. I have a feeling . . . some danger will come to your home tonight."

"What . . . what're you *saying*?"

She let his question hang, listening elsewhere, watching him . . . and smiled sadly. "No," she said. "Forgive me . . . *Sal*. I'm a foreigner. I've said the wrong thing. I'll go inside now. Perhaps I will see you again."

She'd unsettled him so much, that he let her go, though he wanted her to stay, to explain. Dad hired wetbacks. Did *he* know about the dope? Did *everybody*? He watched her walk up onto the back porch. She paused there, seemed to muse a moment, then decisively twisted the knob and thrust herself inside.

Uneasy, Sal plucked apricots. Had to concentrate, to pull at the correct angle—ninety degrees off what his long-trained hands had learned with vertical trees. The fuzzy heft of the fruit seemed even more unpleasant than before. His fingers twitched them into the paper sockets of the crates, glad to be done with each one, unwilling to grip the next, and working all the faster for that reason.

QUETZAL WALKED SLOWLY through the kitchen, feeling
already the thing she sought. Such gloom and grief
inside this house! That poor young woman! To have
returned to this place! Quetzal must find . . . *Emily*. The
whole house, whose duena she had so long been in life,
murmured her name. Must find Emily, calm her and
give her courage, alone in the dark as she was, before
her spirit must face what she had still to face!

Quetzal made, in the air before her, the upward-
curving sign of the Serpent, who was both Earth and
Sky. She made the sign of the Cross as well. Why not?
Any of those who loved light, who loved all that was
kissed and encouraged by the sun, these could cross
themselves, too, and what harm?

Here was the dining room and it still reverberated
with a contact between the mother and the daughter.
Here the daughter, Karen, had almost been murdered
and here Emily, already dead, had reached out and
saved her. Here would be the mother's loving, lingering
soul. There. There was what the little witch sought.
There was Emilia herself, framed in a photograph!

She unlatched the breakfront and lifted it out, a
small icon where the woman's tender, undying spirit
still lived. Quetzal caressed the glass that coffined
the face, the face of the soul she needed for this ugly,
bloody war she was about to wage. She could feel the
woman's heart, a steady-glowing coal of grief and love
and steel-sinewed will, hovering in the wind of Time
like an inextinguishable flame, stubbornly haunting
this crude image of herself.

Quetzal looked long into those half-tone eyes. The
photograph had been taken close up, a field of vague

leaves just behind her. Yes. Emily was here now, just behind those gray eyes and was also inhabiting those same orchard leaves outside this house, haunting their sun-struck, breeze-stirred multitude in the latening gold light. Emily was everywhere here, had been dead for scarcely a heartbeat, a mere three years.

"Emily," Quetzal said softly. "Ven a mi corazon. Mi corazon es tu cama, tu casa, tu puerta al mundo. Mis ojos son tus ventanas. Come forth from my eyes. Be born anew from my eyes."

She reached out with her heart, her whole mind, a thrusting-outwards of naked love. Having done this, she sighed and stood relaxed, letting go of her effort, her life-or-death mission, standing slack in the faith that she had reached out with all she had in her and that the answering touch would come.

It came as a shiver like a swift-branching vine up the trellis of her spine and ribcage. She had to unclench from the shock that all her seventy years of witch-work had never dulled—unclench and let the cold, hungry soul writhe up through her, like a long-sounded whale, huge and cold from the arctic waters of death, erupting mightily back up to the sky, to the earth-spanning air.

Quetzal bucked and quivered, and dead Emilia launched out of her, pouring from the windows of Quetzal's eyes in a brutal, icy flux that pulled stinging tears down the witch's gaunt cheeks.

Dizzied, she swayed, struggling to focus her eyes again, to see the inquietude in the air before her, the squirm of an energy twisting this way and that in the dining room's gloom. Afternoon light filled the kitchen, but only a few rays reached in here. In the faint glow Quetzal saw a liquid stir. A few moments later—for the ghost must find its place among the new, more cramped dimensions of this earthly space—the closet door-handle twitched, then twitched more decidedly and, at last, the door came open. A long moment later, a shotgun came out of the closet, moving upright, its stock skittering lightly across the floor as if it were hauled out by an invisible child too short to take it up in arms. It wavered unsteadily upright, as if its invisible possessor were seeking a grip on it. Suddenly, it rose decisively into the air, hanging horizontally some four feet above the floor. The slide was worked, a live shell jacked out clattering onto the floor.

And only then, as she bent to retrieve it, was Emily vaguely revealed, a smoky blur squatting down, reaching a pale arm of faintest mist, plucking up the shell and thumbing it back into the chamber. Then the gun hung there at port-arms, the vaporous shape that held it thinner than the mere memory of smoke, no shape at all, really.

"My daughter," said Quetzal. "Mi hija. Put it down. We need a weapon more potent and primitive. Among the tools of this man—once a man—you married, we will find what we need. Then we must gather your sisters who have died, and who will die, in this valley. And then, we will fight."

OVER THEIR COFFEE, both Karen and Helen were awkward with the conventional pleasantries. Tired and in pain, Karen couldn't understand why she'd gotten herself into this. "So. How are your kids?"

"We just have one. Marty Junior. He's thirteen."

Helen's wan smile touched Karen. How *would* the kid be? Marty Junior! Karen took a chance. "I'll bet he likes to be called something besides Marty. Does he have a nickname?"

"His friends call him Skip." Helen's eyes winced saying this, but they held Karen's, who saw this worn-down woman might be submissive to her martinet master, but her spirit was not broken, was perhaps just in hiding. Karen decided to take a chance.

"Helen. I'm a crazy dyke drunk, right? No—please, I'm not fishing for kindness. I'm just trying to open your ears to me, because I want to help you. Just listen a moment, okay?"

Helen surprised her, reaching out and gripping her forearm with an unexpectedly strong hand and looked at her with a directness for which Karen was unprepared. "I don't think you're crazy, Karen. I think you've . . . suffered a lot. I've always liked you. Always . . . *admired* you."

Tough old Karen Fox—as she'd always thought of herself—this touched her so sharply that actual tears jumped into her eyes. "I was never very nice to you," she blurted. "I remember when I came up to you and Marty at your table in the restaurant that time, with my lover and I acted so—"

Helen's grip on her arm and her steady golden eyes, stopped her. "I *always* liked you, Karen. I thought you were brave. You know why I married Marty? Basically, because he told me to and I didn't have the backbone to refuse. I mean, it was what I was *supposed* to do. An eligible guy . . . . But you were the opposite of me and I always admired you for it."

Karen had to wipe her eyes on her sleeve, but felt no embarrassment. Even the cracked bone in her hand seemed relieved by this sweetness. Somebody she'd never even troubled to think about had been out there

in that earlier world of hers—that world so full of
nightmare and pain—thinking of her, *liking* her. She
started to speak and had to clear her throat. Grinned
crookedly.

"That means a lot to me. Look. What I have to tell
you will make me sound crazy, but please try to hear it.
First, don't eat that fruit, not even a bite. I think Marty
will want you to . . . and— Marty is dangerous. I don't
exactly understand it myself, but he was like . . . my
father's *apprentice*. My father is . . . my father was a
very dangerous man. My lover, Susan, was killed three
days ago. They said it was a traffic accident, but I think
Marty had something to do with it. I'm so sorry, but I
truly think it. I think my *father* had something to do
with it . . . . You'll know I'm crazy now, I guess, and
I guess I just can't help that. I just saw my bus pull in
down there and I have to go, but I couldn't leave without
trying to warn you. I know I sound insane . . . but *leave*
him, Helen. Take your boy and leave him." She rose
and, impulsively, kissed Helen's cheek. Then stumbled
out to catch her bus.

RAUL AND ISAURO, in the cab of their rusty old Chevy
pick-up, glanced back simultaneously at the knock on
the cab's rear window. The old woman they'd picked
up a few miles back up the highway was standing there
in the truck bed as easy as you please, balanced against
the truck's rocking and swaying—standing there
perfectly poised though she was so skinny, so old—and
motioning for them to pull over.

Isauro did so, at the rusty gates and mossy old
wooden sign of the Spaith walnut orchard. They
watched the old woman take up the pair of axes she'd

been carrying when they picked her up and, gripping the hafts of both with one sinewy hand, jump out of the bed, incredibly spry for her apparent age. Spry, but surely addled in the head, because once on the roadside, she made a strange gesture towards the bed she'd just jumped out of, seeming to beckon . . . and a moment after, gently touched the air beside her. Then she shouldered the axes, saluted Raul and Isauro, and walked down the road into the orchard.

"Una vieja loca," said Isauro, as he whipped the Chevy back onto the highway.

"Una bruja," said Raul, somewhat dreamily. And Isauro nodded.

"Hija," said Quetzal, speaking to the empty air, it seemed, as she walked down the lane so profusely littered by the narrow golden leaves of the walnut trees. "My daughter. We are seeking one of your sisters."

When she had walked perhaps a quarter mile, she stopped. "We are near," she told the air. "I will dress you now, daughter. It will help you to take hold of this world you have returned to."

She gestured and a little wind-devil rose, snatching up a whirling cone of leaves, which began to snag on a vertical core, creating a patchy mosaic of yellow leaf and empty air. The shape of a naked woman stood beside the witch and wonderingly raised leaf-fingered hands before her leaf-sketched face. "You are clothed," said Quetzal, "in the flesh of our enemy. Our enemy is Xibalba, the green god who blankets this earth, piercing its soil with his roots, who feeds on its rain and its sunlight, and who has been the cradle and the shelter, the food and the clothing of our race since our beginning. He who now would feed on us and destroy us utterly. Xibalba has learned to steal our minds and our eyes, the better to hunt us. But it is we, your sisters and I, who will go hunting Xibalba. Take this, Emilia, and follow me."

She held out one of the axes. The ghost, with leafy fingers, gripped the haft. The autumnal mosaic of her face . . . smiled. The strange pair left the road and stepped into the lane between the trees.

"You see?" said Quetzal. Ahead, the stark ranks of autumn-denuded trees filed down to a small swamp. Black muck, a big pond of inky mud, spanned the lane, and the trees flanking it were bannered and festooned with vines and lianas. Thick moss wrapped the trunks and webs of creepers wove a velvety green fabric that tented the whole zone. Just beyond this uncanny micro-bog, a brown Dodge with front doors hanging open sat with its front bumper wedged against a tree-trunk.

Quetzal led the ghost to the brink of the muck. Mosquitoes and dragonflies clouded the air, their wire-thin song stitching the silence of the leafy acres. The witch gestured at the bog, where a serpentine trunk or massive root threaded through the muck, thick as a man but sinuous, its bark so rough it seemed like scales. "A limb of the green daemon. Daughter, we must strike it till his green blood sprays!" At these words, here and there along the fissured limb, crude black gems appeared, oily-bright knobs that stiffly stirred, that searched for—and seemed to *see*—its enemies. Hoisting her axe, Quetzal shrilled, "With me, child! With me!"

They brandished their axes, ghost with living woman, against the blue October sky and Quetzal cried, "Hunaphu! Ixbalanque! Itzamna! Strike with us!"

In tandem, their axe-heads whickered down, the arcs of their honed bits flashing silver. Green sap sprayed, the limb convulsed. Again the axe-bits rose, flashed down . . . again . . . again, as vegetal tissue and geysering sap arched up from the wounds.

A shudder went through its anacondan length. The eye-knobs dulled, a waxy pallor frosted them.

Quetzal sighed, her shoulders sagged from their militant tension. She reached over and gently touched the back of her hand to the leaves that partially shaped one of long-dead Emily Fox's cheeks. "Sweet hija. Queridita. That man, that lover who killed you with grief. You know now what possessed him. You know what he served and what he—deep under the earth—still serves. You know what your dear daughter fights, y que todavia tiene que luchar—what still she must fight. What *we* will fight. Y mira! Behold! We will not fight alone!"

She faced the swamp—already less black, its tent of vegetation seeming to shrink, beginning to shrivel. Her sleeves fell back a bit with her priestly gesture and showed the stark thinness of her forearms, yet showed withal the tendony strength of those brown limbs.

"Lupe!" she cried. "Tienes tu libertad! Ven a mi, pobrecita! Ven a mi, queridita tontita!"

A muddy shape rose from the drying muck, a woman-shape from which the soil slid off, till she was only a sketchy earthen shadow—a shoulder, a thigh, a pendulous breast. Quetzal commanded a windy cone of leaves and clothed her. The full-bosomed shape staggered, raised the gapped yellow sketch of her face to the blue autumn sky . . . touched with foliate-hands her foliate torso and lifted the voids of her eyes in wonder.

"Mis hijas," said Quetzal. "Vamos a salvar otras, y otras, y otras. We are going to raise an army of murdered women and men! Vamos a matar a nos matadores! We are going to kill our killers and we are going to kill the killer of us all. Will you follow me?"

Airy Emily Fox, a thing of sky and leaves, turned her half-invisible face to airy Lupe. Lupe reached for the second axe that Quetzal held and gripped its haft, brandishing and testing it. A smile spread across both their leafy faces.

"Entonces, que vamanos!" cried Quetzal, smiling a smile of her own, a triumphant smile, her seamed eyes red and wet with tears both of tenderness and a jubilant anger. "Y mira!" she cried in a tone of discovery. "Here is our chariot!" She made one brief, beckoning gesture. The brown Dodge shuddered. Its front doors creaked shut and its engine came to life. It backed off the tree, with a slight creaking of its bent bumper, swung a half-arc in reverse, wheeled round, and trundled over the cloddy earth of the next lane over. Stopped. Both doors on its nearer side swung open.

"Come, my sisters. We have brothers and sisters, who are waiting to join us!"

ASSISTANT CHIEF DEPUTY MARTY CARVER, acting sheriff of Gravenstein County, with one lordly finger on the wheel, steered up the Gravenstein Highway, sifting in his mind, as a miser sifts his wealth, the seeds of power he had planted and was about to plant. Jack Fox's mantle had not been draped upon unworthy shoulders!

The ape Babcock was a done deal, as Rabble and his bitch would shortly be. He'd given Rabble the orders last night and even now the crippled cowboy should be picking up his hooker at the bus station. Once Marty made sure of Babcock, he would check on the retired Chief Deputy. Then his next bit of business would be that dope-growing punk next door.

Babcock's long absence all but assured Marty the ox had accomplished the one thing he was fit for: feeding the green god. Marty prepared his courage. Where the god had been fed, one of his dragons would be born and Marty would finally confront a soldier from the demon army he had been chosen to raise.

Less than a mile from Spaith's, straight at him in the opposing lane, came . . . a brown Dodge, one of the Department's unmarked cruisers. And by the plate, the very one Babcock had checked out this morning! But Babcock was not at the wheel. No, it was some old Mex bitch, with white hair curling out from under a battered gray hat. She glanced and grinned at him as their vehicles passed each other . . . and from her rear window . . . a shape of yellow leaves thrust out! A knot of yellow leaves hung in the air, alongside the window, somehow contracting and clenching? A *fist* of yellow leaves it was, a fist from which a single, jointed leaf rose up. A leafy fist, giving him the *finger!*

He stopped dead, right in the middle of the highway and, in the rearview, saw his slack face was beaded with sweat. He had come braced for awe, but of a marvel *he* had summoned—for a nightmare surely, but one whose horror *he* would harness. Marty fought to breathe. Why couldn't he draw air? It seemed he'd just been inhaling the pure atmosphere of Power, only to have it punched out of him. Because suddenly Power was elsewhere, Power was with that chicken-killing white-haired bitch, Lupe's neighbor. Was she a witch? A bruja? To command a fucking demon of dead leaves? How the hell did they get Babcock's car?

He could not doubt the powers his master had given him, he *dared* not doubt them. He had to shake this trance off and see his mission accomplished.

Accelerating towards Spaith's, he snatched up the mouthpiece and thumbed Central. "Bruce? Sheriff Carver. Gimme anyone northbound on Gravenstein Highway."

"Copy that, Chief."

Marty was pulling into Spaith's acres when his earpiece crackled. "Shurrf? Haynes here. My Twenty is three miles north of town."

"Step on it, Haynes. One of our un-markeds has been stolen, maybe five miles north of Spaith's by now. I want 'em shackled and brought in, do you copy?"

"Copy that, Shurrf. Shackled an' brought in."

"Report on contact, you copy?"

"Report on contact, copy that, Shurrf."

Very slowly, Marty rolled through the orchard, scanning left and right, the disregarded wealth of walnuts loud beneath his tires. Ahead he saw a spray of soil on the asphalt, where someone had accelerated out of the midst of the trees. He turned and rolled downslope between those two rows.

There, a hundred yards ahead. When he emerged from the cruiser, he had to steady himself. A swamp spanned the lane; the swamp already a patch of black, fast-hardening mud. Shriveling festoons, a canopy of vines and creepers, stretched between the flanking trees. Explosive greenery had webbed this lane but was already brittle, gray as ash, its shriveled leaflets drooping like dead fingers. A massive, crooked, crocodilian shape lay half sunk within the hardening muck. As he drew near enough to see clearly, his legs half-buckled and he went down upon one knee.

Brutal axe-wounds bit its scaly dorsum. Hindquarters sunk, its frozen forelimbs clawed the air, stiff as dead branches. The great jaws might have been a lightning-split bough lined with thorns that were all too plainly fangs. What brought Marty's reverent terror to its peak were the pallid fungal nodes that studded the head like a pustulous pox. All *eyes* they were and in the milky spheres of some, the dimming outlines of a human iris gleamed.

The raw shock of miracle—before he could collect his full-grown self about him—threw Marty back in time, far back into a younger self. It was back when he first picked for the Foxes, a gawky pre-adolescent, when he first—come evening amid the sweet-smelling plums—sensed something in that Fox earth, sensed a privilege, a potency, a promise in that soil. Back in those days, he saw a beautiful sinister something in Jack Fox's eyes, eyes that hinted there was a secret in that ground, a precious power, an *immortal* power. That was the year Jack Fox had become, in his heart, his true father.

What Marty remembered, as he looked upon the miracle of his God's murdered scion half-sunk in the mud, was a single fleeting moment in that crucial childhood autumn of his. It was a moment *before* the immortal power had seduced him. In that instant, young Marty Carver had felt only *terror* of the secret he sensed in Jack Fox's earth.

And just for an instant now, as he looked at the corpse of the green god's dragon, that younger Marty cried, "Thank God!" within his heart.

But Acting Assistant Chief Marty Carver was made of much sterner stuff, was far more powerful than that long-vanished adolescent. The treachery of his heart became rage. He towered to his feet and shook his fist. The green god had an enemy, this enemy had power . . . but Marty was the green god's general, his

first in command. That gray-haired bitch, that witch.
She would die in pain. She would die in *pieces*!

He plucked out his cell-phone and thumbed the
speed dial. "Rabble?"

"Hey, Marty."

"Where are we?"

Some throat-clearing. "I'm in town to pick her up,"
Rabble answered. "I think that's her bus that just pulled
in."

"Listen carefully. You fuck this up and I'm going
to snap your spine. You got that, *sir?*" The sneer at
Rabble's nominally superior rank was an infallible
goad to the man's abject compliance. It recalled to him
his last moments as Marty's actual superior, writhing
on the floor of his office, his shattered leg shattered
anew.

"It's a done deal, Marty."

"Make sure you use that piece I gave you. I'm coming
to your place in an hour. I'd better find it done. And
listen. If you see one of the Department's unmarked
Dodges drive onto the property, with a white-haired
bitch at the wheel, you put a bullet right through her
face, no questions asked."

XIX

Sal couldn't believe he was still picking—the sun was halfway down the sky . . . How long since that scary old lady had left? She'd walked out of the house, into the big shed and out of it with a pair of axes over one shoulder, the hafts clamped together in one gnarly little hand. Just walked off the place and seemed to be talking to herself as she went, leaving behind her a weirdness hanging in the air. No other way to put it. The afternoon silence got creepy, the leaves in the breeze took on a muttery, secretive sound, and the fruit felt even nastier, even more like fuzzy skin to Sal's fingers.

And there seemed to be no end to it! Eighteen flats he'd brought in his truck, all filled already and stacked back in the bed. Then he'd gone into the shed and gotten more flats there, had a dozen of *those* filled, and still it wasn't done. Like the fruit was breeding in there in those tangled heaps of lopped-off branches—breeding even while he was picking it. Everybody said the Fox fruit had like special powers, *nudge nudge*. Fine, whatever. Just typical hick-town local lore, but Sal still didn't like the way his old man acted around the stuff. There was something unpleasant in that Old-Country sly look Pop got in his eyes as he set it out on his stands. And that same weird feeling was right here all around him, was in this earth he was standing on, the soil this stuff grew out of. And if that was crazy thinking, then it was this god damned place that *made* him crazy. All he wanted was to box the last of this stinking fruit and get the hell off of Jack Fox's land.

KARL RABBLE LED the skinny whore—Kitty, she called herself—out of the bus station to his Ram Charger, hitching his crooked legs along on half-crutches. He knew she was calmed by his condition. How could an old gimp like him threaten an oblivious meth-head hooker in her twenties, all the world her John? He could almost pity her if he had the time, if his terror of Carver allowed it. Just get it *done!*

Playing the courtly old cowboy, he handed her up into the cab and then clambered up behind the wheel. Ceremoniously propping his crutches on the seat between them, fired up the engine, gave her a smile. A skinny, pale antsy little thing in a loose top string-tied behind her neck. "Three-four miles out of town, dear, I got a nice piece of property. I'm the sheriff here, sweetheart, semi-retired on account of injuries. Check my wallet and take out those three hundreds while you're at it."

She liked the money, but looked slightly worried by the photo I.D. He swung out from the curb, waved ostentatiously to a deputy in a passing cruiser, and told her, "Now don't you be scared because I'm the law, ex-law. It means you're safe with me and safe from anyone else in the department. Out here in the country, we don't pay this kinda harmless recreation any mind at all. And it ain't any big thing either, what I want from you. I mean you can see I'm not in much shape for rough stuff. Fact is—my, you're a pretty little thing!—fact is you just have to help out an old jerk-off. All you gotta do is pose for me. On an inner-tube! Floatin' out there on my own personal trout-pond I got in my yard."

"Ooooh!" she said, giving him a practiced lascivious look. "I love jerk-offs! Say, you mind?" She held up a pocket-rocket she'd plucked from her pathetic bra.

"Not at all! Get happy. Get comfy. We're near half-way there."

Ten minutes later, they were roaring up his drive, parking in a smoke of dust at his rambling ranch-style house. He led her out to the back deck, thinking as they went that his place looked kind of dark and shabby. He tried for a jovial air as they emerged on the deck. "It don't look like much, an old bachelor's digs you know, but looky there! Isn't that the prettiest little pond?"

He gestured grandly at the theater of their tryst: saggy lawn furniture and flattened beer cans on the pond's muddy border, the half-deflated inner tube bobbing at the edge of the water, which was coffee-brown and decked here and there with bubbly green patches of algae. He rubbed his hands together to express gusto. "Well now. I'm gonna get changed and set on that lounge down there. You just get undressed and get on out there on that tube and I won't be a minute. And here's your bonus up front." And he plucked another pair of hundreds from his shirt pocket.

"Ooooh! Thanks. You hurry on out now, big daddy!"

Kitty meandered on down to the pond, honking up an extra big dose of vitamin M from her pocket rocket and thinking, boy, was this something new. That water looked cold and nasty, but it was Easy Money and it shouldn't take long. She noticed, lying by the lounge, an open gym bag, with towels and sun lotion in it. She paused to gratify a life-long petty thief's instinct and bent to rummage in the bag. Her fingers met a dense metal shape . . . .

Well, what d'ya know, an automatic! She could sell
this for plenty to Rafe, one of her connections back in
the city. She decided to keep on her ultra-brief cut-offs
and hid the gun behind her, tucking the blunt square
barrel down there between her buttcheeks, then shed
her top and bra. Eager to hide her prize, she snugged
her rear down into the tube and, with her heels, pushed
herself backwards into the water.

But what if he wanted to see her pussy? She unzipped
the front of her cut-offs and spread them open as much
as she could in front. Well . . . he'd be able to see *some*
of her pussy. Somehow she would persuade him to go
with that—there was no way she was going to give up
the extra three or four hundred she could get for the
piece.

But why would he *have* a gun in that bag? Well, he
was a cop. But why would he have a gun in that *bag*?
Christ. What if he was a hurt-freak? What if he meant
to *shoot* her?

No way. It was just that she'd honked way too much.
She was cranked to the gills and beyond, was truly spun,
disoriented. Even the water beneath her was giving her
a creepy feeling of nasty green things lurking around
below. Get a grip, girl!

Of course she was disoriented, look at how she
lived! Just look at what her life was. And all at once,
unbidden, a flood of memories came to her. Herself
in sordid contortions on floors, on beds, on greasy
Naugahyde couches, in the back seats of cars. Men's
bodies gripping and kneading and twisting and
penetrating her . . . .

This kind of mood had come on her once or twice
in the last couple years. It was rare because she prided
herself on never looking back, never recalling or

dredging things up. Her motto was just keep moving ahead, onward to the next party, the next gram, the next drink, the next pill. But when it hit her as it did now, it was intense. She floated there on the pond, slack and astonished, as the tableaux flashed, humiliation after humiliation.

Out came Karl in black swim trunks, crutching his crooked legs along, the neck of a bottle sticking out of his waistband and a big grin on his hairy face. "Don't you look sexy! Oh, my! I can't wait! Just paddle back here a minute and take a slug of this—it's good for what ails you!"

Look at that potbellied bastard, just like how many other whiskery rank-smelling sonsofbitches who'd mauled and dirtied her over the years, starting with her stepdad before she'd even had her first period. No way she was paddling back in, letting him find his gun and take it back from her.

"No thanks!" she called. "Drink mine for me!"

He did, too, then gave her a genial wave with the bottle and socked down three major gulps of it. Easing himself down onto the chaise lounge, he took three more. Like some guy in a movie drowning his sorrows or something. Looked like his hand there had a bit of the shakes, too . . . . And then that shaky hand reached down into that gym bag. Reached farther in and fished around.

A smile sprouted across Kitty's face. She felt something big rising through her body. A kind of joy, an energy that seemed to well up from the water beneath her. Like the tables were turning. Like the course of her whole pitiful life was reversing and the shit was flowing the *other* way for a change. She took out the gun and waved it in the air.

"Hey, Karl! Looking for this?" She thought her grin would split her face. This was too much! This was wonderful! "Draw, cowboy!" she crowed and gripping her right wrist with her left hand, just like in the movies, she fired off a shot in his general direction. The recoil spun her tube slowly around and when she'd cycled back to face him, lo and behold, there was a spray of red tissue on the top of his shoulder and mucho blood curtaining down over his hairy chest and belly. "Whoa!" she shouted and while there was a tiny corner of her that was stunned and frightened by what she'd done, what she'd gotten herself into, it was dwarfed by this mighty joy that filled her, an exaltation hoisting her high above the dirty struggle of her life up to this moment.

"Wanna see me do it again?" she crowed and *whack*, fired off a second shot as reckless as the first, counter paddling with her feet so that she was not turned away, so that she saw a spray of crimson leap up from his *other* shoulder. Was she dreaming this? It was too perfect to be real!

But what was the man doing with his legs? Something was happening to those crooked legs of his! They were darkening, growing longer, twisting and twining together into a single ropy braid and *snaking*, pouring off the end of the lounge, and sprouting branchlets as they rivered across the mud and into the water. His chest was shriveling and darkening, his arms too, becoming rootlike cables that joined the weave of the rest of him, all of him pouring into the pond, his head shrunk down to a featureless knot, a burl—

Ice pierced the soles of her feet. It was not pain exactly, more like pure power, an energy so absolute it stilled her with its first touch. Was it pouring into her or was she pouring into it? Her body, meat blood and bone, became a cold thick smoke that tendrilled into a new shape beneath the water—coiling, reweaving itself according to a dark green Will almost as ancient as the bones of the planet herself. All that was left of her now was her head sliding under water. Before she sank her eyes showed her a sky of sapphire blue that stretched into two dimming streaks that turned green, turned black, were gone.

"ALMOST FORTY-TWO FLATS," Sal told his father. "Now I'm heading for the hot tub."

"Not so fast." The old man had that gloating look that made his son so uneasy, though he didn't seem as surprised at the volume of the harvest as Sal had expected him to be. Plucked up a slightly bruised peach and pulped it in that skilful, one-handed way he had. "Hot tub. Whadda you, da owner? Your old man goes to da hot tub. I wanchoo here sellin' till sundown."

"Pop! Who's gonna come?"

"You kiddin?" He gestured toward the front of the produce arcade. Sal walked over, saw placards even bigger than this morning's: FOX FRUIT SPECIAL PRICE TO MOVE. And saw at least a dozen shoppers poking around among the other stands, while actually eyeing him and his father and the loaded truck.

"Damn," Sal murmured. "Pop, look. Lemme just grab an hour at home, say hi to Cherry, explain I'll be late."

"Okay. But tonight you spend at her place. I want da tub, want da place ta myself. I got comp'ny."

So ten minutes later Sal, his little clippers in hand, was ducking through the sagging barbed-wire strands of old Mr. Kittredge's fence and weaving his way through the thick bush, the manzanita and scotch broom and scrub oak that covered almost all the old man's five acres. He followed an old deer trail which, for all his goings and comings along it, he had taken care not to enlarge with his passage and found his first patch, five fat dope plants just over six feet tall, buds nodding weightily amid the native foliage. Reminded himself for the hundredth time that his neighbor on the other side, acting Sheriff Marty Carver, was at least a quarter mile away as the crow flew and that all the pungent shrubbery of his own land stood between.

He clipped suckers from the woody stalks and slipped them into a Ziploc. Just one more week and the buds themselves would go into bigger Ziplocs, then straight into the specially sealed trunk of his Volvo. Then just a (clip . . . clip . . . clip) four hour drive down to the city. From bulky agriculture to pure cash. Thirty-five K in pocket had no odor to worry about. Added to what was already in the lockbox, he and Cherry would have title to a comfy little condo in the city.

From his first patch to his second—*clip-clip*—to his third, the Ziploc of suckers swelling in his pocket.

He ducked back over onto his father's property. Cherry already had the hot tub fired up and her bikini on when he got home and now she had some margaritas mixed. "Hey, honey," he told her. "I'm sorry, I gotta go back to the market till dark. And we gotta stay at your place tonight."

"Why didn't you tell me?"

"So I could do this." He wrapped his arms around her and stood hugging and enjoying the half-clothed feel of her. "And this," he added, releasing her just enough so he could grab a margarita and down it with a smack of the lips. Then he gave her the moronic smile that he'd used since high school to disarm all his aggressive corn-fed white-boy schoolfellows and keep them at a distance. It was his and Cherry's private joke now. "Simple Sal!" she smiled. "You sure you won't have a nice bubbly bath? Just a quick one?" She cocked a comic hip at him and waggled her eyebrows.

This led to another interlude of hugging and kissing and fondling, from which, at the last possible moment, Sal disengaged with a groan. "I gotta give Pops a break. He never asks for overtime."

"Okay hon. Can I take a quick dip?"

"Sure, but I think he's got plans for it when he gets back. I think he's having Maureen over."

The hot tub was half screened by potted plants and trellised flowering vines and, as she entered it, Cherry comically half-draped herself with vines, posing as a jungle beauty before she sank into the water. Settled in, she asked, "So how's it looking?" with a nod towards Kittredge's property. Some of her nervousness about the dope showed through, couldn't help it, having been raised a conventional little corn-fed white girl herself.

"'Ey!" Giving her his parody of his old man. "Whatchoo tink? Every 'ting great! Anudda week, tops!"

"You shouldn't make fun of your dad, he's a sweet man."

"I don't know about *sweet*. He's been pretty good to me, sure, but I just don't wanna be *like* him."

"Do you really want to live in the city? I mean, isn't it nice living where everything's green? I know it's Hicktown and all, but . . . look how good *you* grow things. Maybe you just think you'll be happy in the city, but you really won't. I mean, your *roots* are here."

"Yeah," he answered, "but in the city my *roots* will be in a nice safe closet under grow-lights. And there'll

be clubs and restaurants and movies and concerts.
Come on, sweetie. Doncha wanta come with me?"
   "'Course I do. I can live anywhere if I've got you . . .'"

HELEN CARVER STOPPED to pick up her son from Susie's,
where he was "hanging" with his pal Chet. They both
begged her to let him spend the night with Susie sweetly
seconding their plea—her husband was a long-distance
trucker and she "loved the company." Of course Helen
agreed. "Skip can stay," she said, "if Skip does his
homework." It was a love-token she offered him, to use
his *own* name, as he called it, whenever Marty wasn't
around. He vowed prodigies of homework and when
she demanded a hug, he gave it willingly.
   Guilt pierced her as she briefly held him, an irrational
guilt that she had given him Marty for a father. She
walked back to her car grieving and fearing for her
son. It was Karen Fox who had put her in this state. She
had all but said that Marty played a role in the death of
her lover. In the same breath as saying her father had
also, her *dead* father. Karen was delusional with grief,
there could be no other explanation, and yet she had
seemed so present, sad and calm if anything.
   Helen thought of the sexual cruelty of Marty's
fantasies. She had accepted the little rituals he wanted,
they were scary at first, but for all years, she'd never
been really hurt, maybe a bit sore sometimes. And he did
provide for them. But over these last few days, Marty was
different, had a kind of aura about him. Maybe a *scent*?
Very faint, a hot-house aroma with a touch of the bitter
smell of sap, especially when they had sex. So odd, how
it struck her somehow as being a scent of danger.
   She turned onto their own street and got a scare:
fifty yards ahead, Marty's patrol car erupted from the

driveway. He seemed not to see her as he sped off, a man on urgent business.

When Helen let herself in, she confronted something that grew more and more disturbing the longer she stared at it. Down the hall, the door to Marty's study hung open just a crack. Marty's study was always locked, never to be entered by anyone but himself. He must have slammed it behind him in his haste, too distracted to notice the latch hadn't caught. She stepped up to the door and touched it.

She didn't open it, but she knew she was going to, and she stood there trying to decide why it was that all at once she believed what Karen had just told her. Marty was mean, yes, cold and withholding, indifferent to her feelings, but those things in themselves didn't mean that someone was a killer. She'd liked Marty back in junior high, he had an innocent energy, enthusiasm. By the time he started courting her, right after high school, he wasn't so likeable. In her shyness and humility she'd just decided that boys becoming men naturally got less nice. She decided that nicer junior high kid was still in there somewhere and she'd tried to find and love him.

But what it came down to at this moment was that Karen Fox said she was in danger from Marty; now Helen believed her. Just like that. She pushed open the never-to-be-violated door to his sanctum and stepped inside.

There were chests and cabinets, a rack of rifles above a workbench and, on the bench, aside from a stack of bondage porn magazines, nothing but handguns, just lying there spread out on its surface. Revolvers, automatics—beyond this she could not classify them, except that all seemed to be of different makes.

Why did he have all these guns spread out on a bench? Didn't men keep them in racks or cases? Why would they just be lying around in the open air? And the air of the room touched her nostrils. A scent in the air.

She bent above that . . . smorgasbord of pistols and drew the scent into her nostrils. Far stronger than the smell of oiled steel it was. It recalled the smell of newly chainsawed trees on her dad's farm: a bitter whiff of sap and raw plant fiber. It brought vividly upon her, the memory of Marty rutting in her, his invasion like a root breaking cold stiff soil, a brutish green imperialism.

He had rushed in here to choose one of these guns, and rushed out with it . . . .

It was as if a gunshot had shattered a shell that had encased her all her adult life. Without her knowing it, cold new air bathed her and the thought *Why am I here?* slapped her in the face. Look around! A den of ropes and guns and bondage porn. A cop rushing in to grab a surely unregistered gun, and rushing out with it! She almost ran, but a cold, steely thought gripped her spine. Her hand darted out and took one of the pistols, a heavy, blunt-snouted revolver. Her hand, yes, but feeling like someone else's as it hefted the weapon's mass . . . . or the hand of a different Helen, just as afraid as the one she'd been a moment ago, but freer to move—a Helen whose fear *was* the power to move, instead of the paralysis it had always been.

She stood a moment baffled, unable to decide whether to leave the door as she had found it or pull it shut. Surely he had assumed it had shut behind him, so it was safest to close it.

Hurrying to her room, Helen threw things into a suitcase, and ran from there to *Skip's* room—and threw more things in. As she backed out of the drive and swung onto the road, she didn't yet know where she was going, but for now, it was enough knowing where she would never return.

MARTY ROCKETED towards Rabble's place, with a glance at Fratelli's driveway as he passed it. The Beretta he'd just grabbed from his stash of Wands (as he privately termed them) was for his return trip, for Sal Fratelli and his squeeze. As soon as Marty had made sure of Rabble, he'd work Jack's magic on that little dope-growing punk.

"Forgive me, Jack," he murmured, "for the witch's murder of the green god's serpent. I didn't suspect the old bitch's power. Please sustain me in the service of Xibalba." But in his heart, Marty silently withheld a reservation in his faith. For Jack Fox he felt awe and love, and for the green god felt the same. But it was up *here* Marty wanted to wield their power, here under the sun, in the cleanness of the wind and rain, ruling over men and women, constraining them, enjoying and disposing their bodies and lives. He did not want to go under the ground, as Jack had done by his own hand, as Harst had surely done, though far less willingly, Marty suspected. Harst's vanishing had helped him to see his own unwillingness for that last transition. Marty wanted the sun, and humankind to rule. He did not want that empire, however vast, of black earth and root and worm.

He arrived at Rabble's drive and the Chief Deputy's truck was in it. Marty's thundering fist on the front door produced . . . an encouraging silence within. A walk around the side of the house to the back yard revealed . . . emptiness. An unsettling emptiness. That

Rabble and the hooker should be gone was good, but where was the lush, unearthly luxuriance? There was no new growth. Just the empty deck, the littered mud, the scummy pond . . .

He approached the brink of the pond. Sitting open beside his lounge was Rabble's bag, no pistol in evidence. The lounge was collapsed, the aluminum legs buckled flat beneath it. And these . . . these were definitely deep drag-marks, crossing the mud between the foot of the lounge and the edge of the water.

He followed the drag-marks, moving more slowly with each step closer to the pond. Stood right at the brink, his senses radiating, straining outward for the answering touch of what had been seeded here by the fructifying fire of Jack's wand. All the signs suggested success: that the bitch he had shot had changed, seized him, changed *him*, and dragged him under . . . but where was Xibalba's garden and serpent? Where was the flowering the god had nourished on their flesh?

Probing with every sense, he stepped cautiously into the water, stooping to reach his hand down into its dimness . . . advanced another step down its silty bottom, wet to the knees, both hands searching under water for the rough touch of the green god's scion.

Nets seized his legs and arms. Not nets, but snaking vines that poured up from the silt, that laced him in a leafy weave, till he stood like an ivy-shrouded tree-trunk, his human shape engulfed in a dense macramé of stem and foliage. Peering out of this boscage half-blinding him, he saw a luxuriance of vine and creeper and moss radiating everywhere from the pond's rim. It clothed the whole shabby yard in verdure, all of which seemed like a vast extension of his own body, for rootlets pincushioned every inch of his skin and through them he felt the tremor of the whole green weave around him.

He stood there and saw—saw eyelessly, within his mind—the great eye-studded serpent coiled on the pond floor's darkness.

He stood there he knew not how long, for he was under the earth, just where he had feared to be, down in its ancient Darkness where seed and spore and root and filament and sleepless worm commingled, and there he conferred with Xibalba, or rather stood enfolded in that Titan's will, and knew His might, which grips the earth as a hand grips a stone . . . .

Even when the growth that gripped him fell away and joined the green weave as it enveloped ever more thickly the yard, deck, house—even when he moved dazedly from the water and picked his way through the deepening growth back to his cruiser, Marty had not yet returned from that Darkness. He scanned the sky, struggling to believe it was not a hallucination. In his rearview, he studied the micropunctures all over his face, a faint red stippling where the rootlets had pierced him. They itched and it was this that brought him to himself at last. He rubbed his face again and again. It dulled the itch, but not the awe still in him.

HE RADIOED DISPATCH and asked for a report on Officer Haynes, Haynes had been out of touch for some time after reporting a possible sighting of the stolen unmarked cruiser. He'd signed off without giving his location. Marty absorbed this stoically. He told Dispatch that Chief Deputy Rabble was missing from his residence and that a unit was to be stationed there. Two more units were to be dispatched to proceed north on Gravenstein Highway from the Spaith orchard. If they encountered the stolen cruiser, they were to shoot the driver on sight, for she was known to be guilty of a farmworker's homicide, was likely to be guilty of Rabble's as well, and was known to be armed.

Armed indeed, he thought when he had disconnected. He recalled that skinny white-haired bitch in the battered fedora and the thing that rode with her, that thing of leaves and empty air that had gestured its defiance of him. Recalled and shuddered. For his Master had imparted to him, down there under the earth, that the white-haired bitch was raising an army against them.

XX

Quetzal drove the unmarked Dodge down miles of county highway in a manner most normal observers would find strange: she trod the accelerator to the floor, climbed to a hundred, a hundred-twenty miles per hour, and pulled back on the steering wheel as if it were an aircraft's joy stick. And what these observers would have found stranger still, this caused the howling vehicle to lift—just six inches or so—all four of its tires from the pavement and hang there above the blacktop, still doing a steady one-twenty for a hundred yards, two hundred yards—until it dropped back to the pavement again. She would let up on the gas for a moment, scowl, fall back to a speed of fifty or so, tires in conventional contact with the road . . . and then she would try again.

Meanwhile her passengers seemed oblivious to all but themselves. Their leaf-latticed hands touched wonderingly their own and each other's leaf-latticed faces. Their arms and torsos interleaved in fluttering sinuous embraces. They entered and emerged from one another, sharing one another's histories and hearts and hopes of vengeance . . . .

And at length, while their living guide still fought to wrestle flight from earthbound steel, they took flight themselves, poured from the open windows like leafy flames, streamed alongside their chariot like flapping flags, dancing in little whirlwinds on the hood, in perfect spirals of spinning foliage which a hundred miles an hour of onrushing wind was powerless to deform.

But when Quetzal at last let out a howl of frustration, they came pouring back in through the open windows, sat beside and behind her, and touched her cheeks with their feathery fingers, consoling. The witch's Mayan obscenities gave way to calmer speech. "My daughters, you have sisters and brothers buried in these hills. Their lives were taken to feed the power of Xibalba, alimentar su poder, in his house of darkness, his house of seed and root. He grips the earth con manos mas duras que piedra, his hands harder than stone, fingers stronger than steel. It is Xibalba, Emilia my beloved, whom your poor tortured consort served, and still serves within the earth. Y que busca el Dios Verde? What the god seeks is all our lives, todas las vidas humanas en la tierra, because for him human life is a disease, una enfermedad mortal!"

"But from the spirits of these murdered ones, we, too, can raise an army. We must be swift. The more he kills, the more he can. We must find them encontraremos estas hermanas y hermanos, these sacrifices his servants made to him. Where they lie I cannot know unless I can take to the air and for this I need . . . wait— Yes! What I need approaches now! Come close and learn my thought."

DEPUTY HAYNES SAW Burly Babcock drive out this morning in the same unmarked county cruiser that Carver was so steamed about. Well, the missing Dodge Twenty should be somewhere in the southwest quadrant and though this was a very big county, still Haynes thought he might just be the one to spot the Dodge and recoup the ape's fuck-up.

Shit, how he hated that big iron-pumping, steroid-sucking asshole. Because Babcock was one of those guys who thought *his* shit didn't stink, he left it lying in heaps all over the landscape, putting his colleagues at a risk they'd taken pains to avoid.

Haynes was still sweating bullets over that Pakistani fiasco. He had been one of the responding units after Babcock. The asshole claimed a tail-light violation as his reason for initiating contact with the van, but when Haynes arrived, even after the van had hit the tree, both taillights were working fine.

The thing was, you start capping Mexes or Pakis by the side of the road, even if you're a *cop*, and you never know when an investigation might come down. Some goody-two-shoes civil rights lawyers already had a class action pending, accumulated missing persons complaints, mostly from ag-worker families right up here in Gravenstein County. If Babcock's blunder lit a fire under that lawsuit, some *responsible* cops up here could suffer for it, including Haynes himself.

It wasn't enough that Haynes' own trio of brown brothers—two Pakis and one Mex—had no family, no friends up here, because you could never be *sure* what any of these foreigners might know about each other. And it didn't matter that Haynes had been following Marty Carver's orders.

Each time, Harst had met him in the swamp, and each time, had given Haynes the piece that he had used. Brrrr. Just facing that old monster with his blurry bloated eyes made Haynes' balls shrink up in his shorts—all the more since Jack Fox stood behind Harst. Haynes hadn't seen Harst around for a few days, but that didn't matter. Jack Fox was *dead* and *that* didn't make any difference either. If it ever surfaced—

so to speak—that Haynes had put those three men in the swamp, he still wouldn't utter either of those dread names. He'd stonewall it and take his chances. Because Fox and Harst were into some strange, scary shit.

Well, looky here! What a stroke of luck! If that wasn't Ape-cock's stolen cruiser, big as life, headed right towards him! He hit the flashers and the siren, downshifted, braked and went into a sliding one-eighty, meaning to drop side-by-side with the Dodge aimed the same way, catch up with it, and crowd it off the road.

But as he slid screeching through his about-face, he was astonished to see the Dodge brake and swing sideways to meet his car flank-to-flank. And as their flanks hit with a crash, the Dodge accelerated in such a way—but how? It seemed impossible!—that both cars stuck fast side-to side and began a mated spinning, carouselling round and round, faster and faster while remaining poised on the very center of the highway, till Haynes' door flew open and he was flung out. His door was locked, the seat belt buckled, yet his door flew open and he was flung out, the belt snapping like paper, as he went tumbling off the highway, tumbling and tumbling across the grass . . . .

All bruises and dizziness, he got to his knees and was fumbling for his sidearm, when a whirlwind of leaves descended upon him. It seized him like a pair of huge soft powerful hands—seized his body, lifted him high off the ground, and carried him through the air hanging upside down. Carried him back to the highway he'd been thrown from.

The anesthetic of his shock yielded quickly to the flux of his blood to his brain. He tried to thrash himself free, but the spinning air gripped him with a giant's strength. The Dodge pulled away from his stalled cruiser, and then a little old woman with wild gray hair under a battered fedora got out from behind the wheel. Without taking her smiling eyes from his, she made a gesture at the car and, by themselves, its gas-port flapped open and its gas cap spun off.

"I am Quetzal. I am the servant of Itzamna, who brings the dead to life. I am the servant of Itzam-ye, who perches on the World-Tree and summons sorcery." She reached her right hand into the wind-cone that held him and lightly touched his down-hanging head.

Haynes' terror had not left him, but a dream-sensation was enfolding it. He was hanging upside down in the air in a leafy whirlwind! An impossible woman was speaking impossible words to him! Surely he was dreaming.

"You are named . . . Haynes. You have shed human blood into the mouth of Xibalba. Feeding him, you have borrowed his power. Now I borrow it from you." Extending both hands, the old woman held Haynes' face between them. "Forgive me, Haynes. You give pain freely. I do not. But I am afraid you must undergo . . . a violent change." She grasped his head in hands strong as steel and tore it off his neck. Though her palms muffled his ears, he heard with excruciating clarity the snap of his spine and the more complex sundering of skin and muscle. In an instant he was smaller, simpler, lighter and he could feel a cold wet raggedness where his neck should be.

She shifted her grip, now holding the head by hair and scalp. He opened his eyes and saw the world turned right-side-up again. But, though he dangled upright under her fist, he saw his headless body still hanging upside down in that whirl of leaves, which now turned and tilted till the stump of his neck hung just above the opened gas-tank of the Dodge.

From above and behind him came the voice of the little old woman who was holding him. "Be consoled, Haynes. Your transformation will now fuel our flight."

As Haynes watched, the envelope of wind which held his body contracted. A crackling noise of crumpling bones followed and his arms and legs twisted round his torso. His whole body torqued, turning like a wrung garment. A thick braided runnel of blood leapt from his neck-stump and tucked itself neatly, gurgling, down into the port of the gas-tank. At length, his body dropped onto the asphalt.

The whirlwind became two leafy shapes which opened the car's doors and gestured his head and its bearer inside. The old woman slid behind the wheel, saying to him, "Forgive me if I make your hair a bit longer."

Haynes felt his hair pulled long, longer from his scalp, then felt that long lock tied around the rearview, from which he now dangled, gazing out the windshield. Slanting his eyes, he found he could obliquely see the face of his possessor. She smiled at him and fired up the engine.

Haynes watched the highway flow towards them faster . . . faster . . . and awaited the awakening that would surely come, for he must be sleeping in his own bed or perhaps unconscious, knocked out in the crash of his cruiser. Look! The old woman had swung the car off the road, pulled back on the steering wheel, and the car was *rising* from the ground! They were flying, the cruiser's tires spinning on sky! A mosaic of treetops flowed beneath them.

Of *course* it was a dream! He was fully conscious and his head was torn from his body! He was in a flying car!

And he felt so *aware*. Indeed, he knew the terrain below him, recognized that valley. There was the dirt road paralleling the stream he'd driven three times, each time with a brown passenger for Dr. Harst. Both the road and the stream it ran along ended at a swamp just on the edge of Jack Fox's acres.

Oh yeah, for sure and beyond all doubt, this was a dream. Dreams used stuff that had actually happened, like right now they were parking just where he had parked *his* unmarked cruiser.

The old woman unhooked his hair and got out, dangling him from one hand. Flanking them two leafy woman shapes appeared, Haynes' slanting glances told him. The three of them stepped to the brink of the swamp: a big black pond canopied by creeper-shrouded trees, the water scummed over with moss and algae, and crowded with half-sunk rotting logs. Quetzal turned him so he hung facing her. "I send you, Haynes, to your master. Bring him our message. He will dislike the message. I fear I cannot promise you will feel no pain. Tell him, please, that we are coming for him."

She flung him over the swamp. Haynes tumbled through the green gloom—long, long his flight seemed, until he was crashing into fetid water and sinking like a stone, sinking. He saw below him huge shapes stirring, vague, pythonic bodies uncoiling. Fanged jaws gaped towards him and Haynes opened his mouth to scream (though voiceless in that airless deep) that he *had* no message, but when the jaws crushed his skull, and tasted the nutmeat of his brain, his message was delivered.

"OUR ENEMY IS WARNED, my daughters," Quetzal said. "Your flesh is the air! Join your hands and bring us the Vortex! Uproot this swamp!"

Lupe and Emily caught her will like a flame. Standing face to face they linked their leafy fingers and spun, spun faster, sucking the autumn air into their gyration, drifting over the pool. Stripped foliage whipped into their whirlwind. Its tip sank like an auger into the pond and tore its waters spiraling up and away. The black tarn sank, one yard, two yards . . . the slimy bottom emerging into view, a knotted snakes' nest of massive roots was revealed, scaly roots jeweled here and there with crude black eyes. Everywhere in their coils they clamped sodden human shapes, their clothes mostly rotted away, their flesh grown scaly as the unformed dragons gripped them in a sleep of undecaying death. And from the midst of this ophidian tangle one gnarled mass—a grotesque burl at first it seemed—hoisted itself in the gloom. Blistered with black eye-knobs, it unhinged crude jaws fanged with crooked thorns.

"See!" the witch shrilled. "On his feast of prey, they've fed almost to dragon-form. See our danger! Everywhere he feeds and feeding more, the more he takes on the Hunter's shape. Strike! Smite! Avenge your murdered brothers and sisters!"

She flung the axes into the whirlwind, which divided into foliage-clad woman shapes. They bestrode the air a moment, hoisting their weapons, then plunged. Airborne they fought, light as leaves for all the brute bite of their whistling cleavers. Green blood sprayed from every blow. A complex tremor ran through the scaly coils and caused the sodden corpses they clenched to twitch and stir like waking sleepers. The jaws hissed and gnashed the air, but wooden sinews proved too crude and unformed to catch adversaries which its fangs could not have harmed in any case. Sap ran from a hundred wounds; the tentacles slowed, shuddered, and lay still. The onyx eyes dimmed and grew pallid, the jaws hissed wetly, then froze in death.

From her coat the witch drew an obsidian blade. "Daughters," she said softly. "Bring them out to me and lay them in the grass."

A score of dead, like scaly mummies bandaged in black bark, lay beneath the whispering trees, the branches stirring as the sun declined and the late afternoon breeze moved among the hills.

Quetzal knelt by the nearest of the dead and touched her obsidian point to where its heart would be. Quietly she said, "I free you to abide with me, to fight by my side, to know the wind and the sky once more, and the stars and the green hills of earth."

She stabbed the sad shape once and a gust of air breathed from it, stirring the wild white locks that escaped her old black hat. She rose and knelt by the next of the dead.

And so Quetzal moved among them, as the sun declined and the sky turned rosy gold. As each corpse released its ghost, the dark husk began to crumple and its barklike fabric to dry and granulate, collapsing to a fine dust the breezes scattered, while vines and flowers, tiny twisted shoots at first, peeked from the subsiding residue. Morning glories, dandelions, poppies, lupines unfolded in the mellow light, while the breezy air grew busier still, full of a subtle, multidirectional stir. The trees were shaken and jostled, the grasses and shrubs twitched fitfully, and an ever-thickening airy traffic came alive around Quetzal as she knelt by corpse after corpse with her knife and her murmured words.

At length, the witch sat cross-legged amidst the flowery meadow she had made, surrounded by a new, still unseen, congregation.

"Each of you has your own history of suns and moons, of deeds and days, of loves and losses. But Xibalba has taken you from these lives of yours and you have lain since then with him. I must know what you have learned of him. Xibalba the green god is beauty. The green god is life. He has fed us with his flesh, all our millions, time without end. Why does he murder us now? Why does he hunt us? For years I have followed them, the men whose minds he has captured, the men he has sent forth to kill for him, to feed his dragons their human food. Come into me now, my brothers and sisters. Enter me with my breath. Make me know what you have learned of Xibalba's will."

Had some stranger come upon her, he would have seen no more than an old woman sitting in a field of unseasonably blooming flowers, breathing a bit strangely, breathing so deeply, again and again, and staring a bit strangely too, her eyes rapt on the trees surrounding her, the murmuring cascades of their leaves. No more than this would he have seen.

But for the witch those rippling leaves were living mosaics, fluid puzzle-works weaving visions: visions of rainforests writhing in Hell, geysers of gasoline spraying jeweled jungles, replanting them with fierce forests of orange flame rising to the sky, visions of rich wildernesses bulldozed flat, replaced by endless lawns where bulbous monocultures sprawled in their sameness, steer after steer, grapevine after grapevine, horizon to horizon, visions of vast scabs on the planet-skin, concrete and asphalt carapaces where steel monsters swarmed farting up a second atmosphere that diseased the first, that clogged the planetary lung, spreading deserts, spreading flood zones, drowning and parching the green god's children, visions of ancient forest Titans toppled, patriarch after patriarch colliding with the earth, shattering into lumber stacks, mutating into suburbs, suburbs that entombed fertile soil forever, that sucked distant rivers and mountain lakes dry, emitting meanwhile more megatons of hydrocarbon gases skywards . . . .

Quetzal surged to her feet, fighting the air with lifted arms, her head leaned back till her hat fell off, her mouth gaping as if to howl, though no sound came out but something else, the stream of ghosts she had liberated re-erupting from her, her thin chest heaving as the air around her grew fitful in a widening zone of gusts spiraling up from the axis of her slight frame.

She seemed almost drunk for some time after that. Slowly she bent to pick up her hat, swaying slightly, one gnarled hand raking back her frosty curls, eyes staring inward, lips moving vaguely. At length she put her hat on and stiffly lowered herself to her knees. The sun was setting now and brazen light bathed everything. She spread her arms in a summoning gesture and a stir went round about her, a ripple through the flowers that jeweled the grass. The blossoms nodded and trembled as an airy gathering converged to her center.

"El Dios verde es la vida misma. He is life itself. Time without end we have been nourished by his fruits and sheltered by his boughs. Now I see to save his life, he means to kill us all and eat our flesh—take back our flesh. He's learned to use our eyes, our limbs, to hunt us. Xibalba will feed on his killers and so we are at war to the death. I love the green god. Soy bruja! I am his servant, servant of all the gods. But he will feed on the good and the evil alike and by tomorrow night's full moon he will come to birth in the form of many dragons, to scour human kind from the face of the earth.

And so, I stand with you against him. Now, as quickly as he kills, we must take back the spirits of his dead. We must take their spirits back and swell our armies of defense. Emilia . . . ."

The ghost who was her first recruit called flower petals to herself and stepped before her protector, showing Quetzal the smile of love she wore, touching the seamed cheek with a silky fingertip of lupine.

"Emilia, your child will face Xibalba's most terrible dragon, whom you know too well. Whether she will win, or die, is hidden from me. Go to her. Take the green path."

The witch swept her hand at the trees surrounding them, addressing the whole ethereal entourage surrounding her. "Remember. He means to take all human lives, yet the green god is our world still. Leaf, branch, vine, and blossom, they are our Rainbow on Earth. They are radiance made solid to our touch. They are Light itself, Light made solid for our food and drink. Till the moment we die in his fangs, we inhabit the green god's body and his green shade is our proper home."

Emilia stepped into the trees.

XXI

It was windy in Bushmill as the sun sank to a redder phase near setting. The Bide-a-Nite, Karen's motel, was on the burg's northern edge. She stood in its parking lot, watching the light grow rosy on the low wooded hills that flanked the highway out of town. She deeply did not want to go back in that room and read the letter she had left lying open on the desk.

Just to stand out here was a kind of paradise! Her hand not a tape-bound torment, but sedated in a fresh white plaster cast, its trauma in the past, contained and treated. And this place, these trees—*other* than and *elsewhere* from Jack Fox's orchard of nightmares. What a balm to be here, watching a different sun approach a peaceful setting. Just down the highway, a path branched up a hillside. She followed it up through tawny grass, past blackberry vines with a few late fruit, all gilded by the slant sun. A nice view of the rolling hills opened out.

A sneaky sweet feeling of nostalgia came over her . . . and she identified its source: sunny afternoons with Mom in her canning corner came back—the smell of blackberry compote simmering on the stove, the light on ruby jars of strawberry jam freshly sealed in wax, the gems of other jars so warm and solid when Mom let Karen take them in her small hands.

She looked at the hands she had now: usefully callused, neatly sinewy on the backs and wrists. Mom had always trusted tasks to her hands, letting her take hold of her world. She remembered picking those blackberries, greedily reaching on legs not yet quite firm enough and falling into thorny disaster. Remembered Mom hugging her grief away, Mom's comforting smell.

Karen sat on the grass, watching two oak trees ripple in the amber air. For all the terrors in her life, did every life have such sweetnesses as hers had also held? She supposed not, so luckless were many lives. Tears sprang to her eyes. Rising up on her knees, she stared disbelieving at the rippling oaks above her. In their sun-and-shadow dapple the leaves, like Pointillist brush-strokes, held the unmistakable image of Mom's face! The breeze did not destabilize her face, but rippled it with life. There was a special secret glint of brightness in her deep-set eyes and a tender hesitation around her lips, as if she just might speak if she could choose the words.

Karen closed her eyes and shook her head, looked, and saw Mom still, the features crumbling in a stronger gust of wind, but the woman even more piercingly coherent within that commotion. Was Mom *there*? Or only in Karen's own heart? So piercingly real. Look at her eyes—grief in her eyes and joy within the grief!

And then the sun was down. The trees were only trees, alive with wind.

For the first time in many days, terror was at bay. Karen remembered only sweetness and love and felt only sorrow. She knelt there in the grass and let the tears come freely. "Oh Mom . . . sweet precious Mom . . . Oh Susan . . . poor sweet Susan . . ."

The stars were coming out when at last she wiped her eyes and got to her feet. To cry like that! It came so hard to her and seemed to drain her strength so utterly. And yet such relief and something like strength were in its aftermath. She thought of all that had been happening to her and found she could look at it and see it clearly for what it was, despite the fact what she saw was madness itself.

A man had broken her hand while almost raping her. She had killed the man, undressed his corpse, and buried that corpse on her own property. Simple facts, which would simply end most lives, destroy most people's worlds. And yet these facts were not the worst.

Worse was poor Susan dead in a long steel drawer, only her lovely face eerily intact. But looking out of that dead lovely face—Karen saw it suddenly as a mask for another.

Or Wolf's face as he chewed noisily on one of Dad's peaches while, from behind the glaze of the man's own brainless malice, *something alien, something murderous looked out*.

Worse was herself sticking Dad's gun muzzle into her mouth and touching her own blood, still wet on a yellow dress stained a quarter century ago.

There was something in Dad's earth, something in her own home ground, and it stared out at her from the eyes of the dead. It had killed Susan. It had killed Wolf, using Karen as its cat's-paw. It had tried to kill Karen's spirit, through her unripe body, decades ago. And it had tried to blow her brains out, mere days ago.

A monster in the earth. It was *sanity* to face it and *in*sanity even to think it. She needed something—and it surprised her to realize it was not a drink she needed. No, somehow that had been buried in the compost heap in the dead of night. What she needed, she realized, was to hear the voice of a friend. A voice to pull her mind up out of this monstrous darkness.

There were no phones in the rooms of her dirt-cheap motel, only a pay phone next to the check-in desk. Needing to be alone with her call, Karen staggered down the trail and back onto the highway.

On Bushmill's quiet little main drag, she found a gas station and behind the counter of its mini-mart, a big country kid with pale eyes who wordlessly made her change for the ancient pay phone in the corner., He then sat there watching her as she fed in the quarters, watching her as if he'd never seen this done or that there was nothing else in his world to think about. She turned her back to him.

Someone answered with a single word that didn't sound like what Kyle had written: "Hello. I'd like to speak to Kyle, please—I think he just took a room with you today." It stunned her that she didn't even know Kyle's last name, that he hadn't provided it. Didn't know his last name, his age, his origin, though such intimacy lay between them, though she could still see his muscled arms laying a naked corpse in her steaming black compost. A complete stranger had brought a killer into her life. She had killed the killer and he had laid the killer's corpse in her native ground.

"Who?" The voice sounded like an old man, an old man blurred and husky with drink.

"Kyle. He's a big guy, black hair with some gray. Muscular . . . ." There was a mumble at the other end and she thought she heard the phone set down. She had just described a phantom to a phantom. Despair embraced her like rising black water. She looked around and the kid's pale eyes were still adhering to her, so fixed that they seemed inhuman.

"What the fuck are you staring at?" The kid didn't twitch, didn't even blink. Gave the tiniest shrug, turned sluggishly on his stool, and faced the window behind him. The window was filled with the interior's bright reflection and he resumed staring at her mirrored image.

She stared at it too, a shadow-Karen, gaunt-faced and wild-haired, a woman almost gone, eaten away to near-transparency by the night, by the dark earth . . .

The mumbly voice came back. She thought she made out the word *message*. "Please tell him Karen called. K-a-r-e-n. I'm in Bushmill. B-u-s-h-m-i-l-l. Will you please tell him? I'm at the Bide-a-Nite Motel."

There was only what sounded like ". . . tell 'im," and the man hung up.

She walked back through a town that appeared utterly empty, though it couldn't have been later than seven or eight. It seemed she was walking the seafloor under miles of water crushing down her shoulders. Each step sank her deeper in exhaustion, till she felt her walking was an illusion and that she was still bent shoveling black muck, digging a bottomless grave. Stepping at last into her room, closing the door . . . there was the letter on the desk. Let it stay. She would not look at it yet.

Her clothes fell from her. The bed . . . a safe place down at the very bottom of the universe. She dove in.

SHE SAT UP IN THE DARK as a vast uproar shook the walls. Her windows had grown larger, lost their blinds and— right outside them, in a flood of moonlight—blown branches surged against the panes. Deep within the tumult someone cried to her, a woman's frail voice that pierced her heart. Karen saw Susan, pale, naked and storm-tossed in the leaves.

She sprang up and leapt to the door . . . no more than turning the knob when the door was snatched into the gale. Running into the slippery turmoil, she was a leaf blended into the blizzard with the rest. She ran through black and silver jungle after Susan, who twisted to reach her, but was pushed always onward—grass-like cold fur under their feet, cold leaves licking their nakedness.

They erupted into emptiness. Earth vanished under foot and they fell and fell into a vast black pit from whose floor far beneath glistened a huge reflected moon. It seemed they had endless time in that long fall, time to swim the rushing air and reach at last each other's arms. Susan's breasts cold against Karen, the uprush numbing their skin. But their limbs locked at last, at last rejoined, their love snatched back from the night. And thus re-knit, they crashed against and sank beneath the liquid moon.

In their drowning, the moonlight showed them to themselves so clear in the liquid dark, so pale in the perfect black.

They were deep, so hopelessly deep, falling together when an upthrust of seething black roots enclosed Susan and tore her from Karen's arms. Karen screamed for her, desperate to reach her, to pull her from the muck below. She fought, entangled in the roots. She could not lose her again!

Powerful arms dragged Karen upwards. Hot arms burning her, showing her that her own skin was cold as death. Arms and legs doubly clamped her, seared her till the lift and the warmth of them won her will and she became frantic to feel their warmth and rise back to the air.

"Susan!" she cried. All the sorrow on earth in her voice.

She sat up, alone in the dark. Outside, only a moonlit wind moved through the trees. Once again, she'd failed to hold her, to protect her. Karen lay curled in a ball then and wept bitterly. The arms that had saved her in the dream, that had saved her from Wolf's tomb . . . a thousand years ago, seemed for a few seconds more to be holding her still.

Unanchored and strange to herself, she sat up in the bed and saw, under its cone of light on the desk, Dad's letter. There would be no good time to slip her mind into those pages, another black tarn though it lay in the light. She stood and slipped on the jeans and canvas coat, regretting the .357s absence from its pocket, and sat down to the document at last.

My Beloved Emily,

A friend will mail this for me, probably from Mexico City. You must have the truth from me, while I am still resolved to tell it. I want to hide nothing from you.

Something in this jungle has found me and entered me.

We were on a "counter-terrorist" mission, meaning we were neutralizing, or rather killing, impoverished native Mayan insurgents.

I was with two operatives I will call Black and Jack, Company Men, smug because they "had kills." CIA kills, nine out of ten, are inserts with full back-up. Ambushes. These spooks were dry-gulchers and, perhaps because I was Special Forces, they had to keep boasting of their exploits.

The true horror began when we captured two insurgents. One young, the other old, both wiry brown men as lean as coyotes. We put them in shackles. And then Black came out with the inspiration he'd been secretly gloating over, the way to achieve "maximum negative effect" on the morale of the insurgents. I call the younger spook "Jack" because he reminded me of myself when I first went to Nam, not particularly evil, just young and ignorant. But Black, ten years older, had a pouchy face with a half-hidden glee in it that liked killing.

Cenotes are natural wells in the limestone sub-floor of these jungles. The Maya used them for human sacrifice and there was a big one just a few days from where we had taken our captives. We should, Black said, weight and drown one in this cenote and free the other to spread the tale.

I had resolved to free them both on my watch, then kill Black and Jack. Night after night, I took the night rotation and watched all four men in their sleep, but did not act.

Because, from the moment of my picturing the deed that Black proposed, it was as if I stood already there, at the rim of that big watery grave, which held a thousand years of dead in its silty bottom. It was as if I stood there already and I felt its cold green breath welling up around me. More than this, felt in that breath, a consciousness, an awareness of me. As if some huge living thing within the cenote summoned me.

Do you see the strangeness of it? I had only to hear Black's description, a word-sketch of a bizarre homicide, and I was seized—heart, spine and mind.

I've told you how I love our acres, how the feeling of my father's land beneath our feet seizes hold of me sometimes, as I walk between the trees at dusk. I have always felt it in our soil, a kind of sleeping earthquake of life-to-be, a might and majesty older than Man.

Our last night-march brought us to the cenote just before midnight. With every step, I felt that I moved already through the giant's flesh, that every leaf of this jungle was a nerve of him, and the very darkness was his blood.

The dank smell of trapped water reached us long before the sight of that great gulf opened suddenly to our eyes: a yawning stone throat, an eighth of a mile across, its black water seventy feet below the rim. Stepping to its brink was stepping into an awe as old as Man.

We advanced onto a narrow limestone shelf overhanging the abyss. Perhaps it was the ancient platform of sacrifice. I knew only that to stand here was to stand outside myself and, though the private plans I had made for this moment were dim and vague, I executed them ecstatically, flawlessly. Moving back from my partners' position on the rim, I touched my automatic's muzzle to Black's nape and my machine pistol to Jack's. Saying, "Dead still, boys. Not a twitch." And to the prisoners I said in Spanish to take the key, unshackle themselves and go. The old man seized it and the pair of them fled.

The instant the jungle had swallowed them, I said to the great black floor of water far below us: "Take my offerings!" And squeezed my two triggers.

The brief thunder of the rounds hid the report of snapping rock, but not the fact that the shelf we stood on had broken and that I, too, was falling with them into the cenote.

The black water seized us and grappled us under.

But Emily, it was not water! It was a liquid flesh, a green-black smoke of countless generations. Those living dead poured through my skin, and the giant who had taken them poured into me with them.

This machine clatters under my fingers, I am raving. I have been filled with a Titan as cold and slow as the Ice Ages, as unrelenting as the spreading jungles that have broken Earth's stony hide and blanketed her equator time without end. In me now is that Will that seizes the sunlight and binds it to the lifeless soil and raises the hosts of life.

I have sworn to myself to hide nothing from you and I still cling to the hope you will not think I am insane . . .

As I climbed my slow way up those walls, I became aware of two other shapes, inching their way up other crevices. Their progress was no more halting than my own, though the moonlight here and there fell directly enough on one of them to show me that he had but half a skull, the top of his cranium a ragged ruin.

I don't know what has touched me, but even with this horror in my mind, I long to hold you again, to hold our precious little daughter, to come back into the circle of our love, where time can wear away this nightmare I have entered. Emily, I beg you not to leave me. You are my sun and my stars, you are my open sky. Only your love can keep me from sinking completely and forever into the darkness of the earth.

Soon I will be demobilized, debriefed. Before I come any closer to home than this, I will contact you again, my precious love.

                                        Your Jack

Under a night-sky still paved with stars, though the east had just started paling from black to indigo, Karen emerged from her room. She thought she had cried all that was in her—for her father, for Susan—but it seemed there were more tears yet . . . .

But there were deeper things than tears. Things stirring down in the cellar. A skull-blown corpse climbing the wall of a jungle chasm. Dad down in a crypt as garishly colored as any jungle, crushing her wrist in his fingers . . . Susan . . . Wolf.

For the first time she stood in fear of the very earth beneath her feet. For the first time, the stars had become an abyss she might fall into.

Her hand throbbed, her body and her heart ached, but she knew that she must go home. Would she find herself alone there? Would Kyle have returned?

KYLE LIKED SLEEPING in his truck bed. It was small, like his bunk in his cell, but it was roofed by the whole open sky and had wheels, 350 horses tucked under the hood. Lying in the bed of his truck was like lying in an anti-cell, curled on a magic carpet. He felt cozy, naked in his sleeping bag, the restless wind now and then nosing down into his warmth.

His review had gone well. Even though the acne-scarred old mick did nothing but scowl and sneer, he'd given him a late Friday interview, so Kyle had the whole weekend free. His case file revealed the injustice of the seven years he'd done and the man saw it.

He watched the trees rock and sway. The wind was what he'd missed most in prison, the way it stirred things to life, the way it seemed to blow the stars brighter, as if they were live coals it fanned.

If only he hadn't had to leave Karen. He hoped that right now she was safe in some motel far out of Gravenstein. What a heart she had! That soulless loser broke her hand and pinned her down and still she blew his foul life right out of him, saving her own when she did it, because Wolf would have killed her.

Kyle.

"Karen!" Bolt upright, he scanned around him, the blown trees and bushes. The blazing stars, but nothing else.

Kyle.

It wasn't so near this time. Somewhere out among the trees her voice shaped his name. It came to him, a leaf dancing on the wind and touched his ear like a caress. A moment after, something soft and warm touched his lips lightly and vanished.

His heart was an anvil hammered by desire and fear. He stood in the truck bed. Then wind parted the dark foliage of the nearest oak and within that shadowy opening, Karen stood. Terror and desire played across him.

What was happening? He did not *have* hallucinations.

Her phantom roused him to anger at his rebel senses. He bent to where his jeans lay in the bed and took his knife from the pocket and slashed a cut across his forearm. The stab of pain was as real as the wind and stars, and the salt tang of his blood was no dream when he tasted it.

There—moon-white and unclothed—her hair snaking in the wind, stood Karen in the crux of the tree, its branches a riot around her, but not one leaf touching her.

"It wants to kill us, Kyle"—her voice as close as a mate's in bed, for all the gale that blew between them. "Come and hold me and our love will break its power."

Leaping out of the truck he went towards her. His sex seemed a lifted rapier in a war they must fight. And it astonished him, the power of this feeling, that they were in a battle. That the enemy, whatever it was, was all around them, merciless and dire. That he and Karen must cleave to one another for all they were worth.

He climbed into the tree and stood on the great bough before her. She came into his arms, giving him a shock of wonder and recognition as they touched. "Brace your back against the tree. It can't hurt us if we love." Kyle straddled the bough, his back to its bark; she straddled him, her breasts soft against his face. Moving as if within a sky-filling melody, the music of their hearts beat in cadence with the singing wind.

KYLE WOKE SHIVERING. His sex was wet and cold and a scab had formed on his arm. Seated cross-legged on the roof of his truck was a small white-haired figure in a black coat and fedora. She spoke quietly, yet he heard her as if they stood face to face.

"Hombre. You must go through fire and fury to find her, mi hijo. You are not her lover, but you love her and must protect her. Sleep for an hour or two, my friend. You will need your strength. Go to Gravenstein, not to the orchard, for she is not there. Get to Gravenstein by sunrise and be ready to fight."

XXII

In the deep of night Marty rocketed his cruiser down the Gravenstein Highway towards Jack's acres. His face itched with its new pox of piercings, while jubilation twined with terror climbed his spine, like a clinging vine. Jack was *with* him, had been, since his immersion in Rabble's pond. In waves of imagery and understanding, the sequence and reasons of Marty's task had been revealed to him.

He summoned the night-shift's cruisers to the station and let the men know that at their shifts' end they must return to the station for extended assignment. Next he notified the day-shift troops—for troops indeed all the deputies were, an army that Jack now called to fight the witch's army. Marty commanded some to duty at first light and some to stand by during the night "for special ops."

With these redeployments in place, and the whole force poised for muster just after dawn, Marty saddled up his cruiser and headed out to Jack's orchard, with his heart divided between delight and dread. And how not? The aura of this place had ruled his spirit since he was a boy and now, as Jack's living will unfolded in his body, blooming before his inner eye, the feeling was equally of slavery and power. He wore his master's mantle and wielded his might, but his every move was commanded from under the earth by this Master.

He rolled down the long drive, past the black-windowed house—past the vandalism of toppled plum trees, but did not pause—down the lane and into the night army of spiderish branches he went, the trees all gesturing in the starkness of his headlights. At the lowest border of Jack's plantation, he knew the task he was summoned to.

The lights were on in Jack's still shed and he stepped inside, into a gasoline stench. He gazed around at an interior he had beheld only once before, summoned here four years ago, the night he had become a man and seized the reins of power from Rabble. Jack had admitted him that very night, only then had he fully unfolded to him the coming mystery and Marty's role in it. Told him of his power-to-be and the vista of the immortality that was to be his prize. He'd been so proud that night!

Now, knowing what he was about to do, awe was dominant—so much so that he had to struggle to find his breath, to master the galloping of his heart, and wrap his will around the hugeness of his mission here. Now, wirecutters and a hatchet . . . . With trembling hands he tucked both in his belt, and faced the kegs. So many of them! Awkward rather than heavy for his new-grown strength. He found he could hug two at once against his chest.

Out of the shed with them and around the huge compost heap. That black shape seemed like a shrouded giant with something of Jack's power coiled within it. Marty only sensed this without understanding it; some seed or scion of his departed master lay dormant in that fecund mass. He hastened to the acres' barbed wire border. Setting down the kegs, he cut through the wire, resumed his burdens and carried them down a rough and overgrown slope to the bank of the stream that skirted Jack's land. And on this bank, wielded the hatchet, broaching the first cask in two blows and tilted a gurgle of brandy into the stream. Brandy's breath scenting the night air.

A long labor lay before him. Near a hundred kegs remained to be transfused into the valley's water-table. A long labor and a great terror to be subdued in the doing of it, to be bent to his will as he worked, because Marty understood what he was feeding here, understood he was, with this endless libation, awakening monsters from the earth, summoning the green god's army of conquest to the battlefield this valley would become.

But bubbling up beside his terror rose a devilish merriment, a mocking glee for the powerless enemy he knew rode above him, riding the air even now, cruising like a night-hawk or a great white owl. That white-haired bitch-witch whose leafy phantom had mocked him. She cruised up there, but dared not dive, oh no, for there was a guardian giant in this earth. Jack Fox himself, and one greater than Jack even deeper, and she dared not strike Marty, dared not try to kill him as she had surely killed the still-missing Haynes.

So Marty mocked her as he toiled, as he went back and forth trucking kegs, splintering them, disgorging them—mocked her with a work-chantey as he poured the pungent brandy in the stream:
"Here goes the brandy
into the creek
that flows to the swamp
that drains to the stream
that runs to the river
that goes through the town
that *Jack* killed!"

WHEN THE MOON had reached its zenith and its light
suffused the night sky with the power she needed,
Quetzal called her gathered ghosts close around her
around her and spoke to them. "Now you must come
into me, mis Queridas. Stretch these old bones, this old
flesh with your spirits. Ayuda me. Help this old monkey-
body of mine take the shape we need.

"Our enemy's fortress is under the earth, there is
a gate, a door he keeps open. It's the door he'll use to
draw his servants down below. It's the door he'll use
when he comes out to harvest every human life on
earth. Help me find this portal from the sky. Then, if
we can pass through it, we can go down and free your
sisters and brothers taken before you. Come into me,
you spirits of the air, y den mi alas! Make me wings!"

She took off her coat and her coarse-knit sweater and
tied them around her waist. Her chest—lean, indeed, as
a monkey's—with her breasts like winter apples, wore
the moonlight on their Mayan darkness. She spread
her arms and the ghosts around her let their leaf-and-
flower-petal flesh fall from them. Then the moonlit
air round Quetzal's skinny axis grew iridescent, the
witch's skin rippled and dimpled like dark water. Her
chest began to expand like a ribbed cask, her arms
began to thicken and to sprout . . . and moments later,
a gaunt little form in a black fedora rose up on wings
mightier than a condor's, but of a plumage so richly
tinted that even pale moonlight showed its emerald hue
as she hung beneath the silver lunar disc, a huge disc,
one night from full.

Circling upward in a slowly widening spiral, she
sought that vantage where the topography would betray

the green god's hidden workings. She had thought it all but certain that Jack Fox's land must hold a gateway in some secret nook or angle and there, indeed, was . . . the compost heap, a ridged black scar. She sensed beneath the wound it sealed that a titanic malice stirred and smoldered. By that path, she saw, the enemy's realm was near indeed, but his power and watchful hunger held the gate.

Like her sister, the great white owl, she hung there watching the labors of Marty Carver, the flash of his hatchet in moonlight, the glint of liquor falling from his arms into the stream. She watched, too, as a furtive glow began to thread its way along the stream from the point where Marty poured his tribute in. This subtle luminescence moved faster down the stream course than the current's flow could carry it: it moved like a spark down the length of a fuse.

In the water-table of this valley, amid the branchings of its aquifers, there had to be another portal, and surely it would be downstream from here, perhaps right in town, where Xibalba's harvest would be richest when, in his power, he rose with tomorrow's moon.

"Look," she murmured to her brood of spirits. "See how this beast in uniform toils to prepare his god's coming. See how he fertilizes the whole valley for the birth of Xibalba's dragons and when he returns to his men, he will still be about his master's business. Let's kill him, or at least slow him down. Lupe . . . Lupita, you let him misuse you so. Stay here, my daughter, ride back with him."

Quetzal then tilted her great wingspan and, in a majestic glide, sliced southward across the sky, down along the Gravenstein watershed. When she passed above the portal she sought, she would know, and

down it she would go to free more captive spirits to
her army.

MARTY'S WORK WAS DONE by dawn and not a moment
too soon. He flung himself behind the wheel of his
cruiser and fired it up. Turned on the heat—it was *cold*
in the god-damned car for some reason—whipped it
into reverse, spun around and roared up the picking
lane, pale dust rising behind him in the first gray light
of morning.

He drove the top speed he could survive within the
Fox acres and when he reached the highway, cranked
it up to ninety. So much to do! And by God he was
afire with it, was just the general to lead the conquering
army! He felt like Hannibal, bestriding not an elephant,
but the green god himself, Xibalba his own gigantic
mount, the whole round earth his conquest, the endless
green horizons of Eternity unscrolling before him. Jack
Fox might skulk in the dark below, his deity's minion,
his Morlock, but Marty Carver bestrode the god and
ruled a sun-washed world.

First, by oh-eight-hundred, every last department
cruiser and van must be deployed to every ag-worker
ghetto and labor-camp in the Valley. Marty's plainclothes
people would have to be separately briefed—must be
armed with a "special issue" of Jack Fox's sorcerous
sidearms. He would identify their targets as Terrorist
Sympathizer Mexes and Pakis, all of whom were
armed and dangerous and to be taken down on sight.
These officers would, of course, be utilized along with
the immigrants they took out. It didn't matter where
the green god got his eyes and brain matter, his DNA
for vertebrate structures.

Meanwhile Marty's uniforms would bring in every brown body their cruisers and vans could hold—pack them in the drunk tank and holding cells. He would use the day-captain, Contos, whom he'd put half in the know, to help him start staging the immigrants down to the old foundation, and down into the portal, and put Contos himself down the portal last of all. Well before that time, everyone else on the force would be responding to frantic calls from all over the county. Soon thereafter, every responding officer would have joined the callers in the green god's many jaws.

Oh-six-hundred hours, not a moment to spare. The woods and farms and fields had form, though not yet color, as they flashed past him. Christ, it was so *cold* in here, the cold like a muscled shape clenching his skin, squeezing his bones in an icy slippery grip and, just as he roared onto Fast Creek Bridge, the wheel convulsed hard right, breaking his grip, slamming his cruiser at ninety-plus into the parapet, whipping the whole car up ass-to-the-sky. The car cartwheeled in the gray void like a performing dolphin to slam down into the black surge. Marty was surrounded by dark now and upside down, as he fought to unbuckle his belt with at least two fingers broken, and the windows blown to atoms, and freezing water entombing him in the taste of brandy.

A slick naked shape rubbed itself against his face, rubbing big wet breasts against his drowning face. He blacked out still trapped . . . but still struggling, it seemed, for he came to an eon afterwards, skin and clothing torn, with crippled hands fiercely gripping weeds on the bank, his face barely clear of the current, coughing and sucking air.

Now he remembered his superhuman strength and he called upon it in his wakening rage. Clear enough who'd done this—a dead Mex bitch *not* dead, thanks to a white-haired bitch-witch. Any other man would have been killed, but the hag hadn't grasped the kind of power the god had set against her.

He dragged his stunned mass up the bank, up onto the bridge, knew he had a simple fracture of the forearm, broken fingers, at least two cracked ribs . . . and knew it didn't matter. Fifteen miles from the station and no one on the road this early Saturday and it didn't matter. His legs were mighty, his lungs were mighty, and fuck the pain of cracked bone. He began to jog and then jog faster, feeling a warming power rise through him, like green sap in the springtime sprig. Began to run outright—long, unflagging antelope strides that ate the miles. In less than two hours, he would reach town. He would muster his troops in time and *strike back* for the Master.

THE SUN HAD just cleared the horizon and begun to spread upon the town a peaceful, radiant Saturday morning. The whole Gravenstein Valley—edged and woven with autumn gold—was unbelievably lush and green. A sweet and fruitful smell rode the early breezes and the county's veins ran loud with bright indigo water. As if awakened by the sheer color of the day, people were up early everywhere.

Duina Tyler, coming out of the kitchen to cut back her roses a bit, noticed what a rich blue-green Crabapple Creek was, running along the border of their property, and noted how plump and brilliant her roses were, despite the lateness of the season, and how rich their scent. All around her, in fact, such a smell of . . . fertility in the air!

Glancing back at the kitchen window, Duina saw her husband Ry, still sitting at the table, waving a forkful of last night's peach pie at her and tucking it into his smiling mouth. Duina had to smile, too, and perhaps she blushed just a bit. It was good to be close again and to hell with their age. Neither one of them held much with all these new pills for men—though Duina was not entirely easy in her mind with Fox fruit either, with anything *about* Jack Fox, alive or dead, come to that. Lord, but her roses looked *so* lovely. She had to step close to them again, take and stroke their silkiness between her fingers, just had to place the blossoms against her cheek.

COUNTY CLERK FIONA BILLINGS came out just as early, went down to feed the chickens, and paused by their coop to consider the rich color and sharp scent of Fast Creek, which divided her property from the old Sanders house. She was startled to realize both her neighbors—Phil and Jed, the Coroner's Assistants—were also gazing at the creek from their own bank, still wearing their sweats from their morning exercycle routine. Fiona called, "Morning!" with uncertain cheeriness. She had alerted the pair of them when the Sanders place had come up for rent, but once they had become the Billings's neighbors, her husband Bob had begun to wonder out loud just how "close" the older and younger man were. Then, right after work yesterday, Fiona had been embarrassed to encounter them both at Fratelli's fruit stand, lined up for Jack Fox's peaches and apricots, just like her, there at Bob's behest. "My!" she exclaimed a little uneasily. "Isn't the creek *green* today!"

"Yes!" said Phil. "We were just noticing!" An embarrassed pause. Phil, perhaps just searching for something to say, asked, "Have you reached Dr. Harst at home yet, Fiona?"

"I haven't tried again. Marty Carver says he's heard from the doctor and he's just a bit under the weather, will be taking a few more days off."

"It's just we had an unusual, ah, subject come in after you left. One of our own—Officer Haynes . . . ." Oddly, as his partner was speaking, Jed had wandered abstractedly over to their small vegetable garden, knelt down, and was closely inspecting their tomato vines, sniffing their leaves, and stroking the fruit against his cheek.

From the house, Bob's voice called out, in a parody of seductiveness, "Oh Fi-ooooo-naaa!" She decided she'd better get back to him, before he called out something more embarrassing, though she was intrigued by Phil's news and more than a little fascinated by Jed's strangely intimate behavior with his tomato plants. "You better tell me about it later—I haven't made Bob's breakfast yet."

She made her way back across the yard. As she mounted the back steps, her eyes were drawn to the luxuriant morning glories, so profuse upon their trellises flanking the back door. Their colors and textures seemed irresistibly alluring, compelling her eyes and then her hands, which set to stroking their blossoms.

Closer to the heart of town, at the home of Midge and Kenny Adams, Helen Carver was another early riser. Leaving Skip asleep on the cot beside her bed, she slipped out of the guest room carefully, fearing to wake her hosts, whom she'd faintly heard disporting

themselves last night. She'd flung Marty's peaches out
the window on her way over last night, only to find a
peach cobbler on the Adams' table for dessert.

But, padding into the kitchen for coffee, she was
surprised to see, out the back window, Kenny pushing
a hand mower through the high grass of their big back
yard and Midge on her knees rooting in the dense lush
weeds that choked their plantings. Amazing. In a county
full of green-thumb homeowners, the Adamses—with
their shaggy front yard—were notable underachievers.

Helen felt a pang of envy: to be a real couple! Make
love one night, then get up early on a Saturday morning
and do something on a whim, like groom the yard for
the first time in months. How sweet to live with a lover
and a friend, to have your life blessed like that.

She watched them as she made coffee, just peeking
out now and then. Until, halfway through her first
cup, she realized how long it had been since they had
changed their positions. Kenny knelt by the mower, his
back to her, freeing blades that had been jammed by
the long grass. Midge, too, presented more back than
profile, also kneeling, with her hands thrust deep into
the weeds—even deeper now, it seemed, than when
Helen had first started looking.

Were they moving at all? Yes. They both were,
unmistakably, but oddly. A gentle, reciprocating
movement it was, sort of quietly oscillating backwards
and forwards, their faces aimed earthwards. Some
private game of theirs she guessed. Helen found
herself heading to the back door and stepped out onto
the porch, smiling a bit uncertainly. "Good morning!
Kenny? Midge?"

Midge answered, but Helen couldn't make it out.
She crossed the lush, dew-drenched grass, "Midge?"

It was so . . . disturbing, Midge on her knees there, making those tiny rhythmic bows towards the ground, her arms sunk up to the elbows in deep weeds, breeze-stirred weeds, though there was no breeze blowing, was there?

"Midge?"

"Helen? Helen, is that you?" Midge's voice sounded so whispery, so far away. Why didn't she turn around? Brought to a standstill, Helen stood there gripped by an inexplicable awe as Midge spoke, still facing away from her, spoke in a faint, amazed little-girl voice, dreamy and enraptured. "Oh, Helen, omigod it's beautiful. It's an Eden under the earth. Omigod, the green eyes like stars winking open under the earth, a universe of wee green lives rushing up to the sun to greet us to touch us to take us to spread us like laughing windblown leaves across the planet. Oh, we're meeting and mingling. I'm tingling, I'm tingling, the trees will be my legs and arms, the forests will dance with me, dancing green jungles we will be . . ."

Fear struck away Helen's paralysis and she lurched forward, "Midge! What's wrong?" Coming to her friend's side, she leaned over her—and felt her legs cut out from under her in terror, dumping her on her side. Looking up into Midge's enraptured face, she saw fine green whiskers of grass sprouting all over it, while rising from the ground, a thick sheaf of grass had entered her chest and was thrusting, thrusting, with a gentle insistence like foliage rocked by a breeze, branching within Midge's thoracic cavity and even now sending up from her spine and out through her blouse a delicate fur of green shoots.

Like an antswarm of tiny sharp jaws, Helen felt the bite of the grass she'd fallen in—and shock thrust her back up onto legs she could not otherwise have commanded. She stood swaying on these unreal legs of hers and looked up at a sky turned an alien, impossible blue as the sun peeked up past the hill. Looked over at Kenny and saw now how the hair spilling down from his head and onto his trembling back was not hair, but a growing mane of grass, a hyena's spiky dorsal crest of grass blazing an unreal green beneath the sky's unreal blue as it visibly sprouted a marching line along Kenny's spine.

Minutes later her car screeched out of the drive, a groggy, scared-looking Skip blinking in the back seat amid the tumbled heap of their belongings. Helen sped back to the house she'd lived in for the last twenty years. She wasn't going home, she was going to get the Acting Chief Deputy Sheriff, because in her terror, she didn't know what else to do.

THE CITY OF GRAVENSTEIN was so *quiet*. Sal Fratelli, stepping out of Cherry's door on her tree-arched block on the old side of town, stood listening beside his pick-up before getting into it. He should have heard birds everywhere and the squirrels chattering, talking about the sun's arrival. Five minutes ago, he'd sat straight up in bed, eyes wide open, Cherry still softly snoring beside him, sat straight up thinking: *I've gotta cut that dope right now and get it bagged and outta here*. Just like that, and here he had his clippers, a heavy-duty trash bag, and was heading out right now. What was with him?

It wasn't *him* though—that was the thing. It was something all *around* him. It was the quiet, partly, but it was also something the opposite of quiet. A sense of movement, that was it, a quiet, crackly, whispery movement—everywhere. It was freaky. He almost never smoked his crop, beyond checking up near harvest time on what he could charge for it. He preferred a glass of wine or beer now and then to dope, but this sense of movement, it was that creepy-tingly kind of thing you might get off a doob, kinda spooky.

Sal fired up the truck and took off. He trusted his impulses. If he felt the itch to harvest early, get his butt covered risk-wise, so be it. When you break the law, listen to your hunches. He would cut it, get it packaged, make some calls and truck down to the big city this very day. He and Cherry could do some serious week-ending down there.

It was too early to go inside the house. Dad and Maureen might be sprawled on the big couch in front of the plasma screen, the two of them snoring on Dad's embarrassing fake zebra-skin upholstery, cocktail shakers and glasses everywhere. Sal went straight around to the back and into the yard.

There was certainly party-debris out here—pitchers, bottles, glasses on the patio table near the hot tub. But what was wrong with this picture? All the plantings around the yard, had they been this shaggy and overgrown yesterday? Maybe he just hadn't noticed? No! Those trellised vines flanking the hot tub, densely shaggy, shoots thickly dangling into the water—he recalled Cherry very clearly in that tub yesterday: not a sprig of green in the water with her. And as he stood struggling to believe it—two or three feet of growth in one night—he had once more that sense of things stirring *almost* silently, that whispery sound of foliage, yet not a breath of breeze.

He approached the tub. That dense swirl of drowned vine-strands filling it, was it actually . . . *moving*? Yes.

It flexed and twisted slightly, as an arm might do, reaching deeper, deeper, for something sought. Was that some fallen animal or bird he saw there, *snared* in the flexing weave of vines? It was something made of flesh and blood and was coming apart.

It was a face, half a face, one eye, Dad's eye, attached like a little dark fruit to one strand of vine and a bit of cheek and jaw, like a ragged blossom. On another strand, like two parting petals just beginning to sink under the water's surface, Dad's lips, Dad's lips stirring as they sank, whispering as they sank . . . *run* . . . *Sal* . . . *run* . . .

Just as Sal roared out of his father's driveway, Helen Carver roared into the street, headed for her own. They jammed on their brakes, swung screeching through a matched half-spin, and sat staring stupefied at one another from their windows. They encountered their own amazed horror on one another's faces. "What have you seen?" quavered Helen.

"I've seen that we gotta get outta here! Look, I got four-wheel drive and a full tank. Get in with me—I think the roads might be rough."

ALL OVER GRAVENSTEIN, before the sun had half-cleared the hills, a new kind of growth was taking root in the earth. Jesse Rangle, the big-chinned rancher Karen had spoken to so enthusiastically in the 8-Ball, had gorged on juicy Fox fruit all night long and sun-up found him out behind his barn, enjoying one of his sheep. The ewe, a handsome Abyssinian, seemed not much troubled by the high hiking boots into which her back legs were inserted, their laces cross-tied to form loose shackles undisturbing to the animal, as she cropped lush grass, while Rangle grunted astern of her, lost in a dream of bliss. In his transport he was unobservant of how the ewe's jaws had ceased to crop, though still grass entered them, and her throat still worked, still bulged and rippled as insurgent stalks thrust upward from the earth, crowding into the wooly barrel of the animal's body.

As Jesse cocked his head back to yodel his joy, that joy changed timbre, for he suddenly experienced a different kind of linkage to his love. His own torso tremored and swelled with a rippling growth. From his gaping jaws emerged not a cry, but a shock of greenery and his eyes beheld, not the sky, but much deeper things.

ELSEWHERE IN THE VALLEY, Roger Carver made his way out to his prize Black Angus in their feedlot behind the Maitland house. This was Roger's customary morning practice, always involving some private gloating and pipe-dreams of ribbons won at the next Livestock Fair.

Roger moved a little stiffly in his robe and slippers, the back injury he'd suffered at Marty's hands a bit inflamed by his night's work. Marsha's peach cobbler had been prepared with a very strict agenda of husbandly duty in mind. Her motive was dynastic rather than erotic—her father's will had made offspring a condition of her inheritance of his assets.

He was astonished to find his prized herd up to their necks in a lush insurgence of new grass, grown impossibly tall from what was bare-trampled feedlot earth just the night before. The beasts gaped and gasped, their eyes glaring wildly. Alarmed, Roger rushed hobbling among them.

Vigorously he swatted and shooed to drive them out of this frightening greenery from nowhere. Swatted and shooed and shoved at them, till he noticed a furious itch engulfing his legs, an itch that grew suddenly piercing and became a branching, a binding, a threading of thrusting green coolth. His eyes too, then, stopped seeing the sky they glared at. Long he stood there, seeing instead what lay underfoot, seeing the wide realm of weevil and worm, of mole and nematode, the vast dark business of the underground.

XXIII

Contos, the Day Captain, was mad as hell about being summoned to his post before sun-up, but he would never have dreamed of betraying even the slightest indication of his irritation to Marty Carver. Contos feared the Acting Chief Deputy right down to his bones. Three years ago, Contos happened to be just outside Karl Rabble's office during the interview that led to that old cowboy's retirement—had heard the kick that rebroke Rabble's leg. He'd had the sense to grasp at once that a decisive shift of authority had occurred and from that moment had unfailingly presented Marty Carver with a perfectly impassive and obedient expression.

But now, just after sunrise, as the double street-doors of bullet-proof glass were flung open and Carver strode in, Contos let his jaw drop slightly—couldn't help it.

This brought Marty towering near him, leaning close. "*What*, Contos?"

Too late to feign complete blindness. "You're . . . you're wet, sir." That was the least of it. A torn sleeve showed what was surely the bulge of a broken bone in his forearm and the shredded tunic was covered in blood. There were sizable abrasions on his brow and a delicate measeling spread over his face like a freckling of little scabs, except that the color wasn't quite right for scabs . . . .

Desperately Contos kept his gaze glued to Marty's eyes, though these were not neutral facial territory either. An unhealthy tawny light glowed in Carver's eyes, a golden-green shade Contos was sure had never been there before. "I'm wet, Contos, because we're under attack and one of our enemies just tried to kill me. Gimme status. Everyone here?"

"We have both night and day shifts in the situation room, sir. Pearman, Karrick and Mellon haven't responded."

"Activity?"

"Just a drunk, sir. An old woman."

"An old woman?"

"She threw a beer bottle at Spears' cruiser as he was coming in. We put her in the tank."

Carver was really scaring Contos now, very much in his face, golden eyes almost rabid. This close, Contos couldn't help but register the oddity of Carver's little scabs. They were almost green. "Description," Carver hissed. His breath dispensed a smell . . . like a swamp.

"Five-two, skinny, maybe a hundred pounds, white hair, dark complexion, some kind of Native American or beaner." In the silence that followed Carver's face seemed to become a kind of demon mask, paralyzing Contos' will. Voices of the men assembled in the situation room drifted out, a restiveness there, a cautious tone of doubt, complaint beginning to arise.

"Pop the gate. Go in there and shut them up and send me two officers with riot guns. You've put a killer in the drunk-tank, Contos."

Moments later, two men with twelve-gauges at his back, Marty stood in the short-term lock-up wing. The tank was a free-standing cage with no hidden corners. It was empty, its gate hanging open.

Contos came in behind the trio and stood aghast. "Sir. I've been at the desk since we locked her in. No one's—" Marty reached out and gripped Contos' throat so powerfully the man's face turned purple. He stood gazing around him in perplexity and seemed scarcely to notice even when his officers pried his fingers from the gasping Contos' throat and saved his life.

Why would the witch come *inside* here? Why wasn't she taking the field with her damned spooks and fighting the dragons about to be born? Then, as if from under the ground he stood on, an answer came crawling up his spine. *She was after a bigger army.* Right now, all over this great valley, the newly dead were sinking into the earth. Did that sorcerous bitch dare—*dare* to go down here, straight down to Xibalba's realm, and steal the dead as they came sinking under?

"You two. Get down to the garage, make sure she's not hiding out down there, take a couple cruisers out to look for her. Contos, take two men out the entry and search that side of the building. Everyone else stays on post here. I'm going down to the basement—I want everyone standing by when I come back."

If his announced destination surprised anyone, no one dared show it. Down through the morgue he went . . . through the utility plant . . . . If the witch had already gone underground, he could not pursue, but if she went there, surely she would die at the hand of the god himself!

In the shadowy corridor to the building's old understructure, Marty stood staring. The double steel door bulged outward. Its dropped chain and opened padlock showed how effortlessly it had been entered. Force had been exerted from *inside*, the doors were bent and buckled by a powerful impact that had jammed them in their steel frame. Marty put all his strength into a ramming assault with his shoulder. The doors were unyielding as stone. She'd burned the last bridge and gone down Beneath. Well, she'd merely sealed the door of her own tomb behind her.

"Chief Carver!" The voices of two men from the utility plant. Marty heard the note of crisis and ran back up the way he'd come. "Sir!" Webber, breathless, speaking first, he and Graves—two steady old vets whose wild-looking faces promised no good. "The main entry's sealed—we can't get out."

"*What*? You can't get *out*?"

"Not out of the garage either," said Graves. "Both ways are blocked from outside! It's—" Graves' voice failed. He looked to Webber for help. Webber blinked back at him, mouth moving helplessly at first. Then he faced his chief and licked his lips. "There's like these big vines or trees growing up right outside the doors. Right up outta the concrete thick as your legs! Completely blocking all the doors!"

"All of them?" The garage exit had fire-house ports that could admit four or five vehicles abreast.

"It looks like they're surrounding the whole building, sir!" Webber's voice was cracking like a kid's. "I mean they're climbing up the windows, the skylights, you can *see* 'em growing! Right up outta the asphalt! I swear, I came *in* that garage not fifteen minutes ago!"

And new growth was climbing up Marty's spine as well, threading cold and slippery through his very marrow. He knew that what was enveloping his police station was the rising displeasure of Jack Fox, of the god himself. Because that white-haired bitch had outmaneuvered Marty, had outwitted him before he even knew what was happening.

"Show me," he told Webber and Graves, and followed them back up, expecting the worst.

QUETZAL COULD SMELL the tart ghost of the cider kegs that had slept in this cool blackness five generations ago. Over near the farthest wall of the echosome space, she saw, just above the floor, a nimbus of green light staining the darkness. Within the faint light she could just make out the mouth of a pit with crumbled concrete lips. She hastened toward this fissure, her ghostly retinue weaving a close commotion of the air around her—hastened because she feared her legs would freeze with dread if she did not.

At the brink she looked down a contorted clay throat all furred with moss and fungi, the green pelt of Xibalba. No less than she feared *where* she must go now, she feared *how* she must go there. "Bind close to me," she whispered to her troop of spirits. "We must flow like water and I in your midst. I am not purified by death, not hard and pure like you. My insignificant life will come apart down there unless you hold me close. My small being can be torn like smoke by wind. Bind close to me and keep me whole. Guide me where this leads us. My will—our will—fixed in *this*."

She drew from her coat her long obsidian dagger. She pressed it once against her chest, and once against her forehead, and at the last held it before her, fixing her eyes upon it. Her gaze locked there, she began a slow side-to-side rocking of her shoulders, as one might do when shrugging off a heavy coat. Her knees buckled and her body slowly knelt, but as her head and shoulders and arms subsided, the knife remained aloft, two hands of faintest mist still holding it up before a face of faintest mist.

The fleshly Quetzal lay on the concrete curled on her side, a white-haired corpse in an old black coat.

The ghostly currents coiled around her misty axis now, sheathing her right up to the wrists, only the knife left naked. They were a muscled snake of braided air poised upright on the green brink, its one black fang aloft, a tooth of stone. It swayed and danced on the brink till someone whispered *now*—and down it dove.

Quetzal was a little girl again, born and raised in La Ciudad de Basura, the vast trash dump, the metropolis of garbage, on the outskirts of Guatemala City. She was a wiry, wily little girl, darting nimbler than the ten-thousand rats that were her townsfolk in the mazes of made-from-trash shanties and shacks she called home. Every day she went off to work in the streets of Guatemala City, pretending to beg while picking pockets, a gleeful little thief so fleet that her speed was a species of invisibility.

People's pockets were like a host of magical doorways swinging and ambling along everywhere at just about Quetzal's own height from the pavements—little doorways her fingers could dart through and grab pieces of the real world, grab wonderful food on plates, and magical clothes, and flights through time and space in taxicabs that set the high mountains flanking the city to spinning, floating past through the smog till the smog seemed the smoke of dreams and the taxi's rattling seemed the song of the angels she'd seen in cathedrals. At the height of her career—she might have been nine or ten—her friends called her Arco Iris, for the multicolored vest she wore under her rags and whose secret beauty she knew made her faster, made her uncatchable by those she robbed . . .

The ghost-snake clenched her, clamped her into herself, and she knew the earth around her, remembered all her long years of life and knew their tininess in this

swallowing earth. This earth was a throat, a knotty
tongue, a root-veined muscle clenching and tasting
her, and Quetzal became a rivering knowledge of
everything within the planet's embrace.

She knew with awe this planet, a Titan's hand cupping
her in the palm of forever. She felt terror and joy at the
wonder of time without end. Dense granite made their
passage through it arctic, almost frozen, till, pierced by
veins of water, the brute rock yielded swifter transit.
Then came strata of clay and coarse jumbled gravels,
gravels even more richly veined with water . . . and
they were in the aquifer, the deepest base of the ancient
river-course. Here was where their Adversary would
be rooted, in this catacomb of waters . . . .

*Little Arco Iris died at the hand of Itzam-ye, a
woman of power from the mountains. For one morning
Quetzal felt her quick little thieving hand—for the first
time—gripped tight by a larger hand lying in wait in
a pocket she'd thought undefended. It wasn't the fierce
strength of the capture that killed the little pickpocket
forever, but Itzam-ye's eyes, when the girl raised her
own to meet them. Great melting eyes flanking the
scimitar Mayan nose. Eyes like a fierce and merry
beast's, though that nose swept down to a bowed
mouth of such age, of such sad knowledge . . . "Little
daughter," Itzam-ye said, "you will come to school
with me." It was Itzam-ye's eyes, and her sad mouth,
and the word* daughter . . .

*"What will you teach me in school?" she'd asked,
her heart already saying yes.*

"Everything," Itzam-ye said.

*They took a camion out of town, bales and caged
chickens and one or two surplus passengers heaped on
its roof. Up and down mountains to one jungle valley,*

up and down mountains to another. That night in a poor farmer's house, Quetzal stood beside Itzam-ye, who had blood up to her elbows as she brought a baby girl from her mother's womb. Later, in the bed the family made for them, their stomachs filled with beans, fried plantains and rich coffee, Itzam-ye said, "Did this child come out watching and listening, daughter?"

Quetzal thought and answered, "She was crying too much to see or hear anything."

"Just so, daughter. And I have taken you with me because I knew, the moment I felt your little hand in my pocket, that you were one who came out watching and listening."

A drumbeat, drumbeat woke her to herself, as the knife she gripped shook in that subterranean thunder. One gaunt old woman-soul at a giant's door, one skinny old *bruja* with a knife and a few dead friends . . . Come back, little pickpocket, bring me your nerve . . . . For here in the water-veined stone and clay, she had come to the mighty trunk of the green god's war-machine. Its rough-barked shaft, thick as a giant redwood, was the green dynamo, the siege-engine Xibalba was raising against humankind. They rivered up along it, the stone knife stabbing upward, sunward, as the shaft began to branch, wider and wider, intricately, slenderly, till they rose through a network of tendriling branchlets.

Quetzal pulled back on her knife, pressing it to her misty center and hung there static amidst the weave. The earth seemed warmer and the faintest honey-tint of sunlight thinned its darkness. So dense was the woody network that it pierced her ghostly substance and she felt what flowed through these small branches: human sentience flowed through them, captured hearts and minds and DNA. These roots reached up into the plant life that clad the whole valley and that plant life at this same moment feasted on the valley's human denizens.

The green god's siege-machine, then, was an *inverted* tree. Its roots fed on the upper world and the dragon-crop it bore would bloom below. That was where she must go, so downwards Quetzal thrust her knife, and downward once again they dove.

By the time they had been six years together, Itzam-ye had shown her chosen daughter the coming-to-birth of every living thing in the mountains, from beetle to jaguar, from toadstool to tree, and in their seventh year together, Itzam-ye showed her what lay beneath all things that came to birth under the sun.

Near a mountain's peak, in the blaze of noon it was. Such a wealth of colors baked beneath a sun of flawless gold . . . the green-robed earth seemed to leap heavenward in sheer rejoicing at its own rich raiment, its own wealth of forms. "Look up into the branches of that tree," Itzam-ye said. Seventeen or eighteen now, Quetzal was not quite still the doting daughter she had been these seven years past. The steely will within her had, in recent months, been flexing like a fencing foil. She wanted to go back to the city, or some other, larger city—to cross a sea or two. Her wits were keen, where might she not go? What not do?

"Look into the branches of that tree," Itzam-ye said again, a new note in her voice, so that Quetzal met her eye. The old woman said, "This is the last thing I will show you, daughter. Your own road begins here and you will walk it without me. And so you must see what I show you when you look into those branches. Your eyes must do exactly what your little hands did in people's pockets long ago. Your hands stole they knew not what—whatever they encountered. When you look

amid those branches, there is a mystery there you do not know and your eyes must snatch it and pull it into the light."

The fear the young woman felt at knowing she would be alone henceforth worked a kind of magic in her mind. She knew with sudden certainty that this earth, this sky swarmed with things she'd never seen, never guessed, and all creation seethed with miracles. She raised eyes of awe amidst the branches. The empty air between them seemed to stir, to hesitate . . . and there it was: draped across a half dozen limbs, its limber length arrayed in graceful arcs, bigger than the biggest anaconda she'd yet seen, was a serpent clad in shining emerald plumage. This feathered serpent seemed to smile, then leisurely rippled and poured its length along the boughs, and off the boughs, rivering gracefully into the air, and away. A young bruja—who in that moment received her name, Quetzal-coatl —was born. A young witch who looked about her, and found her sorcerous foster-mother gone forever.

THE STONE KNIFE DOVE and pulled the old witch back into herself, into by far the deepest place she had ever searched. The great rough shaft sped upwards past her plunge, while the grip of earth grew denser on her, its darkness absolute. Again the great shaft branched and branched again . . . inverted trees and boughs and limbs, rooted in sun and human flesh above.

A dim green radiance glowed with nascent life that drew her stone knife, that began to pull her laterally, out along a branching, toward a constellation of glowing cocoons. These strange fruit stirred, like hatchlings struggling in their shells and she could feel their tremorings on all sides, a thousand distinct hungers clawing their shells from within.

Now the knife rocketed and she streamed in its wake, her allied souls kindled like flames in her jet-stream. The stone fang hungered and, in that instant, fed. A gnarled pod longer than a man, slashed lengthwise, released a dense effusion of green blood. A crooked embryo thrashed in its throes and a soul burst out, a gust of mind and will and hope reborn. Again! Again! Quetzal's ghostly vortex sucked in each soul as the stone blade arrowed on.

But even though the knife went quick as thought about its harvesting, and the rope braid of rescued souls had grown two hundred strong, mortal danger had come instantly awake. For now far more fruit was ripening into dragons than the blade could forestall. Hatchling monsters swarmed from shattered pods on gnarled limbs that clawed up through the earth almost as swiftly as the witch's troops could fly.

Up those Resurrectors sped, escape their urgent mission now, though still the witch searched for the aura of one soul in particular—and just before pursuit grew too lethal to prolong her quest, she found the one she sought, and slashed her free.

"Up into the air!" she cried. "Seize up my body and lift it high as we emerge!" They all geysered up from the seam in the warehouse floor. Their whirlwind snatched up Quetzal's vacant flesh curled on the floor, lifted it to the ceiling and juggled it high. Her form danced laxly on air as she struggled back into it—a bit like dressing in free-fall—as out of the seam the first green dragons swarmed, crooked brutes twice a man's size, lurching along on clawed limbs unequal in length and angle burl-like skulls all crudely jawed and fanged with nightmare thorns and studded with crude black gems for eyes. As they emerged the dragons emerged, clawed the air and hissed—knew their prey and knew it missed the witch afloat above their reach.

"Listen!" Quetzal hissed. "Something else, something much bigger is coming! Smash the doors out! Hurry!"

MARTY WATCHED THE MAYHEM around him from farther and ever farther away. Panic had seized hold of a hundred and twenty men in a moderately spacious but utterly sealed enclosure. Panic indeed seemed perfectly sensible to Marty, from the viewpoint of his men, who were not Jack Fox's chosen viceroys in the surface world. For these men, panic was undoubtedly quite rational. When one gazed, as Marty did, on the front doors, and viewed, on the outside of their bullet-proof glass, a dense screen of gnarly vines, thick as human limbs, sprouting from the concrete, sealing the doors immovably, and sprouting thence out of sight to cover the building's roof just as densely.

That the doors *were* bullet-proof was being deafeningly demonstrated as he looked on, officers discharging double-ought against them repeatedly to no effect, then using SWAT-team door-rams, persisting insanely in perfect futility, as if their repeated blows, by sheer force of protest, could make the impossibility of it all just go away.

Marty stood watching, listening, waiting for his *sign*. He knew Jack meant to recycle the whole department. Marty gladly willed these men underground with himself surely still the chosen viceroy, only let Jack give him that sign, set his mind at rest . . .

A prickly sensation rippled over his body. His

face . . . it seemed to swarm with ants. He clawed it—and found green shoots, young grass under his fingernails!

A mighty *boom!* echoed from the depths of the building, from down below the utility plant. A hundred cop faces turned as one in that direction. A long poised moment of listening—shotguns and battering rams held in suspension—and then the doors to the morgue blew open and a whirlwind came spinning through, a blurred vortex within which an old woman rode standing on air, her white hair unruffled by the cyclone that sheathed her. The witch! "Shoot her!" Marty shrieked.

The cops' astonished faces, turning to him, registered a new amazement. Their chief had become a Green Man furred with grass. He snarled, knocked a man senseless and took his pump-riot, but could not raise it fast enough, as the miniature cyclone rose. Marty had a half-second to see the witch give him the finger and the skylight exploded amid tatters of torn vines, the windblown witch hit the sky and was gone as the vines re-knit and then came dangling down into the station like seeking snakes.

The morgue doors flew wide. The dragons came. Marty stood unflinching, peering from his green mask, refusing to think himself less than the commander of this carnage . . . and was confirmed. The rough-barked, thorn-fanged horrors, spotted with fungoid eyes, leapt on screaming men to either side of him. Shrugging off buckshot, they tore heads from shoulders and wolfed them down. By the dozens they came and Marty's troops fled screaming before them. Those who did not already lie twitching as they were devoured—fled down to the garage, where Xibalba's host swarmed after and whence more shots sounded, more men screamed. All while

Marty Carver stood there, a Green Man now, but chosen still.

Something new was coming from below. A massive tread that shook even through concrete floors. The morgue doors exploded, torn from their hinges by their old master, Dr. Harst. A Dr. Harst how different though, how huge, how rudely sculpted by the green god's hand. He stood a full ten feet tall, his mouldy nudity grown monolithic, shelf-fungi jutting from his brow and jaw, scales of wort and toadstool crusting his cask-like torso, a gnarled mandrake root his crooked sex. His voice was a blurred rumble: "The god awaits— not a bone of you'll be wasted, not a morsel of your brain, dear boy . . ."

He seized Marty whom—calmed by spinal rupture and tucked beneath his arm—he bore below.

In the heart of town the fight raged fierce, Quetzal had conjured up the sirens' voices from the otherwise useless cruisers all driverless in the county garage, and had wakened as well the bull-elephant voices of the fire engines in their station. The smash of shop windows, where her ghost-troops seized up tools and weapons, added to the din, which drew awakened householders from the core of town. Men, women, and children fleeing their panicked neighborhoods, where they had seen neighbors ensnared already, seen every tree, shrub, vine and blade of grass—all writhing, twisting, reaching out green limbs towards human ones. Where they, terror-struck, had seen less lucky friends shriveling like spider-prey amid green webs of stems, fronds, blossoms, branches, their faces fragmenting into the green explosion, their eyes strangely enraptured, their voices lifted eerily to utter visions of a world below, a world of root and spore and worm and seed, a sunless, fecund empire of the Green Titan everlasting, interweaving all.

And as these refugees came wailing, stumbling, grieving to the heart of town, it was only to behold further horror and yet more surreal mayhem, for here the folk of Gravenstein encountered a swarm of different nightmares: elvish leaf-clad shapes erupting from plundered hardware stores, garden stores, gun shops, and all of them brandishing axes and chainsaws, and machetes and shotguns. And among these phantoms, directing them, a witch with stark white hair who stood, as did her troops, upon the air!

But these flying horrors leapt to do battle with the rooted ones. They lopped the grasping branches of carnivorous trees, or swooped to amputate the limber arms of greedy vines that grabbed for the legs of the staggering refugees. And as these fought, the witchly figure cried counsel to the refugees: "Stay on the pavement! Arm yourselves! Take blades and axes and clippers. Hurry! Worse is coming! The dragons are coming! We must stand together! All must fight!"

SAL HAD HELEN AND SKIP in the back of his cab, and Cherry up front. In the middle of the street outside Cherry's, amid greenery writhing on all sides, he siphoned Helen's gas into the ten-gallon spares strapped in his truck-bed. He prayed his four-wheel drive and high suspension would cope with the green cataclysm he saw writhing everywhere. What he and Helen had just seen had put their planning on an end-of-the-known-world basis—not to mention the din of shouts and sirens and gunshots rising from the heart of town not a quarter mile away. There was a desert region a couple hours north of the county. They would head there.

But the moment Sal fired up the engine, the gas was tromped by a foot not his own, and the wheel was wrenched to a different will. Swearing, he writhed helpless in invisible bonds as the truck burned rubber, whipped a U, and headed straight for the center of Gravenstein.

They braked on smoking, shrieking rubber amid dozens of other vehicles crowding the main drag from curb to curb. Got out shakily and stood stupefied, as all the drivers around them had done, all dragooned here, it seemed, and all now utterly forgetful of that strangeness amid this wilder sorcery, these axe-wielding shapes of leaves and air felling trees that bucked and writhed, or pumping buckshot into vines that surged and seized like hydras, while above the battle, an airborne illegal alien perched on a whirlwind.

"Attend me!" she cried. "You are all who have survived in town." It was not a voice she spoke with, for Sal was sure her lips hadn't moved. It was, he felt, the direct touch of her thought, commanding all of them at once amid the din. "And from those doors"— she pointed toward the police station—"something is coming even now! I cannot let you run! We must fight side by side! Arm yourselves and stand to the battle! We compel your cars. If you run, it must be on foot, and if on foot you flee, you'll surely die."

Sal noticed a big man standing near him by a battered pick-up. Noticed him because the guy had slowly drawn his gaze from the impossible warfare all around him, and settled his dark eyes on Sal himself.

Sal had seen this guy around town this last year or so—
doing clearing and firewood cutting. Two big chainsaws
were lashed in his truck bed. The guy said to him, "I've
seen you at Fratelli's over there, am I right?"—pointing
to the market down the block, its tables fruitless, but
the signs still up.

"I'm his son, Sal Fratelli." Unexpected tears jumped
into Sal's eyes.

"I'm Kyle. Did you lose him, your father?"

"Some fucking *plants!* He was—"

The guy squeezed his shoulder with a powerful
hand. "I'm so sorry, man. This is—" he waved his hand
at the environing madness "—impossible. It's just not
happening, but . . . it *is*. I'm sorry. I'm afraid I've lost
someone, too. I have to ask . . . . Your dad's sign says
Fox Fruit. Does that mean Jack Fox?"

Sal nodded, his mind drifting outwards. This
conversation seemed so strange, or any conversation
in this transformed world! At the doors of the police
station, the entire building overgrown with vines, a
violent upheaval had begun. The vines buckled, quivered
and recoiled: the doors' panels of steel and heavy glass
shrieked and cracked and sprayed fragments. Something
was hammering its way out from within the station.

"Yeah. Jack Fox. I picked it there, the fruit. From
cut-down trees."

The man's eyes seemed dazed with the same
unreality that mesmerized Sal himself. What the hell
were they standing here *talking* about? "Karen Fox.
Was she there? Is she there now?"

"I saw her yesterday. I think she said she was leaving
town. I don't know where she is now."

The station's doors erupted. What lumbered out seemed
too crooked-legged to move, till it lurched forward with

the swift, eruptive lunge of a great Nile crocodile. Kyle turned to his truck bed. "You want one of these?" His hands flipped bungees free and he snatched up in either hand his two big chainsaws, as if they weighed no more than five pounds apiece.

"Yeah," said Sal. "Thanks."

"Arm yourselves!" cried the wild woman perched in midair. "Cut them to pieces!"

XXIV

Of perhaps three hundred people assembled there, a few dozen collapsed lying fetal on the ground or stood moaning and shaking, gripping their faces and masking their eyes in denial, or crawling to hide in their vehicles. But the rest of the townsfolk, rudely snatched out of their known world by the sheer power of impossibility, found themselves stumbling to the gutted stores for weapons, and charging—and not just the young and strong among them—charging to the fight with axes high.

The four square blocks around the police station were treeless, though curbside grass and trees surrounded them. The grass now poured into the streets in ropy sheaves near twenty feet long, serpenting across the pavement, so that townsfolk both ghostly and fleshly danced around its tricky weave with flailing machetes and weed-eaters, amputating the leg-seizing, foot-piercing tentacles. Meanwhile from the heart of the embattled square, the police station radiated danger. The vines that engulfed it poured out in all directions, seizing men at the middle and dragging them back into the cubic jungle where they, faces enraptured, melted into the verdant seethe. Ghost-wielded machetes lopped vines almost as swiftly as they grew, but the dragons slithered all the while from the station's front and rear, and before these the human forces, even with ghostly help overhead, had to fight in retreat, axes flashing and green blood spraying.

A lunging dragon engulfed a combatant to his waist. Kyle and Sal brought their chainsaws down across its spine, had its torso halved in moments while, still wolfing its meal down past the kicking thighs, the dragon's foreclaws tore through the pavement, through the earth beneath, and dragged its meal below-ground, abandoning its hemorrhaging hips and legs to destruction. And everywhere, dragons seized bodies and, indifferent to damage, snatched them underground to the green god's smithy, where new dragons were forged and, rising from the forges, swelled the assault. Before such onslaught, ghosts and men inexorably fell back.

Amid green spray, their chainsaws sinking through a dragon's legs, Kyle with his eyes directed Sal's eyes skyward, where the witch had paused, her attention captured by something in the east. There, where the Gravenstein River ran through town, they saw the crests of the big old grandfather oaks that lined its banks, violently quaking and thrashing side to side.

When next they could spare a glance, they saw the witch directing two county buses to the single gas station within their embattled perimeter. Now the witch's will wove through the melee like quick stitchery in a grand tapestry. Others with axes and chainsaws stepped in while Sal and Kyle fell back to the gas station to refill their tanks. A team of women and children worked the pumps there, filling spouted gas-cans which human chains distributed to needy tanks of chainsaws and Weedwackers. "Jesus!" Sal looked river-ward at the convulsing oak trees. "They've grown ten feet!"

"No!" shouted Kyle. "They're climbing the bank. They're coming towards us!"

Lurchingly, seeming to topple leftwards, then right, the oaks advanced. Kyle and Sal saw the witch's fearful look around. From all directions, the riverside trees climbed toward them, shaking the earth with their tread.

Men carried boxes and bags of rags from the stores. Converging on the gas station, from the boxes they drew empty bottles, began filling them with gas, and fusing them with rags.

Two men died blazing before the sparse army got the hang of these weapons. Flame bloomed on the writhing vines that poured from the police station and dragons twisted and thrashed in fire. But though dragons blazed, the flame was smutty, their green blood damping it, as if the green god's vital sap could choke even petroleum's ardor. Fire was everywhere, but no conflagration could take hold.

A forty-foot oak had thundered on clubbed roots within half a block of the fight's perimeter. Stiffly it stooped, seized up a parked pick-up in one crooked bough, and hurled it into the battle's midst, crushing three soldiers with the dragon they were fighting. Blazing cocktails flew like fire-birds into the oak's branches and flame-fruit bloomed there. It swayed and writhed in undiminished strength, even as its fellow giants lumbered nearer. One of these seized a parked car and hurled it. Its landing struck no one, but its gastank detonated and half a dozen died.

The witch on her whirlwind stood stricken and slack, her seamed face wet with tears. She cried out, "Xibalba forgive us! Our race has defaced us, but we must preserve our lives." When men rushed en masse and flung an orange hailstorm of gas-bombs into the oncoming oaks, she said nothing. Drawing her stone knife she swooped down on a dragon Sal and Kyle were sundering from either side, and drove her blade in the base of its skull. As its eyes dulled and it stilled, she gestured at the oaks and shrilled: "They come too fast! Their roots!"

Chainsaw troops, Sal and Kyle foremost, dodged sweeping boughs to amputate the clubbed feet of the giants. Some fell, hammering earth with their boughs, but a dozen thundered forward undeterred. A flying tow truck killed three men, while dragon after dragon dove underground with kicking human food between its jaws.

Near the gas station a woman's scream went up. The asphalt ruptured by her feet, a green tongue wrapped her legs, jaws as long as she was tall engulfed her and pulled her under. Then they were erupting everywhere, dragons larger, quicker than before, eyes less crude, slit-pupiled now, more lethal predators which suddenly accelerated the human harvest.

The witch saw the battle had turned and instantly shared her knowledge. Perhaps two hundred souls survived and her altered strategy swept through their minds. They responded instantly. A gasoline brigade formed chains and sent filled gas-cans to the tanks of the toughest, most terrain-ready jeeps and trucks within the perimeter. The gassed-up buses were brought forward and the convoy-vehicles driven into formation before and aft of them, with a few of the gnarliest flanking them on both sides, the youngest and oldest were conveyed into the buses, many of them lifted by ghosts and borne out right through the air.

Now the trickiest part of the withdrawal: the fighters had to fall back before a phalanx of near a hundred dragons, the green predators grown so quick and fierce that half the fighters would have died in the moment of turning to climb into their vehicles, had it not been for the ghosts, who rained a storm of airborne steel upon those scaly skulls as the axe- and saw-men broke contact and turned for their vehicles. Kyle and Sal were last to turn, falling back, their saws slashing desperately, when the witch dove and planted her knife in the base of their attacker's skull.

As its eyes dimmed, she fixed Kyle's eyes with her own. "I know where you mean to go, but first you must fight for us here. Ella tiene que luchar sola. She has to fight alone. If you go to her before the moon has risen, she will surely die."

He stared at her, trying to possess her mind through her eyes.

"My strong son," Quetzal told him.

"Grandmother," and he fell back with Sal to the caravan.

"What about your women and the boy?" he asked Sal.

"They're taking care of those older folks there."

Cherry gave them a high-sign with her machete from the back of a stake bed. Helen and Skip were similarly armed at opposite side of the bed. A number of graybeards filled the rest of the bed, with their middle-aged wives protectively gathered at the center.

The witch arrayed her spirit-troops above the caravan. The highway ahead was flanked by high trees. Their destination was fifty miles north of the Gravenstein Valley where, on the relatively barren slopes of hardscrabble ranchland, lay the town of Dry Creek. En route they would pass Gravenstein's outlying homes, where scores of citizens might survive.

At Quetzal's signal the caravan rolled out. Their blade-wielding airborne contingent engaged the outreaching boughs and branches of the flanking trees, while from the beds of trucks and the roof-racks of buses, fighters with shotguns and saws sprayed green blood from the viperous vegetation. As the column advanced, the witch hung in its wake a moment, and beckoned one of her spirit soldiers to her. They hung there for a long moment, the leaf-fingered hands in the witch's fleshy ones, face to face, while Quetzal spoke, and listened. They seemed to kiss and the ghost sped southwards through the air, shedding, as she went, her leafy envelope, leaves fluttering from her, till she was nothing visible at all.

For hours, the fighting convoy crept along, evolving tactics as they went. They learned from their first forays up side-streets. At the first, several trucks detached, Sal's and Kyle's among them, to penetrate the extensive cul-de-sac. A bull-horn elicited, here and there, the shouts of residents trapped in their homes. But the first two of the four pick-ups were seized by muscular undergrowth gripping their engines from beneath. The woman and two girls they brought out were crowded into the second-to-last truck, Kyle's. At the last house of the street, a supplicating voice brought them into a living room where a head and shoulders, protruding from the jaws of a dragon, smiled at them. Another dragon dropped from the ceiling, seized one of the rescuers, and took him straight underground.

They got the mother and daughters back to a bus, with only one truck left of their original four, though with the addition of two chopped hogs parked outside a house with no survivors. Kyle and Sal were astride the hogs.

Thereafter, they rode the Harleys with their chainsaws slung from their backs by rope hawsers, and Molotovs and gas cans in their saddlebags. As the hours wore on, the rescuers' casualties diminished as they learned the ropes, and as the caravan crept north, the buses filled with refugees.

IN BUSHMILL, as the sun sank past the zenith, the cottage door at the Bide-a-Nite Motel swung open. A tired-looking woman in a T-shirt and jeans stepped out, untied her honey-blond hair and shook it loose. She stretched and leaned wearily back against the sun-struck stucco wall. Closing her eyes against the brightness, she pressed her arms against the wall, obviously relishing that heat through her thin shirt. It was obvious what Karen was in that moment: a woman who wanted simplicity, escape, who wanted to merge herself with the sunlight, and simply be free of everything else.

A breeze rolled through the foliage near her and stirred her hair. A second later, her eyes snapped open and, wonderingly, she touched her lips. Karen had felt it: a soft contact, cool as a breeze, and yet just like a kiss. She thought of Mom, Mom's dear face in the rippling oak leaves. But this was not Mom's kiss she had felt. It was more like Susan's.

Turning her back to the road, she went to her knees, still leaning against the sun-warmed wall, and she wept, muffling the sound with her hands. At length she got up, dusted off her knees and went back inside. She brushed her hair and tied it back. Took up her little gym bag of belongings, paused to pick up Dad's letter, and folded it back into its envelope.

Karen felt a sudden ache within her cast. Not the cracked metacarpal, but under the cast's sleeve that covered her wrist. Slipping the letter into her bag, an image floated up from it: a skull-blown soldier climbing a cenote wall. And her wrist ached more sharply as she saw then her skull-blown father, face dead as a Mayan mask, while his icy grip crushed her wrist. Was this ache memory, or a new pain? She thrust her fingers into the cast, probed, and could not tell. She was drowning in death, that was the heart of it. The dead had her surrounded. But amidst all this horror, Kyle had come to her, had held and comforted her like he would a child. Thinking this, her tears welled back up, because it struck her that she had loved her sweet Susan, had loved her, but never *enough*.

Once again, she knew that her home was the orchard, she had to struggle to get past the terror of this revelation. Her previous home before had been Susan—not San Francisco, but Susan herself. Now, she must go home and face her dead. Had to wait the weeks or months it took till Wolf was clean bone and then scatter his skeleton far and wide. Had to go home and know that Dad *was* dead, had to know, finally and forever, that he could come to her *after* death only when the brandy's sick magic had given him life. She set out down the street towards the heart of town.

THE MAN in the tiny county bus-line office shook his head when she named her destination. "We're a trunk line from Gravenstein. Nothing's come out all day, so nothing's going back."

"But when . . ."

"They don't answer the phone! I plain can't tell you when the next bus's coming."

Back at the gas station, the same pale-eyed young goon sat at the register, but a different voice answered her ring, a gravelly voice, brusquely alert. "Kyle. Yeah. He left early this morning. Shoulda reached Gravenstein this morning. You *know* Kyle?"

This intrusiveness startled her. "Why?"

"Why do I ask?"

". . . Yeah."

"I felt like it."

"You're a hotel. What do you care if I know him or not?"

"We're not a hotel. We're a halfway house. He puts up here for his parole hearings."

"You're really willing to tell his personal shit to strangers, aren't you?" It was bizarre, how fast this was accelerating.

"Yeah, I am. I guess I just don't give a shit."

"Hey, I know he killed someone who tried to kill him and *I* don't give a shit!" Death. Was she meant to drown in it from here on out?

"Well, of course, he'd blow that smoke up your ass, wouldn't he, honey? But the guy he killed was a friend of mine and what Kyle says is a fuckin' lie."

"I bet you didn't have the balls to tell him that to his face."

"You must be trippin', bitch! I tell him that every time I see him. But if you mean I wouldn't front him in a fight, you're absolutely right, because that fucker is one stone-cold killer. And even though you're sweet on him, sunshine, I'd advise you to keep that in mind." And the guy hung up.

The pale-eyed kid was staring at her. As she looked for her voice, for harsh words, he blinked, the first time she'd seen him do it. Pointed at his front window. "I saw you at the bus station. There's a guy in town got a cab. He runs drunks out to their ranches on weekend nights."

"Thank you. Where could I find him?"

"It's a green an' yella cab, parked on the main street usually."

She found it in front of a saloon, a small joint crudely stuccoed to look like adobe, with two splintery old wagon wheels mounted on the façade. The place was so quiet from the sidewalk that it surprised her on the inside. There were at least two dozen men and women, most of them middle-aged, at the tables and bar. Soft country-western music from the jukebox engaged absolutely no one's attention. Karen had all of that the minute she walked in and had it in spades when she went to the bar and asked the pouchy old guy polishing glasses, "Is the gentleman with the taxicab here?"

When the cabbie was pointed out, he proved to be the only person *not* looking at her: a skinny little black guy with shades and a goatee, wearing khaki, and bent on a game of hearts with two fat guys in CAT caps. *Studiously* not looking at her, it seemed.

"Excuse me."

"I'm off." He didn't look up. "I don't come on till four or five."

"Which will it be? Four or five?"

"Five."

"How much to Gravenstein?"

"'Fraid I don't go that far."

"I'd pay you extra. I'd pay you a hundred bucks." Now everyone's attention was really focused. This was better than TV. You could tell everyone thought it was a pretty good offer.

"Sorry. I don' go that far."

Some real drama developing now. Would the strange, tall, lesbo-looking, muscular blonde offer *more*?

The street door gusted open slightly and sighed shut again. It drew some curious looks, which quickly snapped back to Karen and the driver.

"Sorry, I'm off." He fanned and sorted his hand, still not looking at her . . . and then half his cards sprang out of his fingers. He turned his face to her, blinking, amazed, as if he thought Karen somehow responsible. It turned out he had lovely, limpid eyes, which looked not only astonished, but somehow passionate. After an uncertain pause he rose dazedly, his voice hoarse, "Are you ready?" And he rose, awkwardly.

Everyone was really staring now—at each other, then back at him and Karen. Such fickleness was clearly out of character . . . .

It made Karen edgy, as she followed him out. The little man looked vague; he fumbled as he fished for his keys. Did she really need to go back now, after all? Did she still feel as sure about Kyle as she had before that phone call? But already she was in the back seat. Fuck it! The man swung the car from the curb and rolled out.

She sank back in the seat and attempted no conversation. The sneering voice on the phone nagged at her, describing a man that couldn't be Kyle! She was *sure* of him . . . wasn't she? Oh God! Everything before her was so dark and doubtful. Could she find the strength? She closed her eyes.

And opened them to find herself rolling down the drive of the Fox orchard, the sun edging down to the western quarter of the sky, the spidery plum trees all burnished copper in the slanting sun. How had the driver known where to bring her? She couldn't remember telling him.

He sprang out and opened her door. Stood there offering her his hand. His smile as he did this was

disorienting, so sweet it was, and he gripped her
hand so firmly, so warmly, helping her out. There
was something about his hand in hers, that hand not
releasing hers as she stood before him. There was
something about the *feel* of this hand in hers . . . .

And then his face was not his face, was Susan's face
instead, so dear, so close to hers. Karen scented Susan's
slightly musky smell, like a mink or ferret, and Karen
saw before her Susan's violet eyes and brave gamine
lips. Karen kissed those lips, kissed them fiercely in
her terror that this dear face would vanish before she
could do so—in her dread that this irreplaceable little
woman, not seized, would die again at once.

Deep within that kiss, Karen discovered joy and
grief exactly equal, because as their tongues found each
other's, Karen knew past doubt that this *was* Susan,
was the living Susan, present and knowing her now,
knowing and kissing her in this instant. And at the same
time Karen knew that within *this* Susan's mouth, her
lips and tongue were tasting only sky, were tasting only
cold, fruitful October air. Karen knew that within *this*
Susan's face, her lips tasted all eternity, all blue space,
all stars, but no longer tasted someone that she could
hold, or have. Karen knew she was kissing a Susan who
could only be with her in the way that sun on leaves,
or snow-melt foaming over rocks could be with her—
glories for the heart and mind to hold, but never again
for her hands or her arms or her lips to possess.

"Yes, sweetheart, yes," said this Susan of sky to her,
answering her thoughts. "Sweet Karen, I am elsewhere,
I am everywhere now. You don't have me, but *I* have *you*,
I have *everything*, as long as this earth spins. I am in and
of its glory, because I have known love, which is always—
whoever it is for—a Love of the World and Love of the

World does not die. Be free of grief for me, my darling Karen. But listen to me—listen for your very life, listen for your everlasting soul. Though the green god took me, the witch saved me because the god's power over our lives was not yet fully grown. But if the green god takes *your* soul, he will grow too mighty for the witch. And you, if he takes you, will dwell in the bowels of his world forever. You will dwell with Xibalba, in Xibalba forever. Don't try to grasp it, just believe it, for you are *living it now* with each beat of your heart, and he is coming for you, coming for you in all his Power, with the fall of this night, and the rising of this full moon."

"How will I fight? What will I fight with?"

"Whatever comes to hand. All this is hidden from the witch, as it is hidden from me. The witch is locked in battle. The whole valley south of here is the green god's, and all things rooted in earth have power to hunt and devour you now. Fight *here* and fight with your very soul. Don't leave these acres! If you don't conquer here, you die, and you become flesh of the green god's flesh, and flesh of his high priest, your father . . . ."

"Susan! Stay with me! Please!"

But Susan was already gone and in her place stood the lean little black man, his face struggling out of a trance-state, so that when she took her arms from around him, he almost fell, and she had to seize his shoulders and steady him. Their eyes were locked, but both of them were looking inward, not outward, were seeing strange landscapes new-opened within them, scarcely seeing each other at all.

"Where've I *been*?" Terror was in the cabby's voice. Then he answered himself, his voice lower, awed. "I was . . . I was in the *sky*. I swear I was in the fuckin' *sky*! I was somewhere up in the sky and all the trees

under me an all the grass was shaking and dancing."
Then at last, finally seeing Karen, he said, "You came
into the tavern—" glanced at the sky "—hours ago!
Where are we?"

"*You* drove *me*! Maybe you were . . . drunk?"

"I don't drink! I just play cards there!" But he said
it dazedly, as if he too felt forced to at least entertain
that hypothesis.

"Look. You drove me here. We're about twenty
miles out of Gravenstein. Would a hundred bucks do
it?"

"I guess so . . . ."

"Hey. I'm kind of confused too. I mean, I just woke
up! Maybe there's something . . . in the air?"

"There is. Smell it? Oily smoke. Gas-fires.
Somewhere down-valley . . . ."

"Here—" she remembered Susan's words of war to
the south "—take this. Don't go into town. Get straight
back to Bushmill, that's my advice."

He stood as if harkening to something in the
remote distance. Then he pocketed the money without
answering at first. "Something going on down there.
Don't you hear it?"

"No."

"It's like . . . underground. Like voices. Underground . . . ." He shook himself, then looked at her
suspiciously, as if all of his disorientation came from
her. He got into the cab and spun it around. Spat gravel
pulling out, raising a rooster-tail of dust behind him.
She heard him hit the highway and accelerate to a
howl. Karen listened till he'd vanished from hearing,
then realized she was clinging to the noise until it was
utterly gone, because now she had to hear the silence of
the acres she stood in.

Hello old house, old trees . . . Why, I've cut a bunch of you down! But then, this is a strange place however you slice it! I mean, someone's blown his own head off hereabouts and that would be you, Jack Fox! And down in the basement, someone *else's* throat got blown out two nights ago—by a crazy old dyke, who would be *me*, in fact! And, just before that, *you* killed a young woman in a truck—just smashed the life right out of her. But you know what, you black-browed son of a bitch? *Her* spirit is still *alive*, she roams the sky and knows the sun and stars and loves me still. But you, *you're* still alive too, aren't you? You want my life now don't you? And you're coming to take it tonight.

Lord, what a strange awful place for a girl to grow up in! In this very ground I stand on there are things that live forever and can be killed without dying and can bruise my flesh from the grave and can take me down to live forever in terror under the earth. And I must believe these things because I've just kissed Susan and heard her speak inside my heart and mind, and Susan's body is dead.

Look at that sun, just beginning to redden, maybe an hour before it's down. Time's running out, because time is *always* running out, and the darkness is always coming down, and then coming down again. And she said I must stay right here. I've run from here my whole life and *spent* my whole life here just the same, right where hope was first stabbed to death. All my life, I've never left this nightmare. So tonight I might as well bet the farm, and stand right here, and try to kill it.

LATE AFTERNOON SHADOWS in the living room. Cold ashes in the fireplace, darkness in the doorframe down to the cellar, late sun in the backyard beyond the kitchen windows, heaps of lopped fruit trees, just peeking up into view above the window sills.

So. Slip on the nice canvas coat again . . . and tuck thirty or forty double-oughts in its roomy pockets. Hang the pump twelve-gauge by its strap from your shoulder and . . . why not this nice U.S. Army 1911 model Colt .45 semi-automatic? And look, it's got ten loaded clips for spares! Rack one in the pipe . . . pop the magazine, *voilà*!

Wow! The brandy cannon by the fireplace, full as ever! Seems I can't empty it no matter how hard I guzzle.

Well, why not have a jolt, Bitch?

Dear Jesus. You sneaking son of a bitch! You murderous boar! Just like you, a scuttling bug, to lurk and mutter in my brain! Stand out here and face me, you brutal piece of shit! Step out here and face me and take a swig yourself, I dare you. Do it and I'll match you drink for drink and then blow your *crotch* out with double-ought! I'm not leaving here.

She cried aloud and was terrified to realize that whether she thought or spoke, it rang equally loud in this house, in this silence where long-ago crimes still echoed. Whether she thought or spoke, here and now it was *heard*.

"I'm not leaving here," she said more steadily, looking around her, seeing the holes her double-ought had made in the walls just days ago. "You want to lurk and put thoughts in my brain, but if you're ready, if you're really here, if you really dare, then *show* yourself. Silence. I thought so. So let's up the ante. Let's mess with *you*, you evil piece of shit. Let's go down to your precious shed and finish what Susan started. See how you like *that*?"

She snatched matches from the mantel, stormed out and fired up the truck. The plum trees sped past, burnished with barbarous color in the ruddy light, their silent thousands standing watch.

She got out at the compost heap—hugely there, hiding homicide in its black belly. To torch the shed, to call any kind of attention to this spot was risky. But did she care? Wasn't she herself, her heart and her hope, buried here? She was dying and she craved the healing medicine of flame. *I will turn you to smoke, I will send your black soul into the sky.*

But at the door she hesitated, and stepped around the building.

At the fence at the foot of the property, she laid her hand on the top strand of barbed wire, and remembered Susan's voice: *Don't leave these acres.* On the woods and the stream beyond the fence, the shadows lay long. The sun had just touched the hilltops. What was it she felt, out beyond the orchard? What was it she felt out there in the shadows? Was there a breeze? The far leaves seemed to stir, and yet she *felt* no breeze. She sensed a hum of power, under her feet, behind her, and in the high black mass of the compost heap. Or was it just the crimes she sensed? Rape and homicide were buried everywhere on these acres.

She walked back to that old creaky-bangy screen door. As she pulled it open, she thought this would be the last time it sounded. And then thought, *Why not—just for fun?* The twelve-gauge blew off hinge number one: *whack.* Hinge number two: *whack.* She kicked the door off the splintered frame. And came two steps inside Dad's shed, his old sanctum.

All those books and papers, snowdrifted on the desk and the shelves and the floor, and the stench of gasoline waited like a promise. All you did to me and I've never struck back! Susan had the nerve, and you killed her for it. She picked up the gas can and a remnant sloshed inside it. She capped it tight, as if this were a bit of Susan herself she'd found. Not much gas, but would this be all that was needed to set the *house* blazing? She put the can in the truck.

She came back inside and stared at Dad's desk. All that printed paper, all those words! She could start sifting through them, for traces of the man she'd once loved more than anyone on earth. Her hot tears spilled, and then hot anger came, and the stench of gasoline waited like a promise. All you did to me, Daddy, and I never struck back! Well, try this on. The struck match hit the floor.

Wood prepared by Susan in the last hour of her life *whumphed* alight and Karen had to jump aside from the scorching tide of heat that swept like surf against her.

Thank you, sweet Susan, thank you! It feels so good, such a relief! Dusty heaps of pages like dirty snow, heaps of dark words written in darkness by a dark man toiling year after year, a man who came out of this hole to hurt his child. Only orange flame was left of all that now. Only raging and roaring! No more dark!

She stumbled outside. The sweat poured like healing tears off her face and she thanked God that, at last, she had *done* something. Broken the ice that had frozen her will. The red light stained the black skin of the compost heap till it looked like some nightmare maggot awash in blood. The sun sank as the shed began to do the same. When the sun had set, the crimson bones of the roof were crumbling down into the inferno that was its foundation.

This is good, but it's only getting ready. After all, it's the *house* that has to burn, if I am to root that cruel bastard out. Well, the dark is coming. Wouldn't some more light would be nice?

XXV

Excitement and confusion in the quiet little ranching town of Dry Creek. Gravenstein's exodus came down through Conejo Pass and onto the arid eastern slopes of the Gravenstein Hills late in the day and a limping, thorn-scarred, flame-scorched caravan it was, windows and windshields starred with fractures, truck beds splashed with blood both green and red . . . and grim-faced were the survivors! The survivors were youths and young women who were somber-faced past their years from the combat they had seen. The survivors were elders whose gaunt visages stared inward. There were stunned children whose eyes had aged a decade in an afternoon. Every smoke-smudged and bloody soul in that convoy had the same strange way of scanning the rocky, sparsely grassy terrain around the town. They seemed scarcely to notice the gathering citizens, but seemed utterly fixated on the dry grass and mesquite and scrub brush growing on the open ground, and on the few sparse plantings along the main drag.

The motorcade usurped half of Dry Creek's central avenue. The motley assemblage of pick-ups and stake-beds and SUVs parked in a strangely defensive-looking circular formation in the big parking lot of the Metro Mart Complex, which also featured a Dairy Freeze, a few burger places, and some hardware and farm equipment stores.

The sheriff of this county, Jim Ruddy, commanded nine vehicles and a staff of less than thirty men. He found no one in particular in charge of the town's strange visitors, though a group of a dozen battle-weary men, conferring in the caravan's midst, gave him their attention when he and four deputies approached them. At Ruddy's questions, they shared a look and seemed to delegate a strong-looking man, scarred about the face and arms, to speak for them.

It was Kyle. "Sheriff, our leader, and a . . . special squadron of our forces, are not here at the moment, are in fact reconnoitering not far off. Apparently there's an old cinnabar mine near here?"

"The Quicksilver, that's right, but the mine's closed down."

"Well, she needed to get underground to check something out. I know she'll want to talk to you first thing when she rejoins us."

"Check something out underground? And *she* has a special squadron of your forces?"

Sheriff Ruddy seemed to be a basically calm, pleasant man who was, at the moment, severely taxed by circumstances. His eyes flitted wildly around, taking in the several hundred refugees filling the largest parking lot in his small town. "Explain to me," he said, "what has happened to you all!"

The men he addressed searched one another's eyes. Sal Fratelli came forward. "It's kind of an epidemic. It's like, all the plant life, the trees and the bushes and the grass—"

Shrieking tires and howling engines came clamoring into the heart of town. Several pick-ups braked just a hair short of collision with the sheriff's cruisers.

"Sheriff! Come quick! Call the National Guard, call the capital—we need help! Get every man you got out to our place!"

On hearing this, the Gravenstein refugees shared a grim but unsurprised look. Kyle told Ruddy, "Let us gas up our trucks and we'll come help you. Because believe me, Sheriff, you're going to need all the help you can get."

Heralded by sirens, a posse of desperate ranchers, sheriffs' deputies, and Gravenstein refugees arrived a short time later at a cattle ranch just outside of town. And every woman and man of them stood speechless in that upland pasture, the astonished cops side by side with the scorched and tattered and *un*surprised veterans of the war in Gravenstein—all stood awed and silent, watching. The pasture's golden grasses had grown so incredibly long, that their mere luxuriance was astonishing, apart from what their golden blades were *doing* to the herds of Black Angus cattle.

The grass seemed to have broken in waves on the hapless herds, pouring down upon, *through* these glossy monoliths of beef. The tawny blades pierced their black bodies, re-emerged, and dove back into the earth. Like little black skiffs on a roiling sea, acres of cattle bobbed in the golden waves, suspended above the earth, canted at this angle or that. Their rib cages fanned out like red combs, they sank into the soil like planted shoots or lovingly planted red tubers. No sound of distress did these brutes make. There was only the sound of breeze-blown grass, the wide whispery noise of the earth at work as the great bovine skulls—with eloquent sad eyeballs—sank like jewels in the gold foam.

As the acres of grass digested the acres of cattle, three-score silent men and women gazed on, meditative parishioners in a Church of the New Earth. And just then, a troupe of mule deer came across the field, leaping dainty-footed through the deep grass, easy dabs of their hooves here and there lofting them effortlessly along in that lovely leaping way deer have.

Kyle alone spoke, "You see? The god devours only the works of Man. No other animal has broken its treaty with him. If these cattle had been buffalo two hundred years ago, they'd be untouched."

A scream went up and a shotgun blast turned their eyes behind them. One of the deputies had fired into the air, blasting a spray of leaves from an airborne, vaguely human shape, which responded by sweeping down, snatching the man's gun, and clubbing him off his feet with the stock. A flock of airborne shapes now hovered near and, as the deputies fumbled for weapons, Helen Carver roared in a voice of command that froze every one of them: "Hold your fire, you fools! They're with *us*!"

Sheriff Ruddy, of Dry Creek, met Quetzal, of Guatemala, who descended to him on a small whirlwind. Ruddy, and the rest of Dry Creek's constabulary, were told a number of unbelievable things, and they found in themselves—rather quickly—the ability to believe these impossibilities.

Returning to town, they found every planted thing in it erupting, growing, carnivorously active. The witch, deep in the mercury mine, had clearly felt the under-earth tsunami of Xibalba's unstoppable advance.

"He's consumed most of Gravenstein," she told them. "We're what's left. His dragons are legion and they are almost at hand. We must have harder earth under us—I believe there is a range of mountains to the east and its rocky ridge will help us. Even hard, dry earth, as you have here, will be no help against the ones who will come above ground to hunt us down."

"*His dragons?*" quavered Sheriff Ruddy. He was speedily enlightened.

The Gravenstein convoy helped to rally and organize the citizens, some two thousand souls. In the heart of town, odd plant-growth or not, there was vigorous public resistance to the idea of abandoning home and property. And then the pavement in front of the Dairy Freeze erupted and a dragon the size of a bull, with wide crooked horns, surged up and half-engulfed two teenage girls where they stood, and dragged them, their legs still kicking, underground. Then the Gravenstein refugees mounted up with a will and all of Dry Creek followed suit. Foothill National Park was six hours away. It had water, was sited on rocky foothills, and its campsites were all but bare of vegetation.

KYLE FILLED THE TANK of his hog, filled one spare gas can for its tank, and another can with oil-and-gas mix for the chainsaw strapped to his back. "You're going to have to run like a demon, man," Sal said to him, a worry and a closeness there, born of a day of desperate battle, and of guarding each other's backs.

"Hey. I'm coming back and I'll have her *with* me."

"I don't like you going without backup."

"You can't leave them." Meaning Cherry and Helen and Skip. "I couldn't go if I didn't know you were watching out for them."

"So. I'll *see* you."

"Damn right."

The sun was getting near the horizon as he mounted the bike.

"I do not see what will happen." It was Quetzal, at his side.

"Then you don't see me dying. You don't see *her* dying."

"I don't see *her* dying in any case. If Xibalba takes her, then, as the green god's consort, she would live forever, underneath the earth."

"Give me some power. Give me some luck."

"*Hijo!* You already have everything I can give! You're still alive, aren't you? Has luchado como demonio and you've survived everything you fought!"

Unable to otherwise express his reverence for the powerful old woman, Kyle reached out and wrapped his arms around her. The witch seemed not displeased by this rude expression of regard. She pressed his craggy face between her palms and smiled. "Hijito! Que coraje tiennes! And you have a heart. I pray you will find her alive. Go swiftly!"

With no intention of bravado, but merely in his urgency for haste, Kyle popped a shrieking wheelie, riding a comet-tail of smoke for fifty yards, before he got both wheels down and screamed off to the south.

Looking after him, the witch made a beckoning gesture at the air and a shape came down and hung close before her. The two of them, the fleshly and the airy woman, conferred a while, before the airy shape sped off, following him.

The witch watched him dwindle in the distance, her seamed smile remembering an early love of her own . . . and then she spoke to the ghosts who bore her. They lifted her and swept her to an already-plundered hardware store. From here, a moment after she flew inside, she emerged holding a sickle aloft like a bright-edged crescent moon. Gripping this tool like a talisman, she came hovering down above the lead vehicle of the departing caravan, the stake-bed truck manned by Sal,

Helen, Cherry, and three other veterans of the Battle of Gravenstein. They were leading their own townsfolk and the hollow-eyed folk of Dry Creek southward out of town.

"Fight as we've learned to do," the witch told them. "If you move quickly, you'll have only dragons to fight on your rear. Use gas and torches and keep moving towards the mountains. If we are lucky, we will win some time. We'll meet you in the mountains near midnight."

"You won't be with us now?" Sal asked. His gesture took in the whole airborne army of ghosts. His and his companions' eyes showed fear.

"The ground ahead of you rises and grows more stony," said Quetzal. "The green god cannot rise through it so quickly. If you push east into the mountains, you can gain ground and win breathing space. With luck, con suerte, mis queridos, we shall all meet again!"

But when Quetzal had led her airy army to its next engagement, it would have baffled Sal and his allies, had they witnessed it. For she and her followers—just outside of town—settled like a flock of birds upon the golden pastures which had devoured the flocks of Black Angus. Here, Quetzal and the ghosts set to work on those long, tawny grasses. The ghosts twisted and braided the growth and the witch, with her stone knife, scythed each twist of grass free of the earth. And soon, each leafy figure gripped one of these tawny fasciae in his or her grip and, just as the sun began to set, the whole fleet of them, their grassy clubs held high, flew south.

As KAREN DROVE back up the acres, the shed's embers glowed behind her in the west, like a second sunset, back where the day had died half an hour ago and sunk below the horizon. The zenith was already darkened to indigo and here and there stars sparked its deepening darkness, while the full moon's upper edge—like a silver scimitar's blade—had inched up above the eastern hills. Her eyes kept lingering on the red coals in her rearview and how their bloody light stained the big black maggot of the compost heap. That was a victory, wasn't it? Those sinking embers of Dad's shed, they were an ancient Enemy laid low.

But now, up there ahead, was the house, far more terrifying. The very temple of her childhood, the place of horror where her new-grown body had been vandalized. How large it loomed! All black-windowed, except for one lamp in the living-room. The shed was an outpost, Dad's sentry-box, a place where he lurked while his poisoned thoughts evolved. But the house . . . .

Getting out of the truck, she hung the shotgun on her shoulder again and patted the .45 in her coat pocket. She took the gas can, went around to the front, and climbed the porch. She would enter here, formally. This place was not her house now, but only the Enemy's, and she had come to call on that enemy, and to administer him his last rites.

Could she really do it? Actually burn this place down? A cold sweat dewed her face. The sheer size of what her heart had chosen to do terrified her. Was she up to this? Big enough? Brave enough? Or was she still Daddy's little girl? Daddy's little victim?

She stepped inside. It was like entering the lungs of some giant alien, breathing the air of a hostile planet, and the breathing giant would kill her if he could. But she had the use of her body and he no longer did. It seemed he'd blown his brains out, poor man. Dear God, this whole place was *unearthly*. The spirit that had ruled it was *not human*. Could she torch it? Yes! It had betrayed her heart, had turned from a home to the lair of a monster. The faint smell of gasoline from the can heartened her. She set the can on the floor.

"Excuse my not knocking!" she shouted at all the shadowy rooms around her. "No, I'll stay armed, thanks. I'm quite comfy with my shotgun and my automatic. I won't be staying long. Neither will *you*, for that matter." It felt good to mock the place aloud—keep it at a distance, keep it from becoming Home again. "Such a pity you're too shy to come out and meet me! *You're* not shy of shotguns? I mean, to judge by how you looked when we last met? And I'm sure you don't mind if I drench the carpet in here with a bit of gas?" Picking up and waggling the can. "It smells bad, but not to worry, it'll burn right out once I've lit the match."

"You know I'm really disappointed in your cowardice, you just skulking around here, not daring to face me!" It had suddenly become much scarier to talk aloud and so her voice grew abruptly shriller. It had begun to seem that her voice, breaking into this silence, was wakening—oh so faintly!—echoes. Echoes of an impatient, heavy tread. Of a *come on down here to me now girl!* Putting her voice out into this air, which she had breathed from her life's beginning, was to shake loose all the sounds that had stirred it back through the years. To speak here was to wake everything that had ever been spoken.

"Really disappointed!" she said even louder, her voice beginning to tremble. "Such a brave brute you were when you towered over a little girl! Where are you now, you piece of shit?"

Almost screamed, this last syllable . . . followed by silence . . . silence . . . and then—a sharp noise, from beyond the couch, from somewhere near the fireplace. Karen's heart was falling, falling, though she stood like stone.

Eeeee . . . eeeee . . . eeeee—a shrill noise of dry wood from the other side of the couch, moving towards her, closer and closer, something small moving with a decided will of its own . . . .

The brandy cannon trundled across the carpet on its wooden wheels, moving all alone, all by itself, its amber contents sloshing gently within its faceted sides. To see this happening was terror itself, but not the worst terror. The worst was the fact that *she* was *not* moving. Not until the cannon came to rest at her feet . . . then the worst was something new. She was bending over, and lifting the cannon, and holding it up to the light before her face. She did this without willing it, without wishing it, without being able to stop it.

Apparently, it was the incised design around the cannon's neck—its *barrel*—that Karen was particularly concerned to study. At first she found the emblem to be just what she had found it to be before: a scaly dragon twisting around the crystal spout, a naked woman clamped in its hind claws, while her loins were plundered by the serpent's loins, and her head and shoulders were engulfed. But now not by a dragon's jaws, no, that had changed. For the monster had a *man's* head now, though his jaws were monstrously large. Now it was this human maw that was swallowing the doubly-pillaged woman. And this monstrous man's eyes . . . Did Karen *know* these eyes?

She raised the cannon's spout to her lips and drank. Smacked her lips and cheerfully cried, "To the bride and groom!" Down in the oubliette of her body, Karen Fox wept and gnashed her teeth and screamed, while her body betrayed no sign of that anguish, but with perfect calm returned the cannon to the hearth and set it down on the mantel. "Love by moonlight among the trees," she said. "A honeymoon, and then, eternal life!"

She stepped out into the full moon's light and walked down the same central lane she had just taken in her truck, when she'd had a body to work her own will. Now she moved solemnly, sedately. Apparently, her captor's mood had changed from what it had been on that first awful night. He did not mock her as he had in her first captivity, with that vile soliloquy and that antic movement of her body. On this night, a strange gravity replaced that hellish satire, although Karen writhed just as limbless, just as helpless, just as hopeless within her paralysis as she had that first time.

The dust beneath her muted her tread. Moonlight lay on not-quite-earthly trees. It felt as if her captor was himself . . . a stranger here, and moved as much in awe as she. She felt as though this rite, whatever it was to be, would change the very earth she walked upon and this moon, this sky would be themselves no longer when the ceremony was done.

The lane steepened downward. She shrugged off the shotgun and let it fall behind her. Still farther down she could see the shed's embers and the moon's milky pallor on the compost's great black slug. She shrugged off the canvas coat, with its automatic. Paused to pull her shoes off next and, a bit farther down, her jeans and her sweater. The night's cold nibbled her nipples hard. She stopped, some two hundred yards from the compost heap. Confronting its blackness naked caused a deep tectonic shift beneath her captive spine. An unspeakable thought stirred deep within her mind.

She must stir. She must not tamely let this come to pass. When her possessor seated her upon the ground and began to lay her back upon the dust of the lane, she understood the pattern and posture intended for her: to lie back, hands behind her head, legs akimbo, voluptuously self-offered on the ground. As her body moved into its position, she desperately thrust her will against her moving muscles and, with huge effort, forced a tiny alteration, such that her broken hand was thrust an inch more deeply beneath her shoulder as she lay back upon the ground. This was all!

Above her, a few stars had sparkled to life within the flood of moonlight. Then, her eyes went to the compost heap at the foot of the lane she lay in. She heard the rip of tearing plastic and understood what she had not dared to understand. Now there existed, in all the world, two and only two places. There was, in a straight line a hundred meters from her, a puncture and a bulge in the plastic flank of the compost heap. A tenting of the plastic and wrinkles radiating from this small peak, wrinkles accentuated by the moonlight. There was this place and only one other place: where her cast-bound hand was wedged between her back and the earth. For in this cramped place, she *must* cause movement. Tears dimmed her eyes.

The plastic ruptured. Flabby black lips puckered out and black sludge vomited forth. Again the wound bulged, the rupture grew, and a more copious feculence slopped out, raising pale dust in the moonlight. Karen's whole universe became a tiny fracture line in one of her carpal bones. Around its littleness she gathered her awareness, to find in the tissue surrounding it some pain, some absence of her captor's will. There it was. Inside that minute pearl of pain was a shred of torn tissue, a mangled muscle-fiber. She could feel it twitch so faintly, unmastered by the Outsider . . . . And inside that damaged tissue was a slender muscle she could move and with the tiny movement, increase the pain!

More sludge extruded from the heap in ropy coils. The rupture lengthened and around one ragged rim, a pallid starfish thrust—a sinewy hand which gripped the plastic, pulled, and dragged a filth-crowned head out into the moonlight. It lifted its eyes to her—Wolf's eyes, but soft as fungi and whitely luminous.

Another muscle fiber woke within her zone of pain. She tensed it, tore it, as the pain bloomed, her whole hand twitched within its cast and with that freedom she moved it with all her strength within the vise formed by her shoulder and the ground. A blessed bright crimson awoke her arm and galvanized her shoulder. Karen thrust the wounded arm out and hammered it against the ground. Pain like a lightning-bolt flashed through her frame and she wrenched her back away from the earth and struggled to her knees.

Wolf slithered from the black heap's steaming cloaca. His lips and eyes and ears were fat glowing fungi, his sex a plague rod all furred with mold.

Again Karen hammered her cast on the earth, crying out in agony and triumph as she surged to her feet. Her legs, so stiff, so slow, but at last she turned and staggered away. Still, Wolf strode with a machine-like tread, devouring the distance faster than Karen could stumble. She seized up her jeans and dragged them on and staggered forward, desperate to reach her canvas coat, as she heard Wolf's soggy tread grow louder at her back. Where was the coat? It should show dark against the pale sand of the lane. Her legs, still sodden, *would* not waken to a run . . .

There! A dark shape on the grass by the lane. She almost toppled bending for the automatic lying near the coat, but then straightened, the gun held two-handed.

It almost flung from her grip in her terror, as she fronted Wolf not two strides from seizing her, his face a seething moon aswarm with tomb-life, his tongue a forked black thing that strained for her as avid as his phallus.

She emptied the clip into his mouth and eyes. A blow-back of hot tissue sprayed her arms and writhed there. But for all this havoc she dispensed, still she must back-pedal, still he pushed robotically into the storm of lead till she was almost toppling backwards, his skull in shards and tatters. Yet he *would not fall*!

Turning around, she bounded from him, forcing a miracle from her rubber legs and, in that slender interval, spun again with just one heartbeat's clearance, and into the wet hiss coming from his mouth, an almost-speech of obscene solicitation, thundered more bolts of devastation. Still, he came on as relentless as before. Though he was just a jawbone, one cheek and a shard of cranium above the neck, still he came. Karen whirled and ran—*could* run now, or nearly. There! The twelve-gauge lying in the lane. She had it! Swung it round—he was almost on her, his black hand inches from her hair—and she fired the first round point-blank in his chest. He catapulted backwards and she pumped five more point-blank at his knees. He struggled to rise on legs with damaged hinges. She ran back down the lane, seized her coat with all its shells, and shrugged it on. Ran back up reloading, and blew both his lower legs off at the knees.

"Catch me now!" she shrieked. "Come on! Let's see what you've got! Get up!" Stood there swaying, panting. Feeling a chill on her breasts, absently she buttoned up her coat. "Look at you twitching! Bet you're sorry now you tried to rape me! Twitching corpses! Undead rapists! You think I give a shit?! *I'm* not insane! The *world* is!" Still, adrenalized, enraged though she was, it seemed that this obscenity should not *be* twitching. Should lie still. She threaded more shells into the twelve-gauge. If she had to pulverize him piece by piece to make him still, then by God—

His body had begun to melt, to flatten and spread and soak into the sand—seemed not to have a single bone inside it! In moments it became a dark stain, vaguely man-shaped. And then became nothing, just dark soil.

And then Karen understood: it had not yet even *begun*.

"You've never left me," she said, her voice suddenly so faint, a long-ago grieving child's voice. "You've never let me go and now you want to drag me underground, forever . . . ."

The ground that had swallowed Wolf trembled, cracking into a network of fissures. Karen stepped backwards and backwards again. The fury that was coming, that was making this broken earth tremble, had crushed her life almost from its beginning. She saw a young girl with wounded eyes and a blood-stained dress. Saw a young woman fighting her way through a decades-long darkness of booze and anger and grief. Remotely she mourned for this girl, this young woman.

She had this shotgun. She had a short time left to live. Okay.

Head and shoulders erupted from the ground. Twice as big as life Dad was, his blown skull grown high-crested, twined boughs and plumes of vegetation grandly back-swept, nodding like a classic Mayan headpiece. His arms were great braided cables of green muscle, his hands gnarl-knuckled as an ancient oak-tree's roots. He had new eyes of onyx, and a beard of vines, and incessantly, all the root and stalk and branch that he was woven of twined restlessly within its living braidwork. He seethed with growth.

He surged out of the earth, a full twelve feet tall, and stood merely surveying his daughter while she fired five rounds up into his face. His face re-knit as swiftly as the double-ought could spray it into sap and shredded tissue. Then his hand shot out, took the shotgun and crumpled it within his endlessly re-woven fingers. She saw there in his onyx eyes that gulf of hopeless distance she had learned to fear when his abuse of her had first begun.

From behind her, there came a roaring sound, a swiftly growing howl. Just as she turned to see, a motorcycle leapt into the air, soared over her, and crashed into Dad's chest. The man who had dismounted just after he launched it—Kyle!—regained his feet at her side, and fired up a chainsaw. Dad caught the Harley in swift-sprouting fingers and flung it—tumbling, chrome flashing—into the orchard. The snarling chain swept through Dad's outstretched hand, both hand and wrist flew off, and a new hand, larger and gnarlier, instantly sprouted in its place. It made a fist and swung a killing blow, and Kyle ducked under it and sank the chain-saw's blade into Dad's leg. Before the limb had toppled, a mightier foot and calf thrust out and gripped the ground, and Dad's hand seized Kyle and held him fast, gripped Karen too and lofted her as well. Wrapped tight as mummies in his branching fingers, they hung before his eyes.

His eyes, dark stars, or frozen planets, were bare of any human history. He tilted his head back, opened his jaws, and a hiss like an arctic wind came out of him. His face, agelessly superhuman as a temple frieze, beheld his child and her defender, and his jaws gaped to consume them . . . and then his eyes were drawn from the eternity they scanned. He saw a frail shape moving through the moonlit air towards him. A slight form, moon-white leaves her sketchy flesh, riding the night-wind, her foliate garment fluttering, as she came to stand upon the air, eye-to-eye with her huge consort, seeming softly aflame in the flutter of her borrowed flesh. Her eyes, mere moonlit gaps, fixed her husband's onyx orbs.

Long they paused there, gazes locked while, within the gnarled hugeness of Dad's face, a subtle sundering occurred, a loosening of the brute weave of braided root and vine. Grief came to haunt the Titan's face, and tender remembrance, long lost, returned to it. He raised his daughter closer to his gaze.

And far down the lane—for they were halfway up to the house now—far below, that black slug in its bath of moonlight shuddered. A ripple went through the compost heap's plastic skin and tires slid off it. Something moved *within* it, something as big as the heap itself. And moved again. A tear began along its dorsal crest, a rupture a hundred feet long.

A sinuous scaly mass erupted from it. Most like a great wingless dragon it was, save for crude crooked scorpion's legs all down along its flanks. Its eyes were myriad, amber-orange, the largest clustered on its huge-jawed head. It reared this head, and beckoned its servitor, and the sacrifices his minion held. The thing that had been Jack Fox obeyed and took one step downslope towards his master . . . and stopped.

His wife's form now had turned from him, and touched her daughter's face, and stroked her cheeks. For all Karen's dire extremity, her tears fell like blood from cuts, a hot effusion she was powerless to stanch. "Mom," she whispered, and felt love crack her heart like an eggshell. This pang went through her father's hand and found his heart and mind in turn. And what had been Jack Fox stooped and set down Karen and Kyle upon the ground. As his titanic master rounded on him and surged upslope towards him in his wrath, Emily Fox's ghost made to her husband a staying gesture and sped through the air, towards the house.

Meanwhile Jack Fox turned to confront the Titan he'd defied, a monster twenty times his size. The black voids of Jack Fox's eyes were now lambent with rekindled self and flashed forth the spirit of a long-ago man with a heart and a mind of his own . . . .

The green god's legs, like the oars of a trireme, rippled as they smote the earth. His fanged jaws flashed in the moonlight and his dragon's body, thrashing, seemed to lash the earth as he swarmed upslope, his serrate tail a wrathful scourge, enraged enough, after centuries of insult, to scour mankind utterly from the face of his plane.

And then it was, between the ascending dragon and Jack Fox, his rebel servitor, that a wheel of fire was kindled in the sky. Seven hundred ghostly hands held forth torches of braided grass which, like a mosaic of flame, kindled a blazing puzzle in the sky. And the green god, gigantically cringing, like a commanded worshipper before the image of its deity, crouched and cringed, its dinosaurian tail thrashing, felling fruit trees right and left. Quetzal, a torch in either hand, bestrode the air. Stepped out above the crouching dragon, her voice like fine steel ringing in the shock of battle.

"Great god! Hear us! Behold! See the wheel of Time! Read the writ of the assembled gods in script of fire across the firmament! Here is the ancient, long-forespoken wheel of man's destruction! Behold it! The time for Man to die has not yet come. You rise in rebellion against all the universe!"

For a long moment the dragon, three hundred feet long, coiled and thrashed and rippled in the moonlight. It seemed no wonder that even such a reptilian monster should pause in a momentary paralysis. For that wheel of fire, hanging just above the newly risen moon, had such an intricately epic swarm of symbols, it seemed a text as dense and cosmic as the constellations themselves, when they blaze thick on moonless nights and fill the dark with intricate hieroglyphs.

"Behold what all the gods have joined to write!" the witch cried. "The death of Humankind is not yet arrived!"

The raging deity twisted in the moonlight, roared defiance, and started once more upslope towards his human sacrifice. The ghosts rained down their torches on him, but they sizzled powerless on his scaly hide. On he surged towards his priest and the priest's daughter. Then Jack Fox saw where his ghostly wife sped back to him, a glittery object in her leafy hands. Karen and Kyle were slow to understand it, but Karen's monstrous father seized it like a sword of salvation, seized the brandy cannon like life itself, and drenched his grotesque body with satiny, gurgling sheets of hundred proof. Soaked and shining, he reached down and seized up Karen's dropped twelve-gauge, even as the dragon surged still closer to striking distance. Karen looked up into her father's eyes and touched her fingers to her lips. He reached a massive hand towards her and touched her face as gently as an alighting butterfly. Oily tears leaked from his night-black eyes. After thirty years, Karen looked into her father's eyes, her *real* father's eyes, while from his inhuman jaw, a hiss emerged, a gasp of grief unutterable, a whisper of farewell.

And then his massive hand found strange finesse— sneaked a tendril through the trigger-guard and replicated his first suicide. The self-aimed salvo sparked to flame the brandy shroud he'd donned. Ablaze now, Jack Fox, a burning giant speeding towards a greater giant, leapt flaming down the slope, the greedy fire he wore towering from his mighty shoulders as he sprang to meet the green god, whose onrush set the orchard earth trembling under the impact of his crooked legs.

Kyle seized his chainsaw in one hand and with the other helped Karen, barefoot and limping, to the truck. "You'll have to drive. I'll need to run the saw. We've got to clear our pathway as we go."

They stood a moment, looking back. Her mother hung above them, looking too. The green god in its wrath, jaws agape, leapt upon Jack Fox, but as they closed, reflexively the dragon recoiled from the flames. The rebel priest leapt high, seized his master's fangs, and hauled his flaming self within his master's maw. Now the dragon coiled and writhed and hammered the earth with its tail, and dug with its claws in its jaw to dislodge the agony of this flaming meal it had been forced to eat. Xibalba bit and chewed to quell the stubborn meal, to sunder and extinguish in his own sizzling throat what fought too powerfully to be expelled, even as it was divided and re-divided, within those colossal fangs. Oblivious in anguish and agony, the green god devoured his blazing servant and, in his agony, clawed at the earth, and dragged his hugeness underground once more.

Now Karen's mother's foliate fingers touched away her tears, and told her, in that touching, they would meet again. There was a gentle leaf-fall, and a parting movement of the air as she joined the ghostly wheel. The ghosts also shed their raiment, and bore the witch away thorough the moonlight. She raised her hand, saluting Kyle and Karen, and was gone

"Karen. We have to go. Can you handle the wheel? The highway is . . . alive."

"I can handle the wheel better than that chainsaw." She fired up the truck, and rocketed them out to the highway. "Thank you."

"For what?"

"For coming to help me."

"What else was I going to do? Just be ready to steer."

THUS IT BEGAN, and was beginning elsewhere in the Midwest. Jack Fox had not climbed from that cenote alone, nor indeed had he and his companions been the only ones to enter it and re-emerge. Scores of men, zombied remnants, or apparently intact, had radiated from that focus. The CIA had seeded the region with thousands trained to spread mayhem and murder, and a surprisingly large percentage of these had found their way to that fertile pool, or to its equally fertile environs. And all of these had brought back to their homeland a

mission as ruthless and murderous as they had taken
with them, though a mission far more "global" than
they'd previously had any conception of.

Late on the following morning, Karen and Kyle
reached Foothill National Park. The refugees of
Gravenstein and Dry Creek filled the campsites, the
great majority still sunk in the sleep of exhaustion.
A couple dozen sat awake at an impromptu council
spot where park benches had been dragged together
and a low fire kept a kettle of coffee hot. Helen and
Skip Carver, Cherry and Sal rose from this group to
embrace these last arrivals. Karen held Helen hard, and
lost herself in tears it seemed would never end.

And when at last she wiped her eyes on her sleeve,
and with a wry smile looked at the exhausted faces
around her, she was struck by something puzzling in
this scene of snoring families and dazed-looking coffee-
drinkers. "So . . ." she said, looking at her companions.
"We're not running. Kyle's told me what you've been
through. Is this . . . safe? Everyone . . . lying on the
ground like this?"

"That . . . witch was here." This was Sheriff Ruddy.
Karen had no way of knowing what a plump, comfy-
looking lawman this gaunt, haunted refugee had been
just yesterday afternoon.

"Quetzal," Helen Carver gently amended.

"Yes. Quetzal. Came back to us here late last night.
Her and her . . . soldiers, I guess you could say. God
knows a lot of us owe them our lives . . ."

But the strangeness of that salvation seemed to
distract the sheriff from his train of thought, and Sal
finished for him. "She told us the rock is deep here
in these foothills and hard for it to travel through.
She also said that it, the thing in the earth and its

demons . . . that it's going to keep changing its path. Going to start *dividing* and *spreading*."

Kyle cleared his throat and said, "This is all-out war."

"*La guerra a la muerte*." This unexpected Spanish came from Sheriff Ruddy. "Everywhere. Everywhere green things grow . . . ."

"For right now," Helen said, touching Karen's cheek, "you two can rest. You both look utterly exhausted. Come on, here's a pair of bedrolls. There's still an empty campsite up on that hill there and a faucet you can wash up under."

There were no trees or any green cover at all, but the site lay in a fold in the terrain and for all they could see of their fellow refugees, they might have been alone on the planet.

"I'll take a hike and you wash up first," Kyle said.

She crouched by the faucet, rinsing her body, drenching her hair and wringing it out. She was utterly alone on the face of the earth, in a hollow under a stark blue sky. To know that Mom and Susan—and Dad now, too—in some way, still lived in that sky did nothing to heal that perfect solitude. The sun and the earth were two tiny cogs of an immense machine. What difference did she or anyone she had loved make in that vastness? What weight did her pain have? Or the slight understanding it had brought her? One naked woman, crouched on a naked hill under a silver stream, beneath an endless blue?

She stood up, shivering in the morning air, the only warmth about her the heat of her tears running down her cheeks.

Then it dawned on her that in fact, she had, in fact, found a treasure, that she possessed something after all, possessed something of great value. She had met a man with an upright spirit and a caring heart who, without a moment's hesitation, had risked his life to save hers.

"Kyle!" she called. She had to keep wiping her eyes, because tears kept streaming from them. "Kyle, come here."

He appeared on the ridge and stopped, seeing her naked and weeping. "Karen? Are you all right?"

Still wiping her eyes, she unrolled the sleeping bags and spread them in the sun. "You bathed me when I needed it, Kyle. Remember?"

"Yes," he said gravely. "I would do anything for you, Karen. You know that, don't you?" He had not taken a step towards her. As if he feared this moment, if he tried to enter it, would vanish.

"I know you are a good man. I know that . . . I love who you are. Come here, undress, and let me bathe you. Let's lie in the sun, side by side . . . ."

And they did that.